No One Will Know

Also by Rose Carlyle

The Girl in the Mirror

No One Will Know

A Novel

Rose Carlyle

wm

WILLIAM MORROW

An Imprint of HarperCollins*Publishers*

NO ONE WILL KNOW. Copyright © 2024 by Rose Carlyle. All rights reserved. Printed in the United States of America. No part of this book may be used or reproduced in any manner whatsoever without written permission except in the case of brief quotations embodied in critical articles and reviews. For information, address HarperCollins Publishers, 195 Broadway, New York, NY 10007.

HarperCollins books may be purchased for educational, business, or sales promotional use. For information, please email the Special Markets Department at SPsales@harpercollins.com.

FIRST EDITION

Interior text design by Diahann Sturge-Campbell

Library of Congress Cataloging-in-Publication Data has been applied for.

ISBN 978-0-06-337993-0 (trade paperback)
ISBN 978-0-06-341115-9 (hardcover library edition)

24 25 26 27 28 LBC 5 4 3 2 1

This novel is dedicated to all of the mothers of the world, especially my mother, Christina, and my late grandmother, Eileen Celia Mansfield.

PART I

CHAPTER 1

Eve

I'm swimming in a sea of dreams when a kiss pulls me into wakefulness. Xander's face is an inch from mine, his blue eyes sparkling, sorry-not-sorry for waking me. He's drawn the blankets over our heads against the cold of early spring, and we're cocooned in dewy light. How blissful it is to wake and not be alone.

"Morning, beautiful," he says, kissing me again.

"What time is it?"

Xander laughs. "Very romantic reply, Eve."

"I don't want to be late, that's all. Today's the big day, and I'm terrible at first impressions. I'm sick with nerves."

"We don't need to hurry." Xander runs his fingers down my spine. "I know just the thing to help you relax."

Xander and I arrived in Sydney yesterday after sailing down from Fiji, completing the last leg of our six-month Pacific Ocean crossing. As soon as we cleared customs, we taxied to Xander's apartment, tumbled into bed, and fell instantly asleep.

I love that he brought me to his home. I want every day to start this way. I want to wake up in Xander's arms every morning for the rest of my life.

Xander nuzzles my neck, his hands roaming over my body. "You're so gorgeous."

I refrain from replying that nobody else has ever said so. I haven't shaken the nagging fear that maybe Xander and I got together during our voyage purely because I was the only woman within hundreds of miles. I'm skinny, with light-green eyes and a complexion so pale that six months sailing across the Pacific haven't left me with a tan. My one attractive feature is my hair—I'm a redhead, and my hair is unusually dark, almost the color of mahogany.

I roll on top of Xander, and my gaze lands on a framed photo on the bedside table. In the picture, Xander embraces a smiling, tanned blonde—his ex-girlfriend, Charlotte. I guess neither of us noticed the photo last night. Charlotte and Xander broke up before I met him, but I still feel awkward romping in bed with a guy before the photo of his previous girlfriend has been cleared away.

Xander follows my gaze. "My bad." He shoves the photo in a drawer and turns back to me, taking me in his arms again. "This is our place now, Eve."

A shrill sound cuts through the air. The landline.

"Ignore it," says Xander.

The answerphone kicks in. It's right beside the bed, and the woman's voice, cool and clipped, kills our vibe in two seconds flat.

"Alexander, it's Mother. I've made a reservation for lunch at Skipper Jack's at noon. Your father had our driver drop the Lexus at your apartment last night. You'll find it in the usual spot downstairs. Wear some smart pants and that white linen shirt I gave you for Christmas, and for Heaven's sake don't be late. I've booked a table for six. Charlotte is coming. She tells me her father is hiring. I think you're on your last chance with that lovely girl, son. Get a wriggle on, and make sure you iron that shirt."

She hangs up.

Xander and I stare at each other, frozen. My first instinct is to laugh. Who in the last hundred years, other than the Queen of England, refers to herself as *Mother*?

My next thought is anything but funny. Xander's mum has invited his ex-girlfriend to his welcome-home lunch—the ex-girlfriend whose father owns a law firm where Xander's parents hope he'll land his first real job.

"I wish you'd told them about us," I say.

"Let's talk about them later—"

The phone rings again. Maybe *Mother* forgot to mention which shoes would look best with that shirt.

This time, Xander doesn't wait for the answerphone. He leans over, grabs the cord, and yanks it out of the wall.

I'M SEARCHING THE kitchen for food that isn't past its expiry date while Xander shaves his sailor's beard.

"What are you going to tell your parents?" I call, adopting a casual tone. "It sounds like your mother thinks you and Charlotte are still together."

Xander appears at the kitchen door, half shaven. "You heard me on the phone to Mum back in Mexico. I told her I was single."

"Is it Mum or Mother?"

Xander points at the fine china I've set out for coffee, as though it's the key to his mother's character. "Mum likes to pretend. She pretends we call her Mother. She pretends to be a member of some imaginary Australian aristocracy. She probably pretends to all her friends that Charlotte and I are still together, that Charlotte got off the yacht because of seasickness."

"That *is* why Charlotte got off the yacht."

When I met Xander, he was inches away from realizing his

lifelong dream. He and Charlotte had recently finished university, and he'd spent a bequest from his grandfather on *Joy*, a small but sturdy yacht that the owners were selling for a song because nobody wanted to fly to a remote part of Mexico to buy a yacht. Xander and Charlotte did exactly that. They moved on board *Joy* and set off for Australia as a gap-year adventure. If Charlotte liked the lifestyle, they planned to save money, upsize the yacht, and sail around the world.

But Charlotte did not like the lifestyle. After their maiden voyage down Mexico's west coast, she broke off their relationship, packed her things, and flew home. I met Xander drowning his sorrows in a village tavern. He considered pulling the plug on his adventure, but with cyclone season approaching, he couldn't leave *Joy* in Mexico. He was facing the daunting prospect of solo-sailing all the way home.

On a whim, I offered to join Xander on board. I'd never set foot on a yacht, but I'd been backpacking around Latin America for months, and this sounded like a more interesting way to get home than flying cattle class. It wasn't like I had anything to rush back to. My parents died in a freak storm in New Zealand when I was four. After a year in foster care, I moved to a small town in Western Australia to live with Nanna, my sole surviving relative, but she died of cancer when I was sixteen. For the past six years, I've moved around a lot. What gave me faith in Xander was that he was honest about the downsides of sailing—the uncertain time frame and the discomfort of bad weather—even though his chances of finding another willing idiot were minuscule.

"Charlotte and I broke up," Xander says now. "She can't expect me to come crawling back. She sure won't after you turn up at this lunch. I can't wait to introduce you to the olds. They'll love you." He runs a hand through my hair, as if to suggest his parents will adore it as much as he does.

A glob of shaving foam lands on the kitchen floor. I shoo Xander back to the bathroom. At times I think my boyfriend is bonkers. No way will his family be happy to swap Charlotte, daughter of a partner in a prestigious law firm, and beautiful to boot, for little old me.

Xander said his mum pretends to be aristocratic, but his parents' wealth is real. This stunning apartment belongs to them. The building was originally a church, and the exterior stone wall stands in bold contrast to the modern lines of the interior. In the morning sunshine, the stained-glass window fills the living room with blue light, making it feel like a magical underwater cave.

When Xander reappears, I hand him the beans. "You're on coffee duty. It'd take me days to figure out how to use this machine."

He grins.

"Your mum booked a table for six," I say, leaping onto a barstool and crossing my legs. "That's your parents, your sister and her husband, and you and Charlotte. Three cozy couples. Will the restaurant be able to fit an extra person?"

"They'll squeeze you in."

This doesn't sound promising.

"Xander, I don't think it's the right time for me to meet your family, especially with Charlotte there. You should go without me. I can't turn up in my grotty travel clothes, anyway."

"We'll buy you something to wear." Xander passes me a steaming cup of espresso. It looks delicious, but when I raise it to my lips, it smells off.

"I spent my last dollar on our groceries in Fiji." The thought of my dire financial situation sends a new wave of stress through me. I sold most of my belongings, even the sewing machine I used in my dressmaking business, to go traveling. In Fiji, not only did I run out of money, but I also lost my phone overboard. Xander is in a tight spot, too. His parents have told him they won't give him any more money, and they want him to start paying rent on this apartment.

"We have five hundred bucks." Xander reaches into his pocket and pulls out the fistful of bills he exchanged yesterday.

"That's all the money you've got. You can't splurge on new clothes."

"You're right." Xander hands me the money. "You keep it. You'll make it last till one of us gets a job."

I pocket the cash. "Could we drive to my old flat and get my dresses?"

"The ones you designed? I do want to see them, but there isn't time to drive to Parramatta. Whale Beach is an hour north of here, and Mum hates tardiness." Xander gestures at my untouched coffee. "What's wrong? Is it nerves?"

"I guess. I just know I'm going to mispronounce my order or . . . I don't know . . . knock over my wineglass."

I place the coffee on the bench and walk to the stained-glass window. In the distance, the bridge arches over the sparkling water of Sydney Harbor.

The truth is my belly is a nest of vipers. Xander doesn't seem to have noticed, but I don't talk the same as he and *Mother*. Xander has a law degree, while I didn't finish high school. When Nanna died, my options were either to move into a foster home to complete my schooling or to find a job and roommates. I'd already lived in two foster homes after my parents died—the authorities had had trouble locating any relatives. I sure didn't want that again. I've been supporting myself with my sewing ever since.

Not to mention that I've moved around so many times in my life that I don't belong anywhere. In my late teens I moved to New Zealand, wanting to reconnect with my homeland, but after a year I was lured to Sydney by higher wages. As soon as I'd saved enough money, I set off backpacking around Latin America. Xander's parents are unlikely to be impressed by my vagabond lifestyle.

Xander comes up behind me and wraps his arms around my waist. "It might be easier for me if you stayed here today, but it would be a mistake. We need to show my family we're serious. That we're a couple."

I sigh, then give him a kiss on the cheek before going to take a shower while he sorts through six months of mail.

As we make our way down to the basement parking garage, Xander uncoils a key from his key ring and hands it to me. "This can be your key."

I slip it into my pocket. *Your key.* Xander's given me his key and his money. As he leads me to the Lexus, my anxiety floats away. He's committed to me. His parents will see that. If today goes well, perhaps I'll start to feel I belong to a family again, something I've missed every day of the six years since I lost Nanna.

We drive out of the parking garage into fresh sunshine. I'm wearing the best clothes I could come up with—a sage-green T-shirt and tan cargo pants. As we cruise over the Harbor Bridge, I open the glove box, and a brochure for Skipper Jack's slips out. Beneath a photo of a bride and groom, the tagline reads: *The perfect venue for your special day.*

"Xander, we're going to a *wedding venue*," I say. "Is your mother hoping to scope out the place for you and Charlotte?"

"Uh, that's probably an old brochure from when my sister got married."

I run over the names of Xander's family in my head—his sister, Lauren, her husband, Niccolò. "What do I call your parents? Mr. and Mrs. Blair or Richard and Patricia?"

Xander snorts. "Dickie and Trish. Don't be all respectful, or they'll go for the jugular."

Whoa. Being polite is a bad strategy? What sort of people are they?

"Xander, I can't believe how relaxed you are. And I just don't understand why Charlotte would come. You broke up months ago. Won't this be awkward for her?"

He shrugs. "There's no point objecting when it comes to my mother. She does what she wants, no matter what other people say. Charlotte's probably coming because it's easier than trying to say no to Patricia Blair. Don't worry. When we get there, I plan to make it clear to Charlotte how I feel, without letting Mum interfere."

I wish we could turn this car around. How does Xander plan to stop his mother interfering? "This sounds like a recipe for disaster. Even if your parents get over me, Charlotte won't. Her dad won't hire you, and your plan to buy a bigger yacht will go down the drain."

"I'll get some other job," says Xander. "Anyway, I only wanted to upsize the yacht for Charlotte. She's used to luxury. You and I can sail around the world in *Joy* as soon as we've saved enough for living expenses."

"Because I'm not used to luxury?" I joke.

Xander gives me a sidelong smile. "We can save up for a super-yacht if you like."

"You know I'm just messing with you. I'd be happy with a driftwood raft."

"I reckon. You wouldn't even get seasick."

It's hard to believe I was afraid Xander would dump me when we reached Sydney. When we were sailing, we were too caught up in the day-to-day magic of our adventure to talk about the future much. Now he's treating our dream of sailing around the world together as a settled thing.

"Have you ever wondered where you would be now if I did get seasick? Or if Charlotte didn't?" I ask as we leave the city behind and Xander steers the Lexus onto a road bordered by eucalyptus. The sight of so much greenery is a stark change after months at sea.

"You *were* seasick, remember, on our last leg down to Sydney. You were throwing up every morning."

I feel as though I'm thinking straight for the first time since we left Fiji—probably because last night was my first full night's sleep since then. Xander's words set off alarm bells. "You're right. I was fine all the way across the Pacific, and then suddenly I couldn't keep breakfast down."

"You felt okay this morning, now we're on land, right?" Xander's tone changes.

"I do feel a little off."

"Eve, you're not pregnant? Are you late?"

My hand moves to my belly. "It's different when you're traveling. I've barely had a cycle since Mexico."

"We were in rough weather the last fortnight," says Xander, "and you're nervous about meeting my parents. I'm sure that's all it is."

He glances at me, his blue eyes full of wonder. What else do I see? If I am just a holiday romance, this is the moment I'll see it in his eyes.

I've got the words ready. *I feel different. It's not just nerves.*

I can't say them. I can't bear for things to change between us. Maybe that's why it happens, because I pause, because I'm afraid to speak, and Xander has taken his eyes off the road.

CHAPTER 2

A horn blares. Silver flashes across my eyes. The world splits, and I scream.

We hit steel.

Silence. Pressure. I'm buried in something cream and soft. A cushion. I draw back and look over at Xander. His face is buried, too.

Airbags.

We're okay. We've been in an accident, but the airbags worked. We survived.

I can't make sense of what I see outside the car. Our windscreen's gone. In its place is silver. A wall of silver.

"Xander," I say, but no sound comes. My ears are ringing, drowning out everything.

Pressure on my shoulder. Something's pulling my arm. The passenger door is open. A big, burly man is wrenching me out of the car.

"Xander," I rasp. "Get Xander."

The man hooks his hands under my armpits and drags me backward out of my seat. My feet slush through shallow liquid. Fumes fill my nostrils. Petrol.

In front of me there's no road, just the silver wall. Sound is returning. People are shouting.

"Get the other guy!"

"Lay her on the curb!"

"Further away! It's not safe here!"

The voices are muffled as though underwater. I'm staring at sky.

"Get my boyfriend," I tell my rescuer. He disappears.

I'm lying on my back. I try to move. Pain shoots through my arm. I reach out with my other hand and feel gravel.

A woman nearby shouts into her phone, "Hurry! There's a helluva lot of hurt people!"

"My boyfriend's still in the car!" I cry. "He needs help."

"Brian's got him," the woman replies, pointing.

Now I see the silver wall for what it is. A petrol tanker. It has jackknifed across the median. The Lexus lies half under it, the bonnet buried.

The big man drags a slumped figure through the pool of petrol.

"Xander!" I scream.

Xander lifts his head.

"Put him beside the girl," says the woman, and the man lays Xander beside me. I sit up and lean over him.

"Xander, can you hear me?"

He looks at me, and I'm staring at a pair of brown eyes.

"Who is this? This isn't Xander!" I turn back to the tanker, and now I see more crashed cars—one smashed into the cab of the tanker, another that has rear-ended the first.

Xander is still in the Lexus.

"It could blow any minute!" the woman shouts. "The forest'll catch fire!"

"You've got to get my boyfriend!" I scream at the man.

"It's too dangerous!"

I gape. *He's not going to rescue Xander?*

I stagger to my feet. "Xander, I'm coming!"

I step onto the road. The petrol has spread.

"Lady, stay back!"

"Xander!" I lurch toward the car.

Hands grab me. The man drags me back from the pool of petrol. Pain shoots through me. Something's seriously wrong with my arm. I jerk free of my rescuer—another bolt of pain—and I'm running toward the Lexus, toward my love, my life, toward everything I care about.

Xander is still slumped behind the wheel, his strong frame so helpless, his blond hair sullied with blood. I'm nearly there.

"I'm telling you, it's gonna blow, lady!"

I'm flying backward, and everything is bright and burning. My world turns to flames.

I don't remember hitting the ground.

CHAPTER 3

Nothing is the way I expected it to be. All I can see, all I can think of, is fire.

For some reason, time keeps passing. The ward grows dark and then grows light again. The hands on the wall clock crawl endlessly around. I don't know why.

The nurses come and go, and they talk to me. They expect me to do things, like eating and drinking and showering, but none of this makes any sense.

Something else is hiding beneath the horror of Xander's death, but I can't remember. It's there, but I won't let it surface.

The police visit me. They've spoken to several eyewitnesses. They tell me the accident killed three people besides Xander. Dashcam footage established the tanker driver had fallen asleep at the wheel.

The nurses talk about Xander, but they get everything wrong. They call him Alexander. They call him "the driver." They call him "your friend." I want to tell them he was my life, but I can't find the words.

They tell me I'm not badly hurt. When the accident happened, I was thrown back by the shockwave rather than burnt. My arm wasn't broken. It was merely a dislocated elbow, which was re-aligned soon after I got to hospital.

You'll be fine, they tell me. They can't see that I died when Xander died. They say I've been sleeping too much. They can't see that sleep is my only respite from a world without him.

I am an elderly woman. I am a hundred years old, and my body is tattooed with grief.

Crossing an ocean is intense, and shipmates get to know every facet of each other's personality. I know Xander loved me for my sense of adventure. He was delighted when I would accept a challenge just for the fun of it—climbing a cliff above a beach to see the view or free-diving in a deep anchorage just to bring back a handful of sand from the seabed. I admired Xander for the resourcefulness that enabled him to skipper a yacht while only in his midtwenties, but I loved him for his kindness. He consulted with me about everything from who should take the night watch to where we should sail next, as though *Joy* belonged to both of us. And he was generous and friendly to everyone we met— something that's always been important to me.

No matter how much I think about him, though, I can't bring him back.

"Eve?"

I'm lying with my eyes shut when I hear the woman's voice. I sense at once she isn't one of the nurses. Her voice is happy, friendly, and fake. She's one of *them*—the people I call vultures.

"Wakey-wakey, Eve."

I want to keep my eyes closed, but the first rule with vultures is to behave the way they want you to. That means being awake during the day. I open my eyes and sit up.

The woman leans over my bed. In her midthirties, she wears square glasses with garish rims and has an aura of frizzy hair. Her beaded necklace sways in my face.

"Lovely to meet you!" she announces, like her whole life has been working up to this moment. "My name is Yasmin. I'm part of the mental health team. The nurses tell me you've been having a hard time."

I should have known this would happen. I heard one nurse tell another my behavior was "abnormal," but after what's happened, only an abnormal person could behave normally.

"I've been in a lot of pain," I say, trying to straighten my inadequate hospital gown. I need to give Yasmin the impression my injuries are purely physical. "I was in a serious accident. My elbow was dislocated, and I was knocked out."

"I know." Yasmin nods enthusiastically. "That must have been distressing."

This woman is a grief junkie. She's desperate for more details. "The young man who died," she says with an insincere frown, "can you tell me about him?"

I want to scream at her to get out. Who is she to talk about Xander? A stranger marches in here and starts asking personal questions, like we're going to have a nice gossip about the latest neighborhood drama.

Yasmin's manner and her appearance—her boho dress with its colorful print, her arms crammed with mismatched bangles—spark a memory. I was so young when my parents died that I barely remember them, but I do remember the succession of foster homes I was moved around after their deaths. Even after the police located Nanna in Western Australia, she had to battle for several months to obtain custody of me because the social workers thought she was too old to care for me. I didn't know at the time that they wanted to keep me apart from my only surviving relative, but I sensed danger whenever I heard their happy-clappy voices and saw their gaudy clothes.

Those vultures pretended to care whether I was safe, whether someone in her late seventies could take care of me, but really, they wanted me to need them. They wanted to believe their nosiness and frowny concern were somehow helping me.

When I don't answer her question, Yasmin tries another approach. "I hear you've been a little out of sorts. The doctors suspected you might have suffered a brain injury, but your scan came back normal."

"I'm fine. I've just had a migraine," I lie. I haven't actually had a migraine for a couple of months, which is unusual for me.

"You've had a migraine for twelve days?"

"Has it been twelve days?" I had no idea I'd been in hospital so long.

"It's difficult to keep track of time after emotional trauma." The corners of Yasmin's mouth droop. I guess this is her empathy face.

"What about Xander's parents?" I ask. "They were expecting us for lunch. Do they know what's happened?"

"It's all been taken care of. The police broke the news to the family. The funeral was yesterday."

My heart drops out of my chest. Xander has been buried?

"Surely they didn't hold the funeral without me."

For the first time since arriving, Yasmin looks unsure of herself. "We're talking about the Blair family, right? Richard and Patricia Blair?"

Can Yasmin be correct? I guess Xander's parents thought I was just a crew member on his yacht. They weren't expecting me at the restaurant, but they must have been told I was in their son's car. Wouldn't they have realized Xander wanted to bring me to this special family occasion? That I must have been important to him?

"I can't think straight," I say. "It's the medication."

"No, it isn't, Eve." Yasmin's voice has a *gotcha* tone. "You're not on any medication, because of your condition."

My condition.

Xander's blue eyes are staring at me, questioning, asking me . . .

Yasmin's voice sounds far away, as though I'm still deafened by the crash. "Doctors run blood tests when a patient is in a state of altered consciousness. When a woman is of fertile age, one of those tests—"

"What are you on about? I'm not in a state of altered whatever. I'm wide awake."

"You're certainly more alert than I expected." Yasmin sounds disappointed. "However, hospital policy requires us to ensure patients have a home to go to. It seems you don't have a permanent address or any next of kin."

"I just returned from overseas, but my old flatmates in Parramatta are storing my stuff. I'll stay with them."

It's as though there are two of me. One is answering Yasmin's questions; the other is back in the car with Xander.

You were throwing up every morning.

I don't want to think. I wriggle to the edge of the bed and plant my feet on the floor. I wish I could make a run for it, but fleeing barefoot through the hospital wouldn't improve Yasmin's opinion of my mental health.

"Yes, your Parramatta address was on your records," says Yasmin, "so I got in touch with the people living there. They said they don't know you. I'm here to help, Eve. We don't like any young woman to be homeless, but particularly one who's . . . You do know, don't you?"

"I need the bathroom." I stand, reach inside the bedside cabinet, and grab a brown paper bag labeled *Patient's Belongings.*

Locked in the bathroom, I open the bag and pull out my clothes. They're a little torn, but they'll do.

I jump in the shower. Perhaps when she hears water running, Yasmin will leave. Perhaps I can get discharged before she comes back.

After drying off, I rub the condensation away from the mirror and turn sideways, looking at my reflection. My belly is flat as a board. And yet.

In the last minutes of his life, Xander gave me something—a chance to absorb the truth before Yasmin came along. He guessed. Xander knew, for a moment he knew, and I have to believe what I saw in his eyes was happiness.

I don't trust this Yasmin woman. I don't know what she wants, but I wouldn't put it past her to get me transferred to a mental health unit where she can enjoy "helping" me more. If I want to get out of here, I have to act normal. I need to convince her I have somewhere to go and someone to take care of me.

I pull on my T-shirt and pants and step out of the bathroom on wobbly legs. This is the longest I've spent standing in a while. Yasmin is sitting by my bed, looking through my file.

I reach into my pocket, and my hand closes on a roll of banknotes and a key. Gifts from Xander on the day he died.

"Lucky I found this," I say, waving the key at Yasmin. "I won't have to beg the doorman to let me in. Thanks for letting me know I'm well enough to be discharged. My fiancé's out of town, and I want to be home before he gets back. I'm glad the accident didn't affect my pregnancy. We'd just found out, my fiancé and I."

"You knew you were pregnant?" Yasmin sounds deflated. "You didn't mention it to the nurses."

"I guess I was shocked by what happened to that Xander bloke, even though I hardly knew him."

"I thought he might be the father?"

"No, thank goodness, or I'd be having this baby on my own, which would suck. He was just giving me a lift that day."

"The medical team said you've been crying over his death—"

"Anyway, I'm going to talk to the nurses about getting out of here. Lovely to meet you, Yasmin, but I'm sure there are loads of people who need your help more than I do."

I'm so faint I'm trembling, but I plaster a smile on my face and march off in search of a nurse.

I discharge myself from hospital and get in a taxi. The last things Xander gave me—the money and the key—are all I have left. So long as the apartment is empty.

CHAPTER 4

I press my ear to the door and listen.

Xander's parents left this apartment empty the whole time he was overseas. Surely they won't be here today.

He gave me the key because he wanted me to feel at home. I'm sure he'd want me to come here.

There's no sound from within, so I enter the apartment and walk around the sunlit rooms, taking in their still silence. Everything's exactly as we left it.

Xander and I spent only one night here, but it makes the place precious to me. When we tumbled in the door after our voyage, I was rattled by the luxury—the bathroom with its multiple shower heads, the kitchen with the coffee machine that looked like it could fly you to the moon. The apartment didn't suit Xander, apart from the wonderful stained-glass window.

Xander told me that, when they demolished the church on this site, they retained the façade. "This unit was the most sought-after in the building, because it was positioned at the rose window."

"There's no such thing as a blue rose," I replied.

"*Rose* refers to the shape of the window."

"But roses aren't circles," I said, and he laughed.

Now, alone, I lie on the carpet in the blue light. If I stay perfectly still, maybe no more time will pass. I can't bring Xander back, but if I could stop time, I wouldn't drift further away from him.

IN THE FOLLOWING days, I wander from room to room in a trance, living off canned food as though still at sea. Each night, I sleep in Xander's bed. Each afternoon, I lie under the window and imagine I'm back in the middle of the ocean. I didn't know until we reached the tropics that the sea truly is blue there. Not green or aqua or turquoise, but blazing blue. Bluer than blood is red. When I sleep, the color invades my dreams.

I think about the cells dividing inside me. I have no doubt that I'm pregnant. The lack of migraines in the last two months is evidence enough—a doctor told me before I left for Latin America that it's hard to predict when and why they come and go, but I do remember him saying that women often find they stop during pregnancy. At the time, I thought the information wouldn't be relevant to me for years.

Since my early teens, my migraines have hit without warning, sometimes two or three in a month. Each time, I have no choice but to put my life on hold until they pass. As a dressmaker, I always stayed ahead of deadlines so that a day or two in bed wouldn't result in disappointed customers. When considering whether to join Xander on his Pacific crossing, I was worried I might be too unwell to stand a watch at times, but he assured me he could sail single-handed until I recovered.

Nobody outside of the hospital knows I'm pregnant. I feel I could go on forever living here, as though waiting for Xander to return. But I need help. I'm twenty-three years old. I have no family and no friends—I never got a chance to get close with anyone before I took off backpacking.

Babies can't be put on hold. Xander won't be around to take over the childcare while I lie in a darkened room, zonked out on painkillers. I'm going to need support.

One afternoon, as I'm watching the sun trace its path across the cold sky, a key scrapes the lock.

I freeze with dread. Xander's family will find me squatting in his apartment like a thief.

"It won't open," a female voice says.

"Wrong floor, silly," says her companion. I hear laughter and retreating footsteps.

My heart pounds as I absorb this unlikely reprieve. Next time someone comes to the door, it won't be a mistake. I check my watch. Four o'clock on Monday, September 29. It's more than three weeks since Xander died. I could drive to Whale Beach to-night. A weekday evening is a good time to visit. The Blairs are likely to be home and unlikely to have company.

Since I lost my phone overboard and Xander's electronics were in the car with him, I can't easily look up the Blairs' address. Fortunately, Xander showed me photos of his childhood home. The stucco mansion stands on the waterfront at Whale Beach, with only a line of Norfolk pines separating it from the sand. It shouldn't be hard to find.

I shower and ferret through my backpack for fresh clothes. I have nothing better than a denim skirt and a tank top. I must get my suitcase from my old flat soon.

Stepping outside, I'm struck by the warmer weather. Spring has advanced while I lay frozen in the air-conditioned apartment. I walk to a nearby car-rental company and rent their cheapest car.

I choose a route that avoids the scene of the accident. I can't bear to see where the tanker crossed the median. Arriving at

Whale Beach, I drive along the waterfront, inspecting the row of well-kept mansions. I'm almost at the end of the road when the house from Xander's photos comes into view.

It looks even bigger in real life—easily three times the size of Nanna's house back in Western Australia. This budget Mazda won't make the right impression, so I park around the corner and approach the high iron gates on foot. Although it's a fine evening, the house blocks out the setting sun, and as I step into its shadow, my courage abandons me. I look back toward Whale Beach, where a few couples are strolling along the golden sand.

I'm walking hand in hand with Xander along the beach. He gets down on one knee. Evie, I love you. I want to spend my life with you.

I turn away from the ocean and press the buzzer.

A frenzy of barking erupts. An overgrown Alsatian hurtles down the drive and jumps at me from the other side of the gates.

I step back. Do I really want to go in there? The dog is actually foaming at the mouth. Before I can decide, the gates open, and it bounds out.

"Hey, doggy. Good boy."

Xander told me the dog's name. Bruno? Baxter? He jumps up on me, his doggy face full of exuberance. I stand my ground, holding my arms protectively across my torso. Soon he drops back on all fours and bounds toward the house. I follow.

The giant box of a house presents sheer walls with vast windows that reflect the sky. The house is a boring shade of taupe, and the wide lawn is unadorned. I guess austerity can be elegant, but if I were wealthy, I'd want my home to sizzle with color and personality. Still, there are worse things than being boring.

I suck in my tummy as I approach, although I'm sure my pregnancy isn't showing. I hope they give me points for fronting up to them.

As I step onto the porch, the door opens. In front of me stands a tall, elegant woman who looks to be in her fifties. Her navy suit with its pencil skirt looks tailor-made. Her blond hair is swept into a French roll.

"Can I help you?"

That voice. *Mother* from the answerphone message. Patricia Blair's expression isn't friendly, but then, she probably thinks I'm a random door knocker.

"Sorry to turn up like this," I say. "I'm Eve Sylvester. I was on the yacht."

CHAPTER 5

Patricia's smile is shiny and tight. "How do you do, Eve? You weren't at the funeral, I don't think?"

"I didn't know about it."

"Well, I appreciate you wanting to pay your respects. Unfortunately, now isn't a good time."

This is a bad start.

"I've been in hospital since the accident," I say. "I didn't know your phone number, so I couldn't call. I had to rent a car to come here."

"I don't understand." Patricia lifts her chin. "You were in the accident, but you were also Alexander's crewmate? That's a coincidence."

"Mrs. Blair, I was in the Lexus with your son." Damn, Xander told me not to call his mother Mrs. Blair.

Patricia shakes her head. "Nobody else was in the car. If you had been, you couldn't possibly have survived."

"Someone pulled me clear before the explosion."

"What? I didn't realize there was time for that."

We stand staring at each other. What can I say? Patricia must be thinking that the choice to pull me from the car first cost Xander his life. And she's right.

So, nobody told Xander's parents I was injured. They didn't

know I was in Xander's car. This is why they didn't visit me in hospital.

"If this is true, you must be disappointed to have missed the funeral," Patricia adds.

If this is true. I try not to flinch. It's just a turn of phrase.

"My daughter, Lauren, thought we should try to find Xander's crewmate," Patricia continues, "but we couldn't remember your name, and with the turmoil of organizing the funeral . . . I never considered you might have been in the car. Alexander was on his way to a very special reunion with his girlfriend. Why would he bring . . ." The question hangs between us.

I'm not sure where to start. Perhaps by pointing out Charlotte wasn't Xander's girlfriend anymore—but I don't want to get into an argument with a grieving mother.

"Was there anything else?" Patricia asks.

Wow, she really wants me gone. "No. Sorry for disturbing you. Can I please get your number and phone you tomorrow?"

"I suppose. I'll get a pen." She disappears, shutting the door behind her.

Should I say anything more? If I leave without explaining where I've been staying, it'll be even worse if Patricia finds me at the apartment, but surely I shouldn't start such a serious conversation on the doorstep.

The door reopens, but it's not Patricia. This woman is also tall and blond and dressed in a designer suit, but she's much younger.

"Hi, I'm Lauren. Come in." She gives me a friendly smile.

"I think your mother's busy . . ."

"No, it's fine. Please, come and meet my father."

"Uh, okay." I follow Lauren through a featureless foyer in

which every surface is taupe, just like outside. The sole ornament is a stone vase that stands empty on a side table.

In my childhood home, every room was crammed with knick-knacks. Nanna's sewing machine lived on the dining table, and the floor was always covered with fabrics and yarn. I used to long for more space. But this house is so blank; it feels as though nobody lives here.

And yet Xander grew up here. He should be here now, introducing me to his parents, bringing his family together.

Don't think about Xander.

We enter the living room—another taupe panorama. Patricia stands at a desk, a notepad and pen in her hands, presumably jotting down her phone number. On the sofa, a middle-aged man sips red wine.

Patricia's face falls when she sees me.

"You've met my mother, and this is my father, Dickie," says Lauren. "Dad, this is Eve, Xander's crewmate on *Joy.*"

Dickie stands and shakes my hand. He's shorter than his wife, clean-shaven and bald, his face as round as a plum pudding. I'd never have picked him as Xander's father.

"Would you like a glass of wine, Eve?" Lauren lifts a crystal decanter off a sideboard and fills a glass.

"No, I can't."

The way she sets the decanter down, the crystal almost shatters. Patricia looks offended. Is it a faux pas to refuse wine?

"I'm driving," I explain. "Sorry, I'm not really here to socialize. I need to talk to you about something."

"Yes, you've been through quite an ordeal." Patricia turns to Lauren and Dickie. "Eve just informed me she was in the car with Alexander at the time of the accident." Her tone is oddly loud, and she speaks slowly, as though they might have trouble understanding her. "She's been in hospital. Now we know why she didn't come to the funeral. I'm annoyed the hospital didn't tell us about her."

Lauren and Dickie exchange puzzled frowns. It's so quiet in the room that, through the open window, I can hear waves crashing on the beach.

"Um, that's terrible," Lauren says, sinking into an armchair. "Were you badly hurt, Eve?"

Patricia sits on the sofa beside Dickie. Should I stay standing? I perch on a nearby stool, hoping this is less rude than taking a seat on the sofa without an invitation.

"I'm okay physically, but it's been tough. Since they discharged me, I've barely gone out. I've been lying on the floor all day under the blue window."

"The blue window?" Patricia looks startled. "Do you mean you've been staying at our apartment on Saint Mary's Street?"

"Yes. That's why I've come to see you. I wanted to explain."

"I was hoping you'd get in touch," says Lauren. "I want to know more about my brother's last few months."

"Not now," says Patricia. "I need a quiet family evening. Anyway, we should think twice about prying into Alexander's life. We should cherish our own memories of him, not ask other people to share theirs." She takes a gulp of her wine.

"Actually, this is why I've come," I say. "I need to tell you Xander and I were in a relationship. A serious one."

Lauren's jaw drops. "What? Since when? I thought he and Char—"

"I told you we shouldn't get into this," says Patricia. "Eve, excuse me. I choose to grieve my son in my own way. I don't need to know what happened on the yacht. We had a beautiful funeral with Charlotte."

I expect Patricia to leave the room, but she remains seated. I guess "excuse me" means she wants me to leave.

I stand.

"We don't mean to be unwelcoming, Eve," says Lauren, "but this is a lot to drop on us."

"Ultimately, it doesn't matter." Dickie's voice is so loud I almost jump. "People remember things differently. If Eve had a summer fling with Alexander, it didn't hurt anyone. Charlotte believed Alexander was coming home to marry her. That's what she said at the funeral. No harm done. We'll let sleeping dogs lie. Eve, I hope you brought the key to the apartment with you. Lauren is moving in."

The floor seems to sway. This isn't going well—but I knew it wouldn't be an easy conversation. Once they hear about the baby, they'll be friendlier.

"I can't give you the key right now. All my stuff's in the apartment."

"Hmm," says Dickie. "It was a bit presumptuous of you to stay there without our permission. However, one more night won't hurt. We'll pick up the key in the morning."

"Xander gave me the key. We were planning to live there together."

Looks are exchanged.

Dickie clears his throat. "The apartment belongs to me and my wife. You must understand your fling with our son isn't a legal relationship. It doesn't create obligations. The yacht is ours, too, as we are Alexander's heirs. We've already put it on the market, so don't get any ideas about moving on board."

"I—I understand." I look outside. The beach is now in shade, but the sun is still sparkling on the water.

They want me to leave, and I want to leave, too. I long to stride down their taupe hallway and through their taupe foyer and never see any of them again. I long to slam their taupe door on my way out.

But I can't. I'm here for something more important than my pride or the thrill of a satisfying exit. However rude these people are, I owe it to them to tell the truth.

"I have important news." The words come out in a jumble. "I hoped we'd get to know each other first, because this will be a shock. I thought if I explained everything, you'd let me keep the apartment, but more importantly, you deserve to know this."

"What are you on about?" Patricia's tone is outright hostile.

"Xander wanted me to come to lunch at Skipper Jack's that day. He wanted to introduce me to you all because we were planning to save up and sail around the world together. We would have had a family together."

"Even if that's true, why bother saying it?" asks Patricia. "None of it can happen now."

"That's the thing. Part of it *has* happened. I'm pregnant."

Silence.

Patricia is frozen in place, her eyes wide. She's clinging to the arm of the sofa.

"If this is a joke, it's in extremely poor taste," says Dickie.

"I wouldn't joke about something so serious." I clasp my hands together to stop them from trembling.

Lauren rushes to her mother's side and rubs her shoulder. "It's all right, Mum. Just breathe."

Patricia tries to speak, but only a croak comes out.

"You'd better be telling the truth, young lady," says Dickie. "You've upset my wife. Alexander was the apple of her eye."

"I'm sorry, Eve," says Lauren. "This is huge news. Please, go back to the apartment, and I'll phone you tomorrow. What's your cell number?"

"I don't have one. My phone fell in the sea, and I can't afford a new one." Damn, I might as well have said *I'm penniless trash.*

"I'll call you on the landline."

I look at Dickie, but he doesn't suggest I stay. Don't they want to know anything more? I'd prefer to leave on good terms, but Patricia looks as though she's about to have a stroke.

"I wish I could have found a better way to tell you." I stumble out of the house and along the driveway, my cheeks burning.

Surely this isn't as bad as it feels. They need time to process, time to realize I'm family now and that they're going to have a grandchild. When Lauren calls tomorrow, we'll patch things up.

Luckily the gates are open, because I've already walked through when I remember I wanted to ask where Xander was buried. The Blairs probably chose a cemetery near here. The Mazda's due back tomorrow, so tonight might be my only chance for a while to visit Xander's grave.

Patricia never gave me her number. Perhaps I can ask Lauren at the front door without disturbing Dickie and Patricia. I turn back toward the house. The dog pricks up his ears, but he doesn't bark. I'm almost at the door when I hear a voice through the open living-room window.

I can hardly believe it's Patricia. She sounds so different. There's no tremor in her voice, no grief. She's taking command of the room.

"Lauren, I know this girl's game," she declares. "She wants

to live rent-free in the apartment while we wait for this baby to make an appearance. Then, oh tragedy, she loses the baby. We won't be the least surprised—and we won't get our money back."

"What if she's telling the truth?" Lauren's voice is plaintive.

"I suspect the girl wouldn't lie about a pregnancy," says Dickie. "She might gain in the short term, but I reckon she's playing a longer game."

Patricia scoffs. "I've never seen such a skinny girl. She barely looks capable of carrying a child. How old is she, I wonder? Alexander and I were so close. If he were in love with this tramp, he'd have told me."

"Mum," Lauren says.

"My son was a responsible young man," Patricia continues. "He knew not to leave contraception to the woman. I don't believe it."

"Mum, Eve *is* pregnant. When she came through the gate, Buster jumped up on her. I saw from the window. She put both hands over her belly. I knew she was pregnant right away."

"Good acting," says Patricia.

"No, Mum. She didn't know I was looking. It was pure instinct."

"Suva's a party town," says Dickie. He has a weird way of talking as though he's carrying on a separate conversation from everybody else. "Who knows what she got up to there? Maybe the real father doesn't have much to offer, so she's trying her luck with us, seeing if grief makes us a soft touch."

"If it's not Xander's baby, we don't need to worry," says Lauren. "A DNA test will prove that."

"Not until after she's had months of free accommodation," says Dickie.

"Women are devious," says Patricia. "They'll prick holes in

condoms, pretend to take the pill. Are we responsible for a child conceived in these circumstances?"

Dickie answers, "Good point. Better not seek a DNA test. Not that we'd have any financial obligation to her or to *it*."

"The simplest thing would be for her to get an abortion," says Patricia. "You must tell her that, Dickie. Make our position clear. Alexander wouldn't have wanted this child, and an unwanted accident isn't our grandchild in any real sense. It would be different if it were Charlotte who'd made a little slipup and had to hurry the wedding. But this girl? We'd never met her, and she's not our type. Lauren, what does that scowl mean? You're not going to be sentimental about this?"

Lauren's going to speak up for me. I feel as though the small soul inside my belly leaps with hope. Aunty Lauren cares. *Yes, Mum and Dad, this is your grandchild. Eve is family now.*

Instead, Lauren says, "I told you that you should have told the police and that social worker that you knew who Eve was. The police asked you three times, and you lied through your teeth."

Her words flash through me like a bolt of lightning.

Lauren continues, "If you hadn't pretended not to have heard of Eve, we could have found a way to avoid her turning up out of the blue like this. It was so awkward having to play dumb."

I'm holding my breath. Everything the Blairs said to me wasn't what it seemed. That's why Patricia didn't want me in the house. Why Lauren and Dickie looked puzzled when Patricia told them I was in the car with Xander at the time of the accident.

She wasn't giving them news. She was filling them in on the lies she'd told me on the doorstep, getting them to play along. They *did* know I was in Xander's car, and they guessed that his bringing me to their lunch meant I was more than a crewmate.

I should have realized Patricia was a liar. I remember that phone call Xander made from Mexico. He told his mother he'd found a crewmate and would be continuing with the sailing plan despite Charlotte's departure. It seemed Patricia objected, because he said in a firm tone, "I can do what I like, Mum. I'm single." Yet Patricia has maintained the pretense that he was committed to Charlotte when he died.

"Nonsense, Lauren," Patricia says now. "Imagine if we'd had that little tart at the funeral, stealing all the sympathy with her sob story. She'd make Alexander look bad, too. Remember Charlotte's parents are donating a lot of money to establish a memorial scholarship in his name. If they hear about this baby, I'm sure they'll find some other use for their cash. Thank goodness Alexander didn't have money of his own, or this tramp would be after that, too."

I can't bear to hear another word. I creep away from the house. The dog barks furiously, but nobody comes after me.

CHAPTER 6

Back at the apartment, I crawl into bed. I might be able to shake off my awful encounter with the Blairs if it weren't for one thing. What if Xander did want Charlotte back?

Xander told me he loved me. He wanted us to sail around the world together. Xander wasn't the type to marry the boss's daughter and seek a corporate career. He was an adventurer, like me.

I close my eyes and let memories of our Pacific crossing fill my mind. Villages of laughing children, coral teeming with bright fish, electrical storms that set the sky ablaze. I feel as though Xander and I lived a lifetime together, but as I toss and turn in my lonely bed, one memory stands out.

It was a few days after leaving Tahiti. Xander and I weren't yet a couple. I felt something unfolding between us, but it was too new and tremulous to be given a name. The wind had been dying a slow death, and one morning, I woke to complete calm. The ocean was a mirror. The sky, dotted with clouds, was still as a photograph. *Joy* seemed to hover in midair.

We stood on the foredeck and watched as nature slept. And then out of the limpid water came the sound of someone breathing, and the yacht rocked as the surface was disturbed by an upswell. A black shape appeared.

"A humpback!" Xander's eyes were wide.

The dark hugeness beneath the surface resolved into a living creature. Only its blowhole was above water. Its breathing sounded so human.

Xander leapt below deck and emerged with a mask and snorkel, which he threw to me. "Jump!"

I gaped in disbelief. Xander had drilled into me the importance of never falling overboard. Now he was suggesting I hurl myself into the water? When an enormous wild animal was a few meters away?

"I'll make sure you get back on board," said Xander. "Do it now. You might never get another chance."

I felt as though I was in a dream. Pulling on the mask, I slipped, fully clothed, into the water. I didn't want to disturb the whale, so I floated in place, watching her.

The whale, however, had other ideas. If I would not approach, *she* would come to me. For one terrifying moment, I thought she meant to ram me. But with perfect precision, she turned at the last second, passing so close I could see the barnacles on her skin. In the blue water, she seemed as vast and dark as the night sky. Her single, massive, unearthly eye gazed at me and filled me with a sense of the unknowable mystery of her world.

I broke through the surface. *Joy* had drifted a short distance, and at once I felt how thin was the membrane between life and death. Without *Joy*, there was nothing around me, nothing beneath me, except miles of water. My breath came fast and shallow. I was an astronaut untethered from the spaceship.

I swam for the yacht as if racing for my life. Xander caught me in his arms and lifted me on deck.

"She looked right at me! She's beautiful! You have to do it, Xander." I handed him the mask.

Xander shook his head. "Look at the ocean."

Water that had been glassy a moment ago was transformed. A light breeze drifted across the sea, ruffling the surface. The orb of the reflected sun shattered into a thousand shards of sunlight, dancing gold amid the blue.

"The wind's come up," said Xander. "You've never practiced getting someone back on board. We can't risk it. I'm glad you had the chance." He grinned. "We'll just have to teach you the man-overboard drill and keep sailing till we next meet a whale on a perfectly still day. It'll probably only take another twenty years."

I wrapped my arms around him. "If you're serious, I'm keen."

"I've never been so serious." He kissed me, a deep, soulful kiss.

It was as obvious as the sea was blue that he loved me. So why am I having these doubts?

I'M UP AT first light, determined to clear out early so as not to risk another encounter with the Blairs. I'll simply leave my key on the dining table. If the Blairs don't have their own key, the doorman will let them in.

I'd better write them a note explaining that Xander's other key was in his pocket when he died. I don't want them to think I've kept it.

Looking around for a pen, I remember Xander going through his mail at the rolltop desk in the spare room that morning. Opening the desk, I brush aside a crumpled scrap of paper and catch sight of the words *Dear Charlotte*.

My heart almost stops.

I tear my eyes away from the page before I can read on.

That morning, Xander was writing to Charlotte. Why? He knew she would be at the lunch. Did he have something to say to her that he couldn't say in front of his family? In front of me?

Xander always wrote rough drafts of letters. Even a simple note to customs requesting clearance in or out of a Pacific nation he would scribble on scrap paper first. This must be a rough draft of a letter that was in his pocket that day. I saw he'd made several crossings out. And I remember him saying he planned to make his feelings clear to Charlotte at the lunch "without letting Mum interfere." I wondered at the time how he planned to do that. Giving Charlotte a note to read in private would have been the best way.

Everything inside me is screaming, *Read the letter!* But I shouldn't. It's not my business, and if it says what I'm afraid it says, I won't be able to bear it.

I force myself to return the letter to the desk and close the lid. I set about packing my things and cleaning the apartment, but I can't stop thinking about it. Twice I find myself with my hands on the rolltop, about to snatch it up and read.

What is the right thing to do? The letter isn't addressed to me, but if I leave it here, the next person to find it won't be Charlotte but the Blairs, and everything I learned about Patricia Blair last night suggests she'll read Xander's mail without hesitation. After all, she and *Alexander* were "so close."

Perhaps the best way to respect Xander's privacy would be to burn the letter . . . or do I owe it to Charlotte to give it to her? But how awkward that would be. I'd have to explain how I came to have access to Xander's belongings after he died. Charlotte doesn't even know Xander was in a relationship with me.

I clean the apartment from top to bottom, even pulling several long auburn hairs out of the shower drain. I don't want the Blairs to have any further reason to criticize me.

I place my key on the table and return to the spare room. I open the desk. The letter lies there like a piece of decaying food.

Without knowing what this letter says, I can't give it to Charlotte, I can't burn it, and I can't leave it here. I can't live the rest of my life not knowing how the father of my child felt about me when the answer might be in this letter.

"Forgive me, Xander," I whisper. I smooth out the paper and read.

Dear Charlotte,

It's awkward meeting like this in front of my family. ~~I wanted to message you but since you unfriended me I~~ Given that you're coming to lunch, maybe you're thinking we might get back together.

You're a wonderful person and I've always cared deeply for you

The words blur as tears well up. My temple throbs. This is my punishment for reading other people's letters. I stifle a sob. I know what it's going to say. He should have followed her home from Mexico, please will she take him back. Just say the word, and he'll break up with . . .

Stop reading. Stop, stop, stop.

I can't stop.

but I think we both know we were never in love, and on my Pacific crossing I realized I want to ~~spend~~ be with Eve. Eve and I are planning to sail around the world together and perhaps even get married one day. I want to. I'm not telling you this to hurt you but so you can move on. I know you'll find a better guy than me and be happier than we ever were. If you choose to leave don't want to stay for lunch after reading this I understand.

Xander

I can't move. The wild joy that should have me leaping around the room is negated by fresh grief. I've lost so much. If Xander hadn't died, he would have married me. We, together with our baby, would be a family.

Now I feel sorry for Charlotte. The pain I felt at the thought that Xander chose another woman—this will be her pain once she reads . . .

I can't give her this letter. It would be cruel. Nor can I keep it. It's not intended for me. I commit those sweet words to memory— *get married one day*—and burn the letter in the fireplace. I write my note to the Blairs, thanking them for the use of the apartment, and place it on the table beside the key. I sling on my travel backpack and open the front door.

Patricia Blair's words are playing on repeat in my head. *An unwanted accident isn't our grandchild.* I dart back to the table, grab the pen, and add one further sentence to my note *P.S. Last night I miscarried the baby.*

I pull the apartment door closed behind me before I have time to reconsider the lie.

CHAPTER 7

I step outside into the fresh morning air with an odd sense of satisfaction at the thought of never seeing the Blairs again. They will probably consider this all-too-conveniently-timed miscarriage to be proof I was lying about the pregnancy all along, but I don't care. My lie ensures they'll never come looking for their grandchild. Surely keeping Xander's child away from such toxic people is the best way to honor his memory. How he turned out to be such a wonderful guy is a mystery.

I have a couple hours until the Mazda is due back. I need to go to my old flat, collect my suitcase, and see if there's room for me to stay.

Rain begins to fall on my drive to the flat. As I knock on the door, it strikes me: *What if no one's home?*

I should have called ahead. In the year I lived in Sydney, my flatmates became friends, but I've been overseas for a long time. Yasmin from the hospital said the people at the flat didn't know me. Perhaps new people have moved in.

Sure enough, a stranger answers the door, a skinny guy in his late teens who emits a pungent smell of marijuana. I run through the names of my flatmates, but he blinks at me without recognition before launching into a meandering story about people cheating on each other and then scarpering, leaving rent unpaid and drug money owed. My hopes of moving back in melt away.

"Is my suitcase still in the crawl space?"

"Dunno. Look for yourself." He closes the door.

I retrieve my suitcase from the cobweb-ridden space under the house and drive back to central Sydney in torrential rain, tears streaming down my face. It seems as though everything falls apart. People cheat, people get hooked on drugs, friendships break up. People lose touch. People die.

Who can I ask for help? When I moved to New Zealand in my teens, settling in Napier where I'd lived as a baby, I lost touch with my Australian school friends. If I flew to Napier, I could maybe reconnect with friends there, but the flight's expensive, and the career opportunities aren't great. The friends I made in Mexico were only travel buddies—besides, who knows where they are now?

I've never put down roots. Now I need to create a stable world for my baby: find a flat and a job here in Sydney where the pay's good. But first, there's something I must do.

Downtown, having returned the Mazda, I find a pay phone and start phoning cemeteries. A few calls later, I've learned Xander is buried at Grayfriars Cemetery, an easy bus ride away. I wheel my suitcase along the footpath to the bus stop, my backpack weighing more heavily on my shoulders with each step. I'm carrying all my worldly goods. It would be sensible to find accommodation for tonight, but I can't wait any longer.

I have to be near Xander.

The bus drops me opposite the cemetery. The rain eases as I walk through the entrance, but fat raindrops from the trees overhead still land on my face. The smell of damp earth fills my nostrils. I descend into a gully where morning mist lingers.

This place is too quiet and gray for Xander. He never chose to come here yet is here for eternity. I hate the thought.

I soon find his grave. There's no headstone, but a white cross bears his name and the dates of his birth and death, only twenty-five years apart. The grave stands under the canopy of a jacaranda. Its purple blossom is a respite from the gloom.

I'm back with my love.

He's dead and buried. His spirit isn't here. He doesn't know I've come to visit him. Yet being close to what remains of him fills me with a strange and painful joy.

I drop my belongings and sink to my knees. The grass, strewn with windfallen petals, is wet, but I can't stop myself. I fall across the mound of soil.

"Xander, I can't believe you're gone. Part of me feels like I always knew you, but I also feel like we just met. We never got a chance to do what we wanted to do. I wanted more than anything to spend the rest of my life with you—to sail around the world together and to have a family. I would have married you, and not just because of the baby. I would have married you because you made me feel like I was home. You always felt right to me. You felt like family, the family I was meant to have."

I can't believe I'm pregnant. It feels wrong for a baby to be born after a parent has died, like a mistake in the laws of biology, an ugly cosmic joke.

"I'm sorry, Xander. I tried to save you, but it all happened too fast."

I roll onto my back and lie beside the grave. The jacaranda stretches its branches in a wide circle above me, its flowers vivid against the sky. The sun is peeking out from behind the clouds.

When I lay on the floor of the apartment, I would wait for the moment when the sun was centered in the rose window and lit up the room. For those few moments, I would be transported back to the blue ocean where Xander and I were happy. Now I let the dappled light dance across my closed eyelids. I press my palms against the earth.

A cool shadow passes across my face.

I open my eyes and nearly scream. An old woman is standing above me.

"I'm sorry." Her voice is husky. "I didn't mean to startle you, but you looked so sad. Tell me if I'm intruding, but I thought you might appreciate some company."

The woman looks like she's time-traveled from the 1930s. Her gray twill jacket matches her long skirt. A cameo is pinned at the neck of her blouse. Her hair is drawn into a schoolteacher-tight bun, and she's holding a black umbrella.

"I saw you get off the bus," she says. "Did you realize you walked in front of traffic? I was worried for you."

I glance at the entrance to the cemetery, visible in the distance. The bus stop is on the other side of a road I don't remember crossing.

"Did you follow me here?" I ask. "Or are you visiting a grave, too?"

She nods. "I know it's hard to believe, but one day you'll come here without feeling as sad as you do now. You learn to live with the pain."

"I'm sorry for your loss." I stand, brushing the soil from my clothes.

"It was a long time ago." She gestures toward Xander's grave. "Was he your husband, dear?"

"No. He's the father of my child." In a strange way, it feels good to say the words.

"Oh, you're so young. Your child must be just a wee babe."

"Actually the baby's not yet born. I'm pregnant."

The story comes pouring out of me. I tell her how wonderful Xander was. I tell her about his eyes as blue as the sky on a summer morning, about his mischievous sense of humor, about his floppy blond hair. I tell her about the accident.

"Is the baby a boy or a girl?" she asks.

"I don't know."

"You must have family who can help."

"I don't." The words sting. How naïve I was to think the Blairs could become my family.

"What about your friends and colleagues?"

"I don't have close friends here in Sydney." I don't want to say that I don't really have close friends anywhere. That would make me appear too pathetic. "I'm about to start looking for a job."

She glances at my belly. "That might be difficult in the circumstances. I presume you know unemployment is high."

I'm silent.

"Perhaps you could work in a day-care center and keep your child with you."

I shake my head.

"You wouldn't like caring for children?"

"Oh, I love kids. I babysat my neighbor's children regularly when I was in high school, but I'm not qualified to teach."

The stranger touches my arm. "My dear, you seem like a nice young woman who doesn't deserve what's happened to you. I'd like to help."

I study her features. Is she worth listening to, or have I just confided in the local crazy lady? Despite her age, she looks strong and agile. Her face is severe, but her words are kind. I feel pulled in two directions. I hesitate to accept a favor from a random passerby, but for my baby's sake, perhaps I should hear what she has to say.

"My name is Zelde Finch," she says. "I'm the private secretary of Christopher Hygate, the head of the Hygate family. They're a distinguished family who live on an island off the coast of Tasmania. I'm in Sydney to find a nanny for their child. I've tried several agencies, but I haven't had much luck. Because of the Hygates' wealth, it's a challenge to find a suitable girl." She pauses as if searching for the right words. "This might sound old-fashioned, but they don't want a nanny who is a social climber. The Hygates prefer employees who keep to themselves. Nowadays, with people plastering their lives all over the internet, we need to be careful. I sense you're not that sort of person."

"You're not suggesting I apply for the job? As I said, I'm not qualified."

"I've had a lot of experience hiring staff," she says, leaning on her umbrella, "and I no longer care about qualifications. I'm more interested in character—and I like yours. Babysitting is good experience."

"Surely nobody wants a pregnant nanny?"

"You might be surprised. It isn't very strenuous to look after one child. Many nannies these days are expected to be the housekeeper, too, but the Hygates keep a full staff including maids, gardeners, and a chef. They're old-style philanthropists who believe charity begins at home. They'll want to interview you themselves, but they'll have faith in my recommendation."

How should I answer? The Hygates sound intimidating. Plus, I expect once her wave of sympathy for me has passed, Zelde will make a more sensible choice, and I don't want to endure a job interview for nothing.

"Come and meet the family," she says. "It's worth the trip to see the beautiful estate. If the Hygates weren't so private, they could run guided tours."

Is she suggesting I would have the job until my baby's born? Her comment about the Hygates being open to hiring a pregnant nanny makes me wonder. Maybe they would want my baby to be a companion for their child.

Zelde hands me a business card imprinted with copperplate script. The address, Breaksea Island, sounds intriguing, but as I tell Zelde, I can't afford to fly to Tasmania.

"Mr. Hygate will cover your travel expenses." She shakes raindrops from her umbrella and turns to leave. "I should mention that the pay is excellent, and the accommodation, for which there is no charge, is lovely. But remember what I told you about privacy. If you want the job, it's important you not talk about it. Not to anyone."

And she's gone, disappearing into the mist as quietly as a ghost.

CHAPTER 8

Three days later, I step out of a plane onto the tarmac of Hobart Airport. The runway is surrounded by hills clad in dense green bush, and a biting wind sweeps away the last of the day's warmth as I hurry toward the terminal. I'm glad Christopher Hygate advised me to dress warmly.

At first, I didn't want to pursue this job. I didn't want charity, I wasn't sure about nannying, and I found it odd that I wasn't meant to tell anyone about the interview. I shoved the business card in my pocket, booked into a youth hostel in inner-city Sydney, and threw myself into looking for work. It would take a while to reestablish myself in the fashion industry, but any job, even low-paying seamstress work, would tide me over.

After a couple of days of hard luck, I'd almost forgotten Zelde Finch. At the laundromat, I discovered the business card in my pocket. As I waited for my clothes, I used the pay phone near the door and phoned the number on a whim. I half believed I was calling to turn the job down.

When Zelde put Christopher on the line, his deep voice was persuasive. His casual references to "our estate here on Breaksea Island" and "the vineyard" and "our yachts" suggested the Hygates were many times wealthier than the Blairs, yet he spoke as though I was his equal.

"I'm worried I'll waste your money, Mr. Hygate," I said when he started talking about arranging my flight. "I'm expecting a baby. I'm not sure how this would work."

"Call me Christopher," came the swift reply. "Zelde mentioned your condition. We want someone who truly understands being a mother. We trust Zelde's judgment. She says you have a certain gentleness that simply can't be taught. I believe my child needs that."

He sounded like an upstanding family man. Maybe I would enjoy a different line of work for a while. Dressmaking requires creativity and mental energy, neither of which I had much of at the moment. Nannying might distract me from my sorrow.

"I grew up with nannies myself," Christopher continued. "They were always leaving for various reasons. My parents didn't give enough consideration to their happiness. That's why we've arranged private living quarters—a beautiful home just for you. But I'm getting ahead of myself. We'll understand if you don't wish to accept the position. We only ask that you come and see for yourself. Come for the weekend so we have time to get to know each other. My wife, Julia, is eager to meet you. She was moved by your story."

Turning down the offer over the phone suddenly seemed rude.

"Can I ask how old your son or daughter is? Zelde said you've just got one child, but she didn't mention whether it's a boy or a girl."

"That's right, just the one," said Christopher, and then he put Zelde back on, and she booked me a flight for the next afternoon.

I still didn't have a phone, so as soon as my clothes were out of the dryer, I made a beeline for the library to research the Hygates. If there was any hint they were snobs like the Blairs, I'd cancel. I found newspaper articles that confirmed Christopher was an entrepreneur and shipping magnate who owned vineyards in Tasmania and Victoria. His company had won an award for social responsibility. Julia was on the boards of two charities: one for disadvantaged children, the other for endangered animals.

I found little about their personal lives, but that had to be a good thing. They didn't lead the kind of life that created fodder for gossip magazines. Anyway, when I arrived on the island, if I didn't like them, I could leave. Zelde had booked a return flight.

Now, outside the baggage claim, a man in a nautical uniform holds a sign with my name on it. He looks around thirty, but his weather-beaten skin suggests he's spent a lot of time at sea.

"Hi," I say. "I'm Eve Sylvester."

The man ignores my outstretched hand, instead reaching for my suitcase. He lifts it off its wheels, turns and hightails it out of the terminal. I scramble to keep up.

"What should I call you?" I ask.

He mutters something. I think I catch the name Joseph.

Joseph's uniform is pristine, but I glimpse tattoos at his cuffs and neckline. They look like prison tats. He leads me outside the terminal, casting furtive glances in every direction as though casing a joint. He gives off an air of having lived hard. He throws my luggage into the boot of a black sedan and asks, "You get seasick?"

"I'm not sure."

He scowls, like I'm an idiot for not knowing. I can hardly say *I thought I did, but it turned out I was pregnant.*

"Hop in the back," he says.

I climb in, and Joseph heads out of the airport at full throttle. We drive in silence, and I'm quickly lost in the scenery. The road cuts a path between rolling hills and an ocean inlet. In the dusky light, the water looks milky and soft. A sense of longing passes through me. Although I've never been to Tasmania before, I feel like I've come home. Everything in mainland Australia is bright and solid. The air here is soft, mysterious, inviting.

Being out in nature, about to catch a ferry to a remote island, makes me think of Xander, and for the first time, I feel something other than pure pain at his memory. I'm grateful for the time we had together. I hope the ocean will always remind me of him.

We pass through Hobart and continue south. We're in the middle of nowhere when Joseph swerves into an empty parking lot at the water's edge. A yacht bobs at the end of a pier—a pretty, old-fashioned sloop.

"This isn't the ferry terminal," I say.

"Ferry goes to the north of the island," is all the explanation Joseph offers. "Mr. Hygate wants *Torrent* brought home anyway."

Torrent is the name painted on the side of the yacht. An odd name. It feels like a bad omen, like an invitation to the gods to send a torrent of rain every time you set sail.

Joseph hurries me on board. "Tide's about to turn," he mutters.

Everything feels a lot more deserted than I expected when I agreed to come for this interview. I thought I would catch the ferry, a regular service carrying passengers to Breaksea Village, which would mean that if I didn't like the place, I could easily return to Hobart.

"Stay inside where you won't get in the way," Joseph says, pointing below deck.

I could say that I know how to sail and wouldn't be in his way, but I'm tired, so I climb down the ladder and settle in for the voyage. The cabin is cozy, about the same size as *Joy*'s, with neat blue-and-white furnishings.

Joseph steers *Torrent* out into the channel while I watch the sea and sky through a porthole. The circle of blue reminds me of the rose window in Xander's apartment, although it's tiny in comparison. As we emerge into open sea, however, and the light fades, *Torrent* begins to lurch sickeningly. The view through the porthole grows dark and is covered with foam and spray.

The ocean here is a different beast from the tropical Pacific or the temperate seas around Sydney. This ocean is cold and pitiless. As we roll and pitch through the chop, I catch sight of a light pulsing with a steady rhythm, a fixed point in a world of chaos, and my heart surges.

A lighthouse.

FOR MORE THAN an hour, *Torrent* motors toward the lighthouse, barely seeming to get closer. The rugged silhouette of an island comes into view, a darkness within a darkness.

Despite the heavy motion of the boat, I feel fine. I guess I'm past the nauseous phase of pregnancy. As the weather builds, waves break over the bow, and Joseph drops the chart into the cabin to keep it dry. He must know the way by heart.

I pick up the chart and study it by the light of my key ring flashlight. Breaksea Island, a few miles off the coast of Tasmania, is long and narrow, several miles north to south but barely a mile across. The only settlement is Breaksea Village at the northern end, but we're heading for the southern tip of the island. We'll sail right past Breaksea Light.

I'd like to go up on deck, but I don't want to bother Joseph. Through the porthole, I catch glimpses of the coastline as we round the southernmost point of the island. Under a fierce moon, sheer cliffs appear, standing staunch against a relentless onslaught of monster waves. I hope the engine doesn't fail. We're so close to land that I can see the great light revolving inside the tower, but no way could we swim to shore. If the ocean dumped us on those rocks, we'd be dashed to death.

Past the lighthouse, we turn and continue along the ironbound coast. Cliffs give way to beaches, but these are equally hostile to a yacht looking for a landing place. Open to the mighty Tasman Sea, they're pounded by constant surf.

A harbor comes into view. Between two headlands, a narrow opening leads to calm water. Joseph steers *Torrent* into the channel. At once, the boat stops being flung about by the sea. The moon disappears behind clouds, and we chug forward in darkness.

Joseph must know this harbor well. I can't see a thing.

A slight bump, and the boat is still. The engine cuts. I hear Joseph leaping about on deck, tying up.

I flick on my little flashlight again.

"Turn that off," barks Joseph, springing down the ladder. He grabs my flashlight, switches it off, and thrusts it in his pocket. "I'll look after this. Don't want it falling in the water. Follow me. I got your luggage. Keep your voice down till we get to the summerhouse. That's where you're staying."

I follow Joseph onto the pier. The night is silent. I have no idea where I am. Is this the part where Joseph takes me to his dungeon?

He leads me to land, and we walk along the beach, arriving at a two-story wooden house standing on the shoreline. Surrounded by blackwood trees, the dwelling looks like something out of a dark fairy tale. Joseph unlocks the door and ushers me inside and up a dim staircase.

At the top of the stairs, I flick a light switch, but no light comes on. Starlight creeps through the windows, revealing an airy room that opens onto a balcony overlooking the bay. I can make out a dining table, sofa, and bookcase. A screen divides the main area from an alcove. I glimpse a bed behind it, neatly made up.

"The light doesn't work," I say.

"Nobody's stayed here for ages. Need to get new bulbs. I'll bring 'em tomorrow."

"Don't you have any I can use tonight?"

"Need to get them from the village. I'd hit the hay if I were you. Go to the main house at eleven tomorrow." Joseph deposits my luggage on the floor.

"Where's the main house?"

"We walked right past it."

I couldn't see anything in the dark, but the house must stand above the beach Joseph led me along. I guess it will be easy to find in daylight.

"What about breakfast?"

"There's grub in the kitchen." He points at a door opposite the balcony. "Help yourself. The door beside it is the bathroom."

"Where are Mr. and Mrs. Hygate?"

Joseph is already heading downstairs. "All I was told is you're to stay in the summerhouse till eleven tomorrow. Reckon you'll meet them then. They're not here anyway. Were meant to be, but—"

The rest of his words are lost as the door shuts behind him.

I open the balcony door and step out. In the darkness below, I make out Joseph's figure retreating along the beach. A few minutes later, he must flick a switch somewhere at the marina, because the scene lights up like a Christmas wonderland.

The balcony, right on the waterfront, almost hovers above the bay. Along the beach, a brightly lit pier extends over the water. I can't see the "main house" or any buildings, because the black-wood trees come to the edge of the sand, but the marina itself is picturesque. Several yachts, held fast by thick ropes, bob and tilt in the night breeze, their movement setting reflected lights dancing in the water. The yachts, all white with a crimson flag at the masthead, exude a sense of energy at rest, like a flock of sleeping swans.

This is what Christopher meant by "our yachts." The Hygates must own a yacht charter business along with their vineyards. And I thought the Blairs were rich.

But something doesn't sit right. Why did I have to walk through the marina in darkness? Why did Joseph tell me to keep my voice down? Why wouldn't they have fixed the lights before I arrived?

I reach for my flashlight. Damn—I didn't get it back from Joseph. I fumble around for a lamp, but I can't find one. There also doesn't seem to be a phone.

Is my presence on this island a secret? There's a ferry service, but instead the Hygates had me collected by private yacht. Zelde told me not to tell anyone about this job interview.

My journey here seems designed to have left no clues. If I were never seen again, would anyone figure out where I'd gone?

CHAPTER 9

I wake to a metallic *clunk, clunk* coming from outside the summerhouse. The pink light of dawn steals through the windows. I throw the heavy quilt aside, pad across the room, and step onto the balcony.

The bay is laid out before me, gleaming in the early light. White sand curves around the water in a perfect arc. Protected from ocean swell, the water within the headlands is creamy blue.

Through the blackwoods I see a parking lot with room for five or six cars. A sign reads "Welcome to Paradise Bay." It's the perfect name.

Along the beach, beyond the trees, I glimpse a gigantic white building. Is that the Hygates' home?

Clunk, clunk. I turn toward the marina. Joseph is at the top of a mast, suspended in a bo'sun's chair, tinkering with a weathervane. He looks the picture of a diligent sailor. Perhaps I was just being paranoid last night.

Back inside the summerhouse, I admire the understated beachiness of the living area with its whitewashed walls and light timber furniture. Spying a door that I overlooked last night, I try the handle, but it's locked. The way the roof falls, I'm guessing a spacious, north-facing room lies behind that door. It's a pity I can't see inside it.

This house is so pretty, just the right size for a mother and child. Would the Hygates want me to continue as nanny after the birth and live here with my baby? Even if the job only lasts six months, with free accommodation and meals, I could save a decent sum of money.

Hours later, I've showered, eaten, tidied the kitchenette, tried the locked door again, and spent far too long choosing my outfit. I check my appearance in the mirror. I've selected a dress I made myself. I hope the cream linen is formal enough, while the Peter Pan collar makes me appear friendly and approachable. Usually, wearing my own designs helps me feel confident, but not today.

At quarter to eleven, I head downstairs, pass the storage area on the ground floor, and set off along the beach toward the house. As it comes into view, I draw in my breath.

The mansion looks as if it's fallen from heaven. A sandstone path leads from the beach to the entrance. One side of the lawn features three turquoise swimming pools landscaped to fit the slope, each spilling water into the next. Steam rises off them. The other side boasts an expanse of lush grass bordered by beds of exuberant pink flowers.

And the house. Three stories of white marble soar into the sky. Ornate pillars stand before the entrance, rising the full height of the building. Arched windows open onto the balconies, where more bright flowers have overflowed their pots and burst through the wrought-iron railings.

The Hygates' child might as well be a prince or princess. I'm not sure I'm posh enough to nanny this child. I'm picturing a youngster named Sebastian or Clarissa who eats caviar for breakfast while discussing stock prices with Papa.

My shoes clack on the terrace as I approach the door. Deep breaths. I ring the bell and wait a solid five minutes. I'm debating whether to ring again when the door opens.

"You're early." It's Zelde, dressed in gray twill again. She looks as forbidding as the first time I met her. "I suppose you'd better come in and wait in the pink room. The weather delayed Mr. and Mrs. Hygate's return to the island."

I step into a bright atrium. Sunlight streams in through skylights three stories above me and reflects off a huge chandelier. To one side, a vast room decorated in brilliant violet opens onto the lawn.

Zelde leads me up the staircase and along a hallway lined with as many paintings as an art gallery. "This is the north wing, where the bedrooms and living spaces are found. The south wing houses the servants."

I glimpse rooms with walls painted magenta, orange, green, their floors adorned with more Persian rugs. I try not to gape. I love bold colors, but it takes taste to use them without being garish—I know from some of my less successful dress designs.

I'm looking for clues about the family who live here, but there are none. The Hygates don't seem to hang family photos. The house is dazzling, but it feels impersonal, like a museum.

Zelde stops at a doorway. "Wait in here." She sweeps away.

I step into the room, then turn back. "Zelde! The child's name—I still don't know it."

She replies without turning around. "I'll let Mr. and Mrs. Hygate explain."

The Hygates really are private. They probably don't want me to know the name until I've accepted the job.

I'd better not be critical. I'd better not even *think* anything critical.

I go to the window. This room is at the back of the house, with no sea view, but what I do see makes my jaw drop. A drive leads up through the vineyard to the ridgeline. Rows of grapevines are awakening to spring, putting out new leaves in an innocent shade of green. A tennis court extends toward a circle of asphalt painted with an *H*. A helipad.

I sit on a chintz armchair, my head buzzing. Silence settles around me. Although Zelde mentioned live-in servants, I can't hear the faintest sound of them.

Half an hour goes by, and my nerves are affecting my bladder. Is there time to dash to the bathroom?

I step into the hallway. "Zelde?" I call. "Where's the bathroom, please?"

No answer. I guess I can find it myself. I creep along the hallway, looking into three or four wondrous rooms before I encounter the welcome sight of a bathroom, all gilt-edged black marble.

On my way back, I glimpse a room at the end of the hall. It looks like something from a dream. I prowl to the doorway.

The enormous room is bathed in sunshine. A rug as soft and golden as butter stretches toward corner windows with sweeping ocean views. Beside the sofa stands a stuffed giraffe taller than me, and in the center, crafted out of deep red jarrah wood, is a crib.

I stand motionless, drinking in the perfection. Everything a child could need is here: a toy chest, a rocking horse, a bookcase crammed with picture books. It's spacious enough for a whole orphanage.

No name decal graces the yellow walls, and nothing hints at

the baby's sex. Before I can stop myself, I've crept to the dresser and opened a drawer. It's exploding with frilly dresses.

A girl. I'll be nannying a little girl.

Now it hits me. I've blundered into somebody's bedroom and rummaged through her things. Sure, she's a baby, but that doesn't make snooping okay.

I push the drawer closed, but it jams on something. I open the drawer below to dislodge the item. This drawer is full of little blue shorts and T-shirts—boys' clothes.

Do they have twins? No, Zelde said there's only one child.

"What in blazes do you think you're doing!"

I spin round.

Zelde stands in the doorway, her face screwed up in fury. "How dare you! After the care I took to explain the need for privacy! After I offered you this opportunity out of pity!"

My cheeks are on fire. How could I be so stupid? "I'm sorry." I ram the drawers shut. I've blown everything. What a fool. I should have known this place was too lovely to ever form part of my life. "I guess there's no point having the interview. I'll repay the plane fare as soon as I can. I'm truly sorry."

"Sorry doesn't cut—"

A thrumming sound from above interrupts her. We both look up. It's so loud, I almost expect to be able to see it through the roof. A helicopter. The Hygates are arriving.

Zelde puts her hand to her head as though her hair is in danger of falling out from sheer outrage. She seems to be holding her breath. At last she says, "Eve, I accept your apology. This incident will stay between us, but be warned, you won't get another chance. Go back to the pink room and stay there. Do not speak a word of this."

"Thank you. That's so generous of—"

"Go."

I scuttle past Zelde to the pink room, where I sink back into the armchair. My heart pounds as fast and loud as the blades of the helicopter.

I'm an idiot. I was told privacy was essential to the Hygates, so I trampled over their privacy the minute I was left alone—just to find out something I was about to be told.

The sound of the helicopter grows to a roar. The craft appears in the window, close and huge, before dropping below my view. If I crept over, I could get a sneak preview of the family as they disembark, but I stay glued to my chair, as if I can make up for my earlier behavior by being obedient now.

Soon, Christopher and Julia Hygate swish into the room, cool and confident. Julia, whose blue cambric dress hugs her willowy figure, extends her hand. I feel like a child as I stand to greet her.

Her aqua eyes gaze into mine. "We're sorry for keeping you waiting, Eve," she says in a friendly tone. Auburn hair frames her heart-shaped face—her hair is as dark red as mine—and she has one of those mouths that turn up at the corners, making her appear to smile as she speaks. "Perhaps it's not a bad thing you've been introduced to the role weather plays in island life. Last night was too windy for the helicopter." She gestures at the cerulean sky outside the window. "Isn't it beautiful now?"

I shake her hand and turn to shake hands with Christopher. Tall and handsome, with ice-blue eyes, Christopher has a smile as warm as Julia's. His height and presence remind me of Xander, but while Xander's hair was golden, Christopher's is strawberry blond. Christopher is older, too. I'd guess a little over forty. He's an age Xander will never be.

"Gosh, there is a resemblance," he says. "Zelde wasn't wrong."

It takes me a beat to realize he isn't talking about himself and Xander. He's saying I resemble Julia. I almost laugh at this flattering claim. True, Julia's and my hair are the same rare shade of deep auburn, and we both have light-colored eyes and pale complexions, but Julia is gorgeous. I hope she doesn't mind her husband's comment.

All she says is, "I'm taller."

"Everyone's taller than me." I shrug.

They sit opposite me, and Christopher takes his wife's hand. I try not to stare at Julia's stunning dress. The scoop neckline and angled skirt are perfectly tailored.

"So, you're expecting a baby, Eve," says Christopher. "Zelde told us you're two or three months along and you don't know the baby's gender. Is the pregnancy going well?"

"Yes, thank you."

"I'm told you plan to put the baby up for adoption," he says.

What? Where did he get that idea? Tears spring into my eyes as the implications of his words sink in. That's why they don't mind hiring a pregnant nanny.

"I commend you for putting your child's needs first," Christopher continues. "Children need two parents."

Of course they don't want a nanny with a baby of her own. How stupid I've been. Zelde is clearly an old-fashioned woman. She must have thought it went without saying that an unmarried mother would choose adoption. I wipe away a tear.

Julia leans forward, and I catch the scent of jasmine perfume. "You don't want to?"

"No. My fiancé and I wanted this baby. At least, Xander would have wanted it, but he died before the pregnancy was confirmed."

Here I am at my job interview already lying. Xander wasn't my fiancé, but it feels embarrassing to say "boyfriend." I already feel judged.

I half expect the Hygates to show me the door at the news that I'm keeping my baby, but instead, Julia says, "Zelde told us about Xander. Christopher and I are sorry for your loss. We hope we can help—"

"Julia," Christopher interrupts. "Not yet." He turns to me with a searching gaze. "Zelde tells us you don't have any friends or family, and you haven't told anyone about your pregnancy."

A prickle runs down my spine. This interview is bizarre. Neither Zelde nor the Hygates have asked any of the usual questions. They're focused on my pregnancy.

"I've only told Xander's family."

Christopher and Julia exchange glances.

"I didn't realize that," says Julia. "What do they think of the situation?"

"They don't want anything to do with me, so I . . . I told them I miscarried."

Great. Not only have I lied to the Hygates, now I'm telling them about the lies I've told other people. I need to be more careful with what comes out of my mouth.

"Smart move," says Christopher. "I hear you're a dressmaker. Why did you choose that career?"

"I've always loved to sew. My nanna raised me, and we spent a lot of time making clothes together. She taught me everything I know."

"It sounds like you were very close," Julia says.

They ask a few more questions, which I manage to answer,

encouraged by Julia's smiles. Yes, I love kids. I've had plenty of babysitting experience.

"Do you have any questions?" Julia asks.

I feel as though I have a thousand questions. My mind whirs, and I blurt out, "Uh, why do you live here?" Oops, that sounded rude. "I mean, it's so remote. Do you have to travel for work?"

"Fair question," says Christopher. "Our vineyards are here, as you'll have seen, and I was lucky enough to buy this house for a good price when I was just getting started in the wine trade. Over the years, I've acquired vineyards in Victoria, but I've never wanted to move. I love the quiet, and I set up the marina as a second business, largely to indulge my sailing hobby—"

"And we think it's an ideal place to raise a family," Julia cuts in. "There's a lovely school in the village, and we want our children to enjoy the beautiful landscape. We travel to Hobart regularly for Chris's business meetings and my charity work, but it only takes twenty minutes in the chopper."

Christopher nods his agreement. "Talking with you has been a pleasure," he says. "Please excuse us. Julia and I need to speak in private." The couple rise and head for the door, still hand in hand.

As the door closes behind them, I overhear him say, "Her looks are just—"

Just what? Just too childish? I'll never know, but from his satisfied tone, I have a feeling he was about to say, *Her looks are just right.*

The room feels colder. Something's going on. Nobody knows where I am. The Hygates don't care about my lack of nanny experience. Zelde has flipped between friendliness and rabid disapproval, and then there's Joseph's secretive behavior.

Charmed by my opulent surroundings, I dismissed last night's worries, but now they all come flooding back. Sure, I wasn't locked in the summerhouse—but there was no need to lock me up. I'm on an island. There's a village somewhere, but I wouldn't know how to get there.

The door swings open, and Christopher and Julia saunter back in.

"Thank you for waiting," says Christopher.

I can't make a run for it. My best bet is to stay friendly and go along with whatever they say. One thing I'm sure of, though.

Christopher and Julia don't have a baby.

CHAPTER 10

I grip the arms of the chair. Half an hour ago, I was afraid I wouldn't get this job. Now I'm almost afraid I will.

Julia resumes her seat. Christopher shuts the door and paces the room. In his Aran sweater and jeans, he looks like a Nordic film star—maybe the kind who turns out to be the villain.

"Eve, I should explain that my wife and I have been unable to be candid about the role we'd like you to play in our lives."

I'm barely able to stop myself from bolting.

"Don't be alarmed," Christopher continues. "We have an unusual proposal for you, but it's your decision whether to accept. If you decline, you'll be returned home at our expense, and we'll pay you one thousand dollars for your time."

There must be no nannying job. I'm disappointed, but if he's telling the truth, a thousand dollars just to fly here and back will be the easiest money I've ever made.

"When can I go home?"

"Tomorrow," says Julia.

"Why not today?"

"Joseph isn't free till morning."

"What about the helicopter? Or the ferry?"

Julia looks at her husband.

Christopher says, "I can't fly you to Hobart Airport. It only takes one person to see you disembarking. And the ferry's out of the question. You'll understand once you've heard our proposal."

My skin prickles.

"There's no easy way to say this." Christopher sits beside Julia and eyeballs me. "My wife and I are happily married, with everything money can buy. Our lives are perfect except for one thing." He pauses. "Your meeting with Zelde was not by chance. We were given your name by a social worker whom we'd asked to find someone like you."

Yasmin. I knew something was off about that woman.

This is why Zelde didn't care about my qualifications. They weren't looking for a nanny.

It all falls into place.

"You can't have a baby," I say.

Christopher nods. "That's right."

Julia leans forward in her seat. "We want to adopt your child."

CHRISTOPHER IS TALKING about the "heartbreak" of infertility, but I'm not taking anything in.

They want my baby. They need secrecy. I'm here on this island alone.

How on earth did they get Yasmin to tell them about me? That must be against the law. And then they had Zelde pretend to meet me by chance? Did she follow me from Xander's apartment, or was she staking out his grave?

"We're prepared to pay a substantial sum for your services as the birth mother," says Christopher.

Whoa. They're jumping ahead. Are they assuming I'll hand over my baby as long as they offer enough cash?

Julia seems to read my expression. She interrupts her husband. "Please, Eve, give us a chance to explain."

"The proper way to adopt is through an agency," I say.

Christopher shakes his head. "Believe me, we'd love to adopt through official channels. Unfortunately, Julia's family places high value on lineage. They care about blood in the traditional sense. If Julia's family knew we had adopted, our baby would suffer a serious financial setback. We're forced to act secretly."

"What sort of setback?"

"Julia was born in Romania, where her family have owned the same estate for centuries. Julia's child is in line to inherit the land, but adopted children are excluded from succession."

"It's not really about the money." Julia's face flushes. "It's the injustice. Although I live here now, a piece of my heart's still in Romania. I can't bear to lose my childhood home."

I shift uncomfortably. "I don't want to put my baby up for adoption, but if I did, I'd choose an open adoption, the kind where the child stays in touch with the birth mother." I'm trying to keep my voice steady. "I can see my baby would have a privileged life with you, but I don't care about money. I just want my child to grow up in a happy home. I'm sure you'd provide that, but so can I. The idea of my child growing up not even knowing he or she was adopted—"

"We plan to tell the child." Julia's cheeks are scarlet now. "We'll explain everything when he turns eighteen. If, as an adult, he reveals the adoption to my relatives and is disinherited, that will be his free choice."

I feel like a farm animal valued for its fertility. "What if my baby doesn't look the part?"

"We've done our research," says Julia. "You told Zelde your fiancé's name, confirming Yasmin's suspicions that Alexander Blair was the father of your child. We know he was a tall, blond, blue-eyed man, a reasonable match for Chris. And you, obviously"—she points at my hair and then her own—"are a perfect match for me."

"I can't just hand my baby over and never see her again and trust that she'll be fine."

"You have all the power here, Eve," says Christopher. "If you don't approve of anything we do, you can claim your baby because he or she won't have been legally adopted. A DNA test will prove your parentage."

I turn toward the window and sink my head into my hands. So, I could pop in from time to time and gaze at my child from afar, trying to gauge whether she's happy? Who would agree to that? I knew this job was too good to be true.

"Please think it over," says Julia. "We would dearly love to be parents. We'd love your child as our own flesh and blood."

Julia's so friendly and openhearted. I wish I could say yes, but the thought of giving up my child . . .

"I don't need to think it over. I can't do it. I've already lost Xander. I can't bear to lose my baby."

To my amazement, Julia bursts out laughing. "Don't you see, Eve? We don't want you to miss out on watching your baby grow. We don't like the absoluteness of adoption either. We want you and the child to be a part of each other's lives. Zelde wasn't deceiving you when she offered you a job. We want you to be the child's nanny."

CHAPTER 11

I'm sprawled on the floor in the summerhouse when I hear a timid knock downstairs.

I've lain here all afternoon, hoping some idea would pop into my brain that would solve my money and childcare woes in one stroke. After I rejected the Hygates' offer this morning, they gave me one thousand dollars in cash, and Christopher escorted me back here. He offered to show me over the grounds, but I saw no point. No landscape, however idyllic, would change my mind.

As soon as he was out of sight, I leaned against the summerhouse door and whispered to my baby, "Your father's name was Xander Blair." I placed my hand on my belly. "Whatever happens, I promise you will know your father's name."

What they were suggesting was horrible. I would see my child every day, watch her grow, but never be able to tell the truth. *I gave birth to you. I'm your mother.* I was sorry to disappoint the Hygates, but I couldn't do it.

They had made a meticulous plan. I was to live in hiding in the summerhouse until my baby was born. Meanwhile, Julia would announce she was pregnant and start wearing a fake belly. Zelde, who's a midwife, is posing as Christopher's live-in secretary, but her real job would have been to monitor my health throughout the pregnancy and deliver my baby in secrecy here in the summerhouse—while Julia staged a fake home birth in the mansion.

Now I understand why Zelde gave me another chance when she caught me snooping. Finding a replacement for me won't be easy. The Hygates want birth parents who match their looks, and they can't exactly advertise. Julia explained that Yasmin is a trusted contact, but even though Yasmin's job involves regular encounters with pregnant women in difficult circumstances, I was the first she found whose baby could be expected to pass as Julia and Christopher's child.

"If you need emergency care during the birth, I'll airlift you to Hobart in the helicopter," Christopher said. "We wouldn't risk your health. We're not bad people."

That's the worst part. The Hygates aren't bad people, just desperate. They're clearly in love and yearning for a family, and although their secretive behavior was unnerving, it's understandable in retrospect. They handed over the thousand dollars without hesitation as soon as I made it clear I wasn't interested. Julia looked heartbroken. I was too stunned to take in the details of why they can't conceive, but it's obviously a hopeless case.

Another knock. I descend the stairs and open the door. Julia stands on the porch holding a platter covered with foil. She looks as though she's aged since this morning. The rosiness in her cheeks has gone. Rich as she is, I feel sorry for her. I've heard infertility can drive people crazy.

"Can we talk?" she asks. "I'm not here to try to persuade you, but I don't want us to part on bad terms."

"Of course." I lead her upstairs.

"I regret that we made you this offer." Julia places the food on the table and sits on the sofa. "I'm mortified."

I sit beside her. "I guess it was Christopher's idea."

"Not at all. This is why I wanted to talk to you. I didn't want you to leave with the wrong impression of my husband." Julia's height advantage is significant even when we're seated, but now she slouches. "I want you to know this is all my fault."

"It's nobody's fault. You're just doing your best to have a family."

"Men sometimes leave their wives." Julia stares at the wall. "Chris always looked forward to being a dad. He chose this house because it has seven bedrooms and island life is wonderful for children. He wanted to teach his son to sail and ride horses and to take over the business." She meets my gaze. "You'd think he'd blame me, but he never has."

"Isn't it old-fashioned to blame the woman?"

"It *is* my fault, Eve. Chris asked me not to ride that day. I thought he was being overcautious. I'd set my heart on it. The whole reason we went to Mongolia was to ride horses."

Christopher said something earlier about this trip to Mongolia, but I didn't catch the details.

"Why would Christopher not want you to ride a horse?"

"He was concerned I would endanger . . ." Julia buries her face in her hands. "I wasn't going to tell you."

The back of my neck prickles. "You were pregnant?"

She nods. "I lost my Angel."

This is why the Hygates have that beautiful nursery set up. I thought it was weird that they prepared it before they found a baby to adopt. All those clothes were meant for their lost child.

"I'm so sorry. Is there no chance of another pregnancy?"

Julia shakes her head. "The horse kicked me. The internal damage was terrible. I nearly died. In the weeks afterward, Chris saved my life in more ways than one. He insisted we could be happy, just the two of us, and at first, I thought so, too, but as time passed, the longing for a child . . ." Her breath catches.

"You don't need to explain. I'm not mad at you." In fact, I feel a pang of guilt. I faked a miscarriage to get the Blairs out of my life. I treated a life-changing tragedy as a convenient excuse.

"We talked about adoption. Chris was torn. He wanted me to have the chance to be a mother but knew how my family would react. Then I had the idea of a secret adoption. Chris told me it was nuts. He never gets angry, but he lost it that day, telling me what a scandal we would face if word got out. When you run a business as successful as ours, anything you do gets into the news. I said I'd drop the idea, but I was so depressed. I tried to hide what was upsetting me, but Chris can always tell what I'm thinking."

"Xander was like that, too. You're lucky to have that sort of relationship."

Julia pulls out an embroidered handkerchief and dabs her eyes. "You're right. I'm lucky. I have a husband who loves me enough to go along with my stupid ideas. Do you know I already bought the fake bellies? Three sizes. I certainly put the cart before the horse. I bought maternity clothes, and I found Zelde. She left midwifery a long time ago, and few people know about her training, so I thought she was perfect for the job, but she was appalled at my scheme. She's such an honest soul."

I guess this explains Zelde's disapproving looks. Maybe she's not as mean-spirited as I thought, just uncomfortable with what she's been asked to do. My attitude toward the thin-lipped woman undergoes another U-turn.

"You're talking as though it's over," I say. "Can't you find another pregnant woman?"

"I'm not putting Chris through this again. I was convinced you'd say yes. Who would say no to being paid to raise their own child? This summerhouse is so pretty, and we did it up specially . . . but when I saw the look on your face, I realized Chris had been right all along."

I wish Julia weren't such a nice person. She's been so candid and made herself so vulnerable. If anyone learned of their scheme, the Hygates could be blackmailed.

The light is fading. I unthinkingly flick a light switch, and to my surprise, it works.

"The light bulbs were missing last night," I comment.

Julia looks embarrassed. "I'm sorry about that. You see, we moved our live-in servants to the village hotel for a few months to make it easier for you to stay hidden here during your pregnancy. We told them we wanted more privacy. Our plan was, once they'd left each evening, you could go outside and get fresh air. We also gave everyone the weekend off, but Antoine, our chef, is such a perfectionist that he stayed behind last night tidying the kitchen. Joseph was concerned Antoine might notice lights in the summerhouse, so he took out the light bulbs."

"I take it Joseph's in on the secret?"

"God, no!" Julia flinches, and her jaw tightens. "It's vital Joseph not find out."

"What does Joseph think I'm doing here, then? What reason did you give him for keeping me hidden from the rest of the staff?"

"Joseph doesn't ask questions. It would have been impossible to conceal you from him because he sleeps at the marina. Someone has to keep an eye on the yachts overnight in case of bad weather. We considered relocating the yachts, but there isn't another suitable harbor on the island."

The Hygates have gone to so much effort. They've upended their lives to make their idea work. If only there were some other way for them to have a child.

"Have you considered using a surrogate?"

"I won't put my marriage under further strain. This is the end of it." Her voice breaks with emotion.

We're both silent. I can hear waves lapping the beach.

"Julia, the house in Romania, you said it was special to you, that it was your childhood home. So it's not about the value of the property?"

Julia steals a glance at me. Damn, I've made her hopeful. She raises her palms. "I won't lie. The land *is* valuable, but that's not why I want my child to inherit. It's about family and belonging. I can't bear him to be unfairly excluded. Some things are more important than money. I feel as though *you* understand that."

I shrug. My clash with the Blairs has left me doubtful there's any relationship between wealth and happiness. Regardless, the Hygates would be lovely parents. They're clearly devoted to each other, and anyone as desperate as Julia to be a mother would surely be great at the role.

Julia's problem is a mirror of my trouble with Xander's family. The Blairs judged me for being pregnant with Xander's child, while Julia's family will exclude her for not falling pregnant. The situations seem equally unfair.

"Perhaps I can reconsider," I say, "but I can't promise anything. I'll give you my final answer tomorrow."

Julia's face lights up. She moves to embrace me, then stops herself. "All right. I'll go." She stands and heads toward the stairs.

I call after her. "One more thing. How long would I stay on as nanny?"

"Stay as long as you want."

"I haven't said yes, remember."

She practically flies downstairs, and I hear the door close behind her.

I lift the foil off the platter. Poached fish, an exotic salad, a crème brûlée.

I can't bring myself to eat. That would somehow seal the deal. Instead, I climb into bed.

Sleep does not come. Dawn finds me wide awake. Only twenty-four hours ago, I awoke in this beautiful place and thought all I wanted was to raise my child here. In truth, my happiness required one other condition: my child must grow up knowing I'm her mother and Xander was her father.

Raising a child alone isn't going to be easy. I'll need to enroll her in day care soon after her birth. She won't grow up with luxuries, that's for sure. As for my migraines, I can't imagine how I'll manage when they hit.

She won't have a father.

As her nanny, I'd spend all day with my daughter. There'd be jobs to do, but there'd also be time to play. Every night she'd sleep in that beautiful nursery with its ocean view. As she grew older, she'd have music lessons and tennis coaching and as many pets as she wanted . . . She'd never have to worry about college tuition . . .

I roll over and plump my pillow for the hundredth time. It's useless to yearn for what can never be. I can't raise my child based on a lie. And I still feel uneasy about being brought here under false pretenses, although I suppose the Hygates didn't actually lie to me. There *is* a nannying position, and they never pretended to have a child. I assumed it. The red flags I saw last night—no light bulbs in the summerhouse, no servants in the mansion, the secretive journey with Joseph—they all make sense now.

I close my eyes and recall the journey here. *Torrent* looked easy to sail. If I could slip out to sea, I wouldn't have to make any decisions. I could travel across the ocean . . .

As early sunshine steals through the windows, I fall into an exhausted doze. I wake a short time later, but something changed while I was asleep. Everything fell into place.

The fish lies cold in its special sauce, but I don't stop to clean it up. I pull on jeans and leave the summerhouse.

I walk along the beach toward the marina, where *Torrent* is tied to the pier. The entrance to Paradise Bay gives promise of the ocean beyond. Gazing at the golden horizon, I imagine sailing toward the sun.

But the real golden life lies behind me.

I turn and walk to the mansion. If I searched for a thousand years, I couldn't find a more beautiful home for my child.

Julia answers my knock.

My voice is quiet but clear. "I get to name the baby."

CHAPTER 12

The brunch laid out beside the pool is a feast of pastries and tropical fruits. Christopher, Julia, and I sit between two open-fire braziers, basking in their warmth. The beach beyond sparkles as though someone has sprinkled diamonds on the sand. I feel as if a new world of luxury has opened up.

"You need to have an ultrasound right away," says Christopher. "Then we can put you on the payroll and cancel your flight back to Sydney."

"An ultrasound already? Why?" I stammer.

"Do you need to return to Sydney?" asks Julia.

"Not really." It feels like an embarrassing admission that I basically had no life there.

"Great. You can simply stay here if you like," says Christopher, loading fresh-cut pineapple onto his plate. He's looking more relaxed than yesterday, dressed in khaki pants and a white shirt. The sunshine brings out the strawberry tones of his hair—even his eyebrows and eyelashes are ginger. "That is, as long as the scan is satisfactory."

Julia notices my puzzled expression. "You said you weren't sure when the baby was due."

"A scan will pinpoint the due date," says Zelde, appearing from inside the house with a pot of coffee. "The sooner it's done, the more accurate."

"Do it straight after brunch, Zelde," says Christopher.

It feels odd being told to have a scan, but I'll have to get used to taking orders from the Hygates. I've agreed this is their baby, not mine. But why is Christopher in such a hurry to get this ultrasound? To determine the gender?

I've been meaning to ask Julia why the house in Romania will be inherited by Julia's child, not Julia herself. She said her family holds traditional values. Is it possible only a male can inherit? Once or twice, Julia has referred to the baby as "he."

I sip my passionfruit smoothie. Maybe the Hygates only want my child if it's a boy. When I met Zelde, the first question she asked was whether I knew the gender. Maybe it wasn't chitchat. Maybe she was pumping me for information.

I guess I'll know soon enough, if it's a girl and they call the deal off.

I reach for a hard-boiled egg and start peeling it. "Could you pass the salt, please, Zelde?"

She hands me a shaker.

"This is the pepper," I say.

"Hmpf . . . Pepper's better for pregnant women. Too much salt can cause high blood pressure."

"Right. Thanks." I reluctantly sprinkle pepper on my egg. I hope Zelde's not going to be obsessive about my diet. Then again, it did seem she gave me the pepper by accident.

I've barely finished eating when Zelde stands and says, "Come on, Eve, let's get the scan over with."

We head for the summerhouse.

"Do you want Mr. and Mrs. Hygate to attend the scan?" she asks as we walk.

I can't stop myself from grimacing. The thought of sharing

my first glimpse of my baby with Christopher and Julia is un-settling. What if they want to attend the birth? That would be awkward.

I should have thought more carefully about my stipulations. I only asked for the right to choose the name. I felt Julia and I had built a rapport and would be able talk through any issues, but what if we can't agree?

"They haven't asked to come," Zelde adds.

"Do we have to do this today?"

She gives me a sharp look. "Mr. and Mrs. Hygate are very trusting, but they're entitled to proof you're carrying a viable fetus. Besides, an inquiring mind such as yours must have won-dered about this room."

We're now in the summerhouse, and she strides to the locked door and pushes a key into the keyhole.

"Get ready. This is something you don't see every day." She opens the door.

My eyes widen. The room is crammed with medical equip-ment. It's a state-of-the-art birthing suite complete with a medi-cal bed.

"No expense has been spared to ensure a safe and comfortable birth," says Zelde.

The Hygates have spent so much money. Fair enough they want me to have a scan, but are they purely checking the baby is alive?

I enter the room, which is bathed in dappled sunlight from the trees growing outside the bay window. I climb onto the bed, Zelde fumbles for the switch, and a monitor flashes to life. Zelde applies gel to my belly and holds a probe against my skin. A small, dark shape appears on the monitor. It pulses rapidly.

Her beating heart.

I didn't truly believe in her till now.

Don't think about Xander. The world blurs.

"Do you see that?" asks Zelde.

"I can't see anything," I try to keep my voice steady.

Zelde hands me a tissue. "You can listen." She presses a button, and a whooshing sound fills the room.

"Is that her heartbeat? It's so fast."

"That's normal."

I dry my eyes, and the screen comes back into focus. My baby, swimming in blackness, is the most beautiful thing I've ever seen.

Zelde sets aside the probe, wipes the gel with a paper towel, and palpates my belly. She holds a tape measure against my skin, her head tilted. "You're eleven weeks pregnant."

"Did the machine figure that out or did you?"

"The machine, of course, but I like to confirm the dates the old-fashioned way. You're due the twenty-fifth of April, Anzac Day. Everything appears to be progressing normally."

Six and a half months away. "She'll be an autumn baby," I say.

"She or he—too early to tell, more's the pity."

"Why is it a pity?"

Zelde shakes her head. "No reason. We'll be able to tell by December. We'll scan you again then. Why don't you go and tell Mr. and Mrs. Hygate the due date? I'll tidy up here."

I walk back to the house. Christopher and Julia are still sitting by the pool.

"Boy or girl?" asks Christopher.

"Zelde couldn't tell."

"When's the due date?" asks Julia.

"April twenty-fifth."

Julia leaps up with a cry of delight. "Perfect! I can't wait! Eve, I can never thank you enough. Let's celebrate!"

"I'm not sure how," says Christopher. "We can't pop champagne or smoke cigars, and we already ate. Perhaps we can show you around the house, Eve?"

I agree, and we set off on a tour.

As we enter the house, Christopher pauses to embrace Julia, and I see she's trembling. That's odd. I'm surprised the due date matters so much to her.

The house is even bigger than I thought. There are rooms I had no idea people needed: a library, a home theater, a music room—although neither Christopher nor Julia plays an instrument. Our voices echo in the unnatural quiet. I feel the sorrow of the large family this couple wanted, which will never be. I'm glad they won't be childless.

Zelde interrupts our tour to report that she's canceled my flight and has some paperwork to go through. She leads us to an office on the middle floor, where we set up automatic payments of my "salary." I can't believe I'm being paid so much simply to stay out of sight. When we're done, Christopher and Julia shake my hand.

"Welcome to Paradise Bay," says Christopher. "Would you like us to show you around the grounds?"

"I'd like to take a walk on my own if that's all right."

"Of course," says Christopher. "Just make sure you stay on our land. Remember, at seven tomorrow morning, the staff arrive, and they leave each evening at seven. Always check whether the minivan is still here before you go outside. You'll be able to see it through the summerhouse window."

Soon after, I'm scrambling up a disused bush track toward the southern tip of Breaksea Island. It feels stupid to seek out solitude when I'm about to begin months in hiding, but this is my only opportunity to explore the island in daylight.

Christopher gave me a map, which shows a single road leading to Breaksea Village, three or four miles to the north. I feel reassured knowing how to find my way back to civilization. Christopher and Julia seem trustworthy enough—a little eccentric, but harmless—but I still get a weird feeling about Joseph.

South of the road, everything is Hygate land. Julia mentioned that a headstone has been placed at Lighthouse Rock in memory of her lost baby, Angel, but I'm not planning to look at the grave. I'm heading for the lighthouse.

I grew to love lighthouses when Xander and I were crossing the Pacific. He taught me never to rely solely on GPS navigation. Xander could measure the sun, moon, and stars with his sextant to ensure we were in safe waters, and whenever we drew close to land, he would look out for lighthouses.

"Each light is unique," he told me one night, his voice warm with enthusiasm, as we sailed toward a lighthouse that marked landfall in Samoa. He flicked on the cockpit light, and his blond hair flopped over his face as he bent over the chart. "See, this light flashes twice every eight seconds, so you can be certain which light it is."

Xander tried to teach me how to calculate our distance from the light when it first appeared, based on the curvature of the earth, but I was too happy to concentrate.

"I wish I could thank the people who built all the lighthouses," I said. "It must have been backbreaking work to build them in such remote places. And people moved to the ends of the earth to keep the lights burning. All to keep us safe."

Xander wrapped an arm around me, drawing me near. "The lighthouses in Oceania aren't manned anymore, but the work of those builders still saves the lives of people who were born long after they died. Humans are awesome."

He promised to take me to visit a lighthouse, but the whole way across the Pacific, we never managed to. Lighthouses were always built on dangerous parts of a coastline—that was their point. It wasn't practical to approach them in a yacht.

Now I emerge from the bush onto a windswept bluff with ocean on either side. The sunny calm of the morning didn't last; the ocean is as tumultuous as on my journey here. Trees don't grow on these blustery cliffs, but some tough shrubs and grasses are clinging to life. Sea and sky are grim, and seabirds circle in search of prey. Ahead of me, standing stalwart against the elements, is the thing I came to find. The red-and-white-striped tower of Breaksea Light.

I want to touch it, and as I clamber down a rocky bank, it seems only an arm's length away, but I'm not going to get what I want. A narrow ravine separates me from my goal. The lighthouse stands on its own rocky islet, as high and steep as Breaksea. Impossible to reach.

I should have realized Lighthouse Rock was a separate landmass. I suppose that's why Julia and Christopher placed Angel's grave there. They certainly are private about their loss.

Turning to leave, I notice a flash of pink and green amid the ferns on Lighthouse Rock. A lizard bright as a jewel scuttles across open ground and disappears into foliage. As I walk back toward the summerhouse to begin my voluntary imprisonment, I almost wonder if I dreamed the creature. To be safe, to know my baby's future is safe, feels like a dream. I only hope that the picture the Hygates painted of my future on this island turns out to be accurate. Something about their offer feels too good to be true.

CHAPTER 13

Being paid to do nothing is harder than I expected. The late spring weather is idyllic, but each day is an eternity of clock-watching and gazing at the blue sky through the window, waiting for the minivan to leave so I can get outside before darkness falls.

I would have thought my time on *Joy* would have prepared me for living in confined quarters, but the situations are very different. At sea, I could always go up on deck for fresh air, and I had a sense of being in a new place every day, even if it was merely another stretch of blue ocean. There was plenty to do on a yacht, from trimming sails to cooking meals, and I had Xander's company. Now I'm stuck inside during the day, twiddling my thumbs, and I am alone. Perhaps I should be pleased I can get my rest, since pregnancy has made me unusually tired, but with Zelde bringing my meals early in the morning and taking away my dishes at night, there's barely anything to do. I go to bed early, I sleep in till late morning, and I clean meticulously every day, but I'm still bored out of my brain.

One evening about three weeks after my arrival, I meet Julia strolling along the beach. The setting sun is bright as a peach, and sea and sand glow with iridescent light.

"You look happy," Julia remarks. "It's a pity you'll have to stop these walks soon. We can't risk Joseph seeing you once you're showing."

The thought of not being allowed outside anymore is too much. "It's a shame you've moved all your other servants off the estate every night, but you can't move Joseph. If only someone you trusted were running the marina, I'd be able to carry on getting fresh air and exercise right up to the birth."

Julia's face turns to stone. "Absolutely not. We cannot replace Joseph, and confiding in him is out of the question. Please never mention this topic again."

She changes the subject, but as we continue along the high-tide line, I struggle to pay attention. The look in her eyes and her abrupt tone have left me wondering. Is she frightened of Joseph? If so, why do she and Christopher keep him around?

"I can't carry on like this," I blurt out. "I have no books to read, nothing to sew. I have no phone, and there's no Wi-Fi anyway. I'm already climbing the walls in that summerhouse, and I'm barely fourteen weeks along—"

I stop. I've said more than I intended to. I *am* finding it a trial to be stuck indoors, but of course I can carry on. I've found a way to give my baby an amazing life. I can handle a little boredom.

Julia stops walking and nods thoughtfully. "I'm sure we can figure something out. I'll talk to Christopher. He's in Melbourne, but I'll phone him. Leave it to me."

I don't hold much hope that Julia will solve my problem, but at six o'clock the next morning, Zelde raps on the summerhouse door and tells me to get dressed and jump aboard *Torrent*.

"Joseph's taking you to Hobart for the day." Zelde's terse tone suggests she has heard about my complaints and thinks I'm a brat. "He's going to take you twice a week until you start to show—which might not be far away, so you'd better make the most of it. Remember not to mention your pregnancy to him. He'll drive you wherever you choose to go in Tasmania. You need to be on board before the minivan arrives. You'll stay away until after it leaves this evening. Don't overtire yourself."

I'm dressed and on board *Torrent* in no time, and before long, Joseph and I dock at the pier in Tasmania. I make the most of my day of freedom. I eat a slap-up breakfast in a city café, take a scenic walk in the hills above Hobart, and go on a whirlwind shopping spree at the bookstore. I can't shop for maternity clothes with Joseph lurking nearby, but I buy a couple of new bras to fit my larger cup size. Finally, I visit a sewing shop and purchase fabric, yarn, and a brand-new machine, which the shopkeeper, a chatty middle-aged woman, offers to carry to the car.

"Thank you." I point through the window at the car the Hygates keep in Hobart, which is parked across the street. Joseph stands beside it smoking a cigarette. "It's the black sedan."

The shopkeeper picks up the machine, I grab my shopping bags, and we leave the shop. We're halfway across the road, pausing for traffic, when she says, "When are you due?"

I almost drop my bags. When am I *due*? Holy crap. How does she know? Am I showing? I checked in the mirror this morning, and there was no bump. Perhaps people can tell I'm pregnant from my complexion. Don't they say pregnant women bloom?

"I don't . . . I'm not . . ."

My head swivels toward Joseph. Did he hear her? He's opening the trunk, having spotted us coming. The traffic has cleared, and it's ridiculous to stop the woman taking the last few steps to the car, but I can't risk continuing this conversation.

"I can manage from here." Hooking my bags onto my arms, I wrestle the sewing machine from her. "I saw another customer arrive. You'd better get back to your shop."

What a ridiculous excuse. The shop's behind us. I'm pretending to have eyes in the back of my head. I leave the shopkeeper looking flummoxed in the middle of the road and hurry to the car, sucking in my belly like crazy.

I glance inside my bags as Joseph takes the sewing machine and puts it in the trunk. The pajama print fabric with yellow ducks is a dead giveaway. Worse, the spines of the books are visible, including one entitled *Pregnancy the Natural Way*. The shopkeeper must have glimpsed inside my bags.

Joseph's hand closes over the bag handles.

"No!" I snatch them away. "I'll keep these with me." I scramble into the back seat.

Joseph stubs out his cigarette, sinks behind the steering wheel, and drives off.

Thank goodness I stopped him from spotting my purchases. But what if that shopkeeper happens to cross paths with him and mentions my pregnancy? After the way Julia spoke on the beach, it seems Joseph finding out would be disastrous.

I take a deep breath. I need to chill. The chances of that shopkeeper speaking to Joseph are a million to one. All the same, I wish the Hygates weren't using someone they distrust to transport me around.

IN THE EVENING, Julia brings my dinner.

"Is Zelde having the night off?" I ask when I open the door.

"No, but I wanted to talk to you. Shall we eat together? Chris is still in Melbourne, and I felt like company. Being alone with Zelde can be peculiar."

When I moved in, I thought I'd dine at the mansion each evening after the minivan departed, but it hasn't worked out that way. Christopher and Julia eat before the staff leave so they can be served at the table. This is the first time Julia has suggested we eat together.

I clear some space on the table, which is covered with my new baby fabrics, and we tuck into cottage pie.

Julia picks up a little pink dress that I've started cutting out. "This is lovely. Can I see the pattern?"

"I don't use patterns. I prefer creating my own designs."

"Amazing! Does it bother you that this dress will go to waste if you have a boy?"

"It's a girl," I say.

"How do you know? Have you had another scan?" Julia's head turns sharply toward the birthing suite as though she thinks I've been sneaking in there.

"Of course not, Mrs. Hygate."

"Julia," she smilingly corrects me.

"Sorry—*Julia*. I wouldn't have a scan without telling you."

"So, it's just a hunch?"

I take a mouthful of pie while I think. I need this baby to be a girl. It can't be a boy. I miss Xander so much. I won't cope if my child is a constant reminder of him. "She'll be a girl with auburn hair and green eyes like me. The hair will be a perfect match, and the eyes will be close enough. Green is close to your aqua eyes. But people might wonder how you and Christopher had such a short kid. Do you think Christopher's hoping for a boy?"

"Darling, Chris just wants a baby." Julia smiles her winning smile. "We'll love your daughter no matter what. We don't mind if she's petite, but we do know your fiancé was tall."

I nod. "He was. Let's hope tall DNA is dominant over short DNA. Speaking of body types, do you think I'm showing? I was worried today in Hobart." I stand and press my skirt against my belly.

"Eve, your tummy's so flat you could moonlight as a bikini model." Julia's eyes twinkle. Her face has regained its happy flush since I agreed to the adoption. "But did you notice I'm wearing the first fake belly? I put it on this morning. We're thinking we'll announce the pregnancy soon, and it would be good if I seem to have gained a few kilos."

Julia stands and twirls. She's wearing a white high-waisted dress with a full skirt that flares as she turns. She could be hiding an elephant beneath it for all anyone would know.

"I didn't notice," I say as she sits back down.

"This belly's too small, isn't it? The next size up is huge. I wish I had a size in between."

"I'm sure it'll be okay. Pregnant women do seem to pop out all of a sudden, don't they?"

Julia doesn't seem to be listening. She chews slowly, gazing at her food.

"Is everything okay?" I ask.

Julia screws up her face. "Not really. I have bad news. Apparently, people suspect someone's hiding in the summerhouse."

"What?" My stomach lurches. "Who? How?"

"My maid, Sarah, left her handbag at the house and drove back to fetch it one evening. She saw lights on. Also, Antoine's commented that we're going through a lot of food. I blamed it on Zelde. I told him she has the appetite of a horse and is fond of midnight feasts. Worst of all, a couple of vineyard workers were on leave in Hobart today. As luck would have it, they were driving along the coastal road when you and Joseph were boarding

Torrent for the sail home. They've been teasing Joseph about his new lady friend."

The atmosphere in the room has thickened. Julia's being nice about it, but this is a problem. If people get the idea that someone's hiding here, some nosy parker is bound to sneak up and spy on me through the windows. If that happens when my bump is showing, it'll be the gossip of the century: a pregnant woman lurking in the summerhouse at the very time Mrs. Hygate announces her pregnancy. That would spark anyone's curiosity.

I was desperate for some freedom, but at what cost? If anyone guesses what's going on, Julia and Christopher will have no option but to pull the plug. This opportunity will be lost forever. I'll never find another chance like this again. I'm so stupid. For the sake of a silly shopping trip I've jeopardized . . .

I drop my fork. It's too bright in here. I place one hand over my eyes, but the light doesn't diminish. It grows brighter. Black-and-white lines zigzag across my vision. A golden orb flashes before my eyes.

An aura. I'm getting a migraine.

What a time for it. This whole thing has turned to crap. I'm going to have to leave and raise my baby alone, and my migraines are coming back.

Best face up to it. Before I know it, I've crossed the room and grabbed my suitcase. I drop it on the bed and open it.

"What are you doing, Eve?" cries Julia. "Wait, are you giving up already?"

I'm scared to speak. When I get migraines, sometimes the wrong words come out. I'll call a toothbrush a pen or say *happy birthday* instead of *hello*.

I haven't told Julia about my migraines. Now feels like a bad time to mention them.

If I take codeine as soon as the aura appears, sometimes the headache never arrives.

"Bathroom," I stammer. I make a beeline for the bathroom. Locking the door, I fish my codeine out of the cupboard and swallow two pills with water from the tap.

I close my eyes and rest my head against the mirror. The golden orb is bright as the sun.

"Are you okay in there?" comes Julia's voice.

Need to tell her I overdid it today. "Just tired. Need sleep." Should I have taken codeine when pregnant? Probably not.

"You've had a long day. I'll come back tomorrow. You rest."

Retreating footsteps. The door thuds shut downstairs. I emerge from the bathroom. Why the heck did I get my suitcase out? I'm so impulsive when I have a migraine. I shove the suitcase on the floor and lie down.

Throughout the night, I drift between wakeful agony and the bliss of sleep, but I daren't take any more codeine.

How my feelings have changed. I can hardly believe I was reluctant to let the Hygates adopt my child. I've got used to having a secure future, knowing I'll watch my daughter grow up with every privilege. If I had any hope I could manage on my own, this migraine has killed it. This adoption needs to happen.

CHAPTER 14

The next morning the migraine has gone. I spend the day desperate to talk to Julia about the problems she raised yesterday, but she doesn't come back until evening.

"Are you feeling better?" she asks, handing me a bowl of Caesar salad.

"Much, thank you." I sit down to eat at the table.

"Great. Listen, fantastic news." Julia walks to the balcony doorway and stands in a shaft of rosy sunlight. "I phoned Chris, and he came up with a brilliant plan. My grandmother's visiting for the weekend, and we know she'd love to be first to hear the news of my pregnancy. We're having a party on Saturday night. It won't be a huge affair, but Granny Meg likes things done a certain way. She's a real lady, the matriarch of the family. I'd like you to meet her."

I sit up straight. "Are you joking? Didn't you say your family can't find out about the adoption?"

"That's why we need a cover story. It's too late to pretend nobody's living here. We need to change tack. Chris decided to tell everyone you're a cousin. You've been living in seclusion because you're on a meditation retreat."

"Your grandmother will know I'm not your cousin."

"You'll be a cousin on Chris's side. I know you resemble me more than Chris, but you're right that Granny would know you're not my relative. She knows the family tree for practically the last millennium. We'll tell her we prefer to have a family member looking after our baby rather than a stranger, so we hired you. After you meet Granny, you 'leave' the island." Julia does air quotes. "We tell everyone you'll return when my baby's born. After we've staged your departure, we'll have to be more careful about keeping you hidden. No more trips to Hobart, obviously."

Living in hiding is turning out to be so complicated. "What about the extra food the chef noticed? And how do I avoid switching on lights in the evenings?"

"We'll think of something."

"Julia, you're no good at subterfuge."

She laughs. "I know! Luckily, Chris is savvier. He's writing up a family history for you, *Eve Hygate*. He's thought of everything. It was his idea for you to meet Granny. Once you've been introduced to her as family, it won't cross anyone's mind that you're not. You must make sure you call me Julia, never Mrs. Hygate, and say Chris, not Christopher."

I'm not at all sure about this development. I thought the Hygates had a meticulous plan. Now they want to make things up on the fly. What other problems have they overlooked?

I push my Caesar salad around the bowl, frowning. "Have you pretended to have morning sickness? Your maid would notice that sort of thing."

Julia waves her hand airily. "I've been turning down breakfast since your arrival. Come to the house, and I'll show you my preparations." She closes the balcony door and walks to the staircase. "Your meditation retreat is over. You need to hang out at the house, be casual, eat with us. Don't be too polite, remember. Act like you've known us for years."

Julia hasn't convinced me that meeting her grandmother is a good idea, but with my cabin fever, the invitation is too good to resist. We head outside. The minivan is in the car park.

"The servants are still here," I say. "I guess we're committed to this new plan. Will you introduce me as Eve Hygate?"

"Staff don't expect to be introduced to guests. Zelde will let them know a cousin has come to stay."

We enter the atrium just as three maids in black-and-white uniforms are leaving. They mumble, "Good night, ma'am," and Julia nods. She springs up the staircase and along the hall to the nursery. We step inside, and Julia closes the door.

I drink in the golden perfection of the room my child will grow up in—the tall windows with their sea views, the butterscotch rug, the towering giraffe.

"I keep the bellies in a secret drawer," Julia says, leaning into the wardrobe. A timber panel pops out, revealing a drawer. Julia fishes out a flesh-colored garment. "I'm wearing the smallest belly. Here's the next size up."

She hands me the garment. The skin-colored mound is held in place by sheer straps that fit around the wearer's back. I almost snatch my hand away from the flesh-like substance.

"It feels like skin," I say. "Very convincing."

"It's silicone, with no seams that could show through clothing. I was so relieved when these arrived. I ordered them from the UK. They're marketed as theater props, but the sellers must know there's a shady side to their business." She hangs her head. "I feel ashamed deceiving everybody. It's a relief to confide in you. Chris doesn't really understand, you know? I mean, he's on board with the plan, but he treats the bellies as a bit of a joke. *He* doesn't have to wear them."

A thrumming sound interrupts her. The helicopter.

"That's him now," says Julia.

"I should go back to the summerhouse." I hand Julia the belly.

"Chris will want to see you. Stay and have a glass of wine."

"I can't have wine."

"Of course not. How stupid of me."

You shouldn't either, I want to add. Doesn't Julia think about the servants finding used wineglasses?

"Is this room the safest place to keep the bellies?" I ask.

"Ever since my miscarriage, I've kept this room locked."

"The door was wide open the day of my interview. Also, I hope you're being discreet about sanitary products. You can't be seen buying tampons when you're meant to be pregnant, and you need to dispose of them carefully. The way you offered me wine just now, it seems you're still drinking yourself."

Julia is silent as I list the ways she's messed up. I can't believe I'm daring to speak this way, but her carelessness is endangering the plan.

"You're meant to avoid a whole bunch of foods during pregnancy." My voice rises. "Not to mention the way you leapt up the staircase just now in front of three maids. You don't seem to realize your staff have eyes. *They're* the people you need to worry about, not your grandmother. They'll have guessed your pregnancy is fake before you've even announced it!"

Silence hangs in the air. I've gone too far, said too much.

Julia bursts into hysterical tears—just as the door is flung open behind me.

CHAPTER 15

Christopher fills the doorway, dressed in his leather pilot's jacket and canvas pants. He takes one look at his weeping wife and demands, "What's going on?"

"Everything's a mess," sobs Julia.

Christopher steps inside and locks the door. As Julia lists the issues I've raised, I squirm. I sound like such a troublemaker.

"This is a serious problem." Chris gestures at me. Is he saying I'm the problem?

"I don't know whether we can fix this," I say, "but I have some ideas."

"Good, because you've hit on something." Christopher's gaze returns to Julia. "Nobody tells the boss the truth. That means you and I have no idea what people think of us. We fire rude employees, so only the bootlickers are left." He folds his arms and leans against the wall. "We've lost touch. Our staff would never dream of telling you not to drink when you're pregnant, so we forget that they notice these details. If things don't add up, tongues will wag."

"Chris, I must have had one glass of wine in the past month—"

"That's one too many," says Christopher.

Julia shakes her head. "This is much more difficult than I anticipated."

Christopher crosses the room and takes me by the shoulder. "Tell us what you have to say, Eve."

He has a firm grip, and even though he's on my side, I find his gesture a little intimidating, but I look him in the eye.

"If I'm going to be seen around the island while I'm not showing, I should behave like a woman who isn't pregnant. Maybe I'll play loud workout videos and be seen on the summerhouse balcony in yoga pants, wiping sweat off my brow as if I've just finished a vigorous workout. I'll go to the village and buy tampons. I'll be seen taking bottles of wine back to the summerhouse. Julia should make a show of drinking nonalcoholic drinks."

"Gold dust!" Chris moves to his wife and hugs her. "Honey, we sure picked a good one. Eve, you're smart, honest, and not afraid to speak your mind. From now on, we consult you every step of the way. Come upstairs, and we'll talk. Looks like Julia and I *can* have that glass of wine, as long as we leave two wineglasses and one tumbler for Sarah to tidy up."

Chris and Julia lead me to the third floor. I try not to gape at the magnificence of the master suite, which dominates this top level. The bed is as vast as a landing field. An open archway connects the bedroom to a living room furnished with a white lounge suite and matching chaise longue. The aqua walls and an aquarium bursting with fish give a sense that the ocean has swept all the way into the room.

Julia ushers me to a seat. I gaze out the window at the soft evening sky.

Christopher strides to the wet bar against one wall. "Orange juice?" he asks me.

I nod.

"I'll have a Chardonnay, love," Julia says. She retrieves a book from a drawer and sits beside me. "This is my pregnancy calendar. I've written in the dates of your pregnancy, based on Zelde's calculations, and the calendar tells me what would happen each week if I were pregnant. How much my waistline would expand, what symptoms I would experience. What's today, the twenty-eighth of October?" She turns the pages. "Here we are. I'm meant to be fourteen weeks along." She reads aloud. "'Morning sickness eases for most women. Many start to show a small bump.' I ate breakfast this morning for the first time in weeks, and as I said, I'm wearing the small belly."

Chris brings our drinks. He produces some handwritten pages from his pocket and tosses them to me. "Here's the family history I wrote up. You'll be my third cousin, so it won't matter if you forget a few family names, as long as you get the gist."

As I read about my great-great-great-grandfather, William Hygate, arriving in Australia in the nineteenth century, I breathe easier. The Hygates are more organized than I thought. Maybe, working together, the three of us can pull this off.

Chris raises his glass. "Here's to Eve, the cleverest girl on the island and the first person in a long time to tell us the truth."

THREE DAYS LATER, I'm lined up outside the mansion with Zelde and the staff. We're facing the ocean, squinting into the morning sun as we wait for Granny Meg to arrive.

Julia's remark that Granny Meg likes things done "a certain way" turned out to be the understatement of the century. I thought the mansion was pristine, but apparently it was a pigsty. Since her visit was announced, everything has been turned upside down in preparation. I've never seen so many scrubbing brushes and feather dusters. The men climbed ladders to polish the great chandelier until it shone so brightly I thought I might go blind. Fresh flowers were placed in every corner, and furniture was re-arranged so the old lady can occupy the red room on the middle floor in the style to which she is no doubt accustomed.

Amongst all this activity, my presence at the mansion was barely noticed. I've eaten with the Hygates each night, taking a crash course in which cutlery to use by observing my hosts. I've watched movies in the home theater and spent hours curled up in the library with a book. I've driven to the village in Chris's car, where I bought tampons, wine, and unpasteurized cheese, like a woman who definitely isn't pregnant.

In a strange way, I've felt lonelier in the past few days than I did hiding in the summerhouse. Zelde was certainly speaking the truth when she said the Hygates like to hire employees who keep to themselves. The maids are mostly older women who fall silent when I enter a room and answer my questions with mono-syllables, while Antoine is the stereotypical grumpy chef, and to top it off, barely speaks English. The gardeners who tend the vineyard and grounds are migrant workers who also speak little English. I'm told a new group is hired every year. As for the Hy-gates, Chris is shut up in his office all day, and Julia is busy with party preparation.

Perhaps the staff are keeping me at arm's length because I'm seen as their employers' family, not a workmate. They're never rude, just taciturn. Sarah, Julia's personal maid, seems as though she could be fun. A plump, energetic woman with sparkling eyes and an infectious laugh, she's younger than the rest of the staff. While we haven't spoken much, she always greets me with a smile.

Now the gravel crunches as the limousine cruises into the marina parking lot. The servants, who have been warned by Zelde to be on their best behavior, stand tall. I'm next to Sarah, and she leans over and whispers, "Does my collar look okay? My baby flicked food on me this morning."

"Oh, you have a baby? How awes—" I stop. I shouldn't appear too interested. For a split second, I felt I'd found a point of connection with someone, but I can't bond with Sarah over being a mother.

"Your collar's fine," I whisper, just as Zelde says, "No chattering."

Our view of the parking lot is obscured by a gum tree, but I hear the limousine door open, and an imperious voice announces, "Stop fussing, Julia. I'm quite capable of exiting a vehicle unaided."

Our guest steams into view like a ship under sail. I was expecting a frail old woman, but Granny Meg is statuesque and svelte with luxuriant dark hair and more makeup than a cabaret dancer. Dressed in a burgundy traveling suit of fine cashmere, she sweeps along the beach and up the path to the house, barely glancing at the row of staff. Julia and Chris follow.

"Who is this little thing?" Granny cries when she reaches me.

"I'm Eve Hygate." I almost feel I should curtsey.

Granny steps forward. "Speak up! I'm a bit deaf."

"Eve Hygate. I'm a distant cousin of Chris's." As I repeat the name, I see the logic of Chris's plan. Now that the servants have heard Julia's grandmother being told I'm family, they'll never doubt it.

"Eve's staying with us till Monday," Julia says as she and Chris catch up with Granny.

"A pleasure to meet you, Cousin Eve." Granny speaks with an upper-class British accent. "You may show me to my room if you please." Her eyes sparkle, and I can't help but smile at her.

"Come this way." I can't believe I have the nerve to saunter off with this grand lady, but wouldn't it be ruder to refuse? Zelde glares at me as I pass. Maybe she was hoping to cozy up with this important guest. I hope she's nicer to me when I'm in labor.

Granny ascends the stairs with surprising speed, but as soon as we're in the red room, she sinks onto the bed. "I'm getting too old to travel. I'd like to throttle whoever abolished first class on domestic flights. Close the door and plump these pillows up for me, darling. I'll rest for a spell."

"I hope the bed's comfortable," I reply as I obey.

"It's too soft."

"I'm sorry to hear that. Shall I ask a maid to come and help? Or Julia?"

"I don't want a maid hovering when I can be spending time with family. I told Julia to go and lie down." She pulls off her burgundy heels, wincing and wriggling her toes. "Darling, you must know Julia's happy news? She couldn't keep it a secret! Told me before we'd made it out of the arrivals lounge."

"You must be delighted. You'll be a great-grandmother." I've spoken before I have a chance to reflect that I'm yet again deceiving somebody I just met.

"Julia's my only daughter. I was beginning to think the family tree would die out."

"Granddaughter, you mean."

"Hmm? Oh, yes, granddaughter. Slip of the tongue. She shouldn't have come all the way to the airport to collect me. Expectant mothers need to take it easy. You won't mind running around for me, will you, little Eve?"

Her remark is ironic, but I like the idea of being kept busy after weeks of lounging in the summerhouse. "I'd love to, Granny."

As soon as the words are out of my mouth, I wish I could cram them back in. "Um, I mean, what should I call you?"

"Since you're family, call me Margareta. Now, have a look in my purse for my pills and close those curtains. I need my beauty sleep."

When I've carried out Margareta's orders, I turn to go. "I'll leave you to rest."

"So long as you come back this afternoon to help me dress for the party. I like having an energetic young thing like you around. We're going to get on like a house on fire. Oh, Eve, I'm delighted Julia's finally going to produce an heir. The thought of nobody inheriting the castle was keeping me awake at night."

CHAPTER 16

I'm drifting along the hall, Margareta's words echoing inside my head. I mount the stairs, passing a maid carrying a basket of laundry. I wouldn't normally approach Julia's bedroom uninvited, but I'm desperate to understand what Margareta just said. Does she truly own a castle, or is she just a bonkers old lady?

I pause at the entrance to the master suite. "Julia? Can I come in?"

"Sure," comes the answer.

I enter and close the door. Julia is sprawled on the bed, a magazine in hand.

"Granny told me pregnant women need to rest," she says, beaming. "I'm fully getting into my role."

"You didn't mention that your grandmother owns a castle."

Julia sighs. "She didn't tell you that, did she?"

"It isn't true?"

"Well . . . yes."

I gulp. This is momentous, but Julia sounds so casual, as if the castle is just a detail she forgot to mention. "So, this castle is the reason you're not adopting openly."

"It probably seems stupid," says Julia. "We already have enough money to meet all our needs, but it's important to me that my child isn't robbed of his inheritance."

"Couldn't you ask Margareta to change her will?"

"It's not up to her. The land's held in a trust written up last century, along with the share portfolio, the jewelry, a pile of old art. She has no other close relatives, so if I don't have a baby, all of it goes to a distant cousin. The rules can't be changed." She lies back on her satin pillow with a dreamy expression. "Eve, don't you think it would be wonderful for our baby"—she points from her belly to mine, as though we're both growing the child—"to spend the Australian winters in a castle in Europe?"

I can't quite believe this is the future Julia is offering my child. There's a lot riding on her fake pregnancy. "Are there any other rules? Like, does it matter if the baby's a girl?"

"No. What gave you that idea?"

"Just checking." I try to sound nonchalant. "Have you considered confiding in Margareta? Then you wouldn't have to lie to her."

"Good God, no! Granny's a stickler for tradition. In her view, if I fail to produce a son—or daughter—my distant cousin is the rightful heir. Besides, it's too late now. We've told her I'm pregnant. She'd never forgive me for lying to her."

Maybe it's because she's reclining on the bed, but Julia seems way too relaxed about deceiving everyone around her.

"Why did you risk introducing Margareta to me? Wouldn't it be safer if we never met?"

"Eve, you're skinny as a reed. How could she possibly find out?"

I'm not satisfied, but I can't see the point in arguing. I head downstairs.

Julia acts as though a castle is an embarrassing secret, but she cares enough about it to go through a fake pregnancy so that her child can inherit. And what else did she mention in passing as though she barely remembered it? A share portfolio, jewelry, art.

She's talking serious money. Christopher's home and business are worth millions, but compared with Margareta, he's a pauper.

IN THE LATE afternoon, Zelde comes over to the summerhouse to repeat Margareta's request that I help her dress. I'm left in no doubt that Zelde doesn't think I'm up to the task. She even reminds me to say "please" and "thank you."

In the mansion, the ground floor is a hive of activity. The doors to the violet room have been thrown open, and enough tables and chairs to seat an army have appeared from nowhere. Maids bustle about making last-minute adjustments.

Upstairs, I knock on the door of the red room.

"Come in," Margareta commands.

Inside, she's in a state of undress. Her hair's a mess, and she's wrapped in a sheer robe through which her purple undergarments are visible. "I'll never be ready in time," she says. "You look pretty, Eve. What a lovely dress."

"Thank you." I'm wearing a green silk dress I made for a friend's wedding. Julia offered to lend me a dress, but this empire waistline disguises my shape. This afternoon, my waist felt thicker.

"Julia found me a better mattress," says Margareta. "It'll be here any minute. I must get dressed." She opens a jewelry box, takes out a glittering tiara, and places it on the dresser. If those diamonds are real, that thing is worth thousands. "Julia thinks this is gaudy, but my dear husband gave it to me. He died years ago, and I still miss him. My son, Julia's father, died soon after. Julia's all I have left."

"I'm sorry." I wish I could tell her I understand what it's like to lose someone, but that would be dangerous territory.

Margareta picks up her evening gown and examines the bodice. "Goodness, the lace is torn. I'll need something to cover that. If only I had my amethyst brooch, but I gave it to Julia."

"I'm sure she'd lend it back to you."

"I'll ask her. Where is she, do you know?"

"You're not dressed. I'll find her."

"Would you, darling?"

I wander along the hall. At the stairwell, I hear soft thuds below me. Joseph is dragging a mattress up the stairs.

On the top floor, the door to the master suite is open. Julia's not here, but on the bed, in plain sight, is one of the fake bellies.

What is Julia thinking, leaving it where anybody could see it? With all the party prep, dozens of people are milling about. They're mostly on the ground floor, but someone could pop upstairs any moment. I rush into the room, grab the belly and stuff it under a pillow. A noise from the en suite makes my head whip around. Chris stands in the doorway, a towel wrapped around his waist, his bare torso wet from the shower.

Heat rises to my face, but I don't have time to apologize for barging in.

"Why did Julia leave that thing in full view?" I whisper-shout. "Why isn't she wearing it? Where is she?"

"She says it's not big enough. She's gone to get the next size up."

What terrible timing to make the switch. From downstairs, Margareta's voice booms. "Young man, do you know where I can find Mrs. Hygate? I need to speak with her."

Joseph replies loud and clear. "Reckon she's in the yeller room."

"Which one is the yellow room?" Margareta shouts.

"Corner room. Right at the end."

I stare at Chris in horror. Julia's so careless. Right now, she's probably in the nursery with the secret drawer pulled wide open and the fake bellies strewn across the floor for anybody to see.

Has she locked the door?

I fly downstairs. Joseph has disappeared, leaving the mattress leaning against a balustrade. Margareta is strolling along the hallway in her robe. I hightail after her, nearly tripping in my high heels. She reaches for the nursery door handle. I grab her by the shoulders and spin her round.

"Granny, please let me fetch that brooch for you! It would be an honor." My words make no sense—I'm not meant to call her Granny—but I'm in such a whirl I can't remember her name.

I hustle her back along the hallway, babbling about how she doesn't want the servants to see her in her robe. I almost shove her back into the red room.

"Where's the brooch?" she asks.

I forgot the stupid brooch. "Wait here! I'll get it this time!"

I slam the door as if that will magically keep Margareta inside and hurry back upstairs. Chris has pulled on some trousers.

"Quick, where's Julia's amethyst brooch? Margareta nearly walked in on her."

Chris strides to the dressing table and flips open a jewelry box. "It's here somewhere," he mutters, lifting a handful of jewels. "What color's amethyst? Is this it?" He holds up a sapphire brooch.

"No! Here, let me look."

As I dart forward, he digs out a massive purple brooch. "What about this?"

"Yes! Chuck it!"

Chris tosses the brooch. I catch it and run to the stairs.

Joseph's voice echoes up from below. "Did ya find her, ma'am?

Lady, are you in here?" He's heading for the nursery. "About the mattress . . ."

I'm downstairs and along the hall in seconds, but I'm too late. Joseph has opened the nursery door. He's standing in the doorway, motionless, his jaw agape.

I rush to his side.

Julia stands in the middle of the room, wearing nothing but her bra and knickers, a diamond necklace, pink stilettos, and a great big silicone belly.

CHAPTER 17

I reach past Joseph and slam the nursery door shut.

"Come with me," I whisper, but he stands stock-still, his face frozen. The key turns noisily in the lock. Jeez, talk about too late. A frantic rustling tells me Julia's scrambling to get dressed.

"Quick, out of the hallway before Margareta spots us," I hiss.

I grip Joseph's tattooed arm and steer him into an unoccupied room. How the heck am I going to talk my way out of this? Hopefully, Joseph was too dazzled by seeing the lady of the house half naked to process the fake belly.

"What was that plastic thing?" Joseph speaks far too loud. "I heard she was pregnant. Is she faking it? Why would she do that?"

"It's not what you think. Keep your voice down." I lock the door. "I can explain, but it's essential Margareta not find out."

We're in the music room. Joseph leans against the grand piano, his brow furrowed. Despite his spotless sailor uniform, he looks out of place in these sumptuous surroundings. His teeth are damaged, suggesting long-term drug use. Why on earth did the Hygates hire this jailbird?

"Does the boss know?" he asks.

"Of course Christopher knows."

"What's her game, then?"

I take a breath. I don't know the deal with Joseph and the Hygates. Best I say as little as possible. I hold up the brooch. "I'm meant to be helping Margareta. She's looking for me. She'll be banging on this door any minute."

"Door's locked, though, isn't it?" says Joseph. "You got all the time in the world to explain." He looks thoughtful. "Rumor is the missus is gonna announce that she's pregnant tonight. Easy to fake a pregnancy but not so easy to fake a baby. What's her plan?"

"It's up to Mr. and Mrs. Hygate to explain."

"The part I want you to explain, girlie, is how come you know all this? What's it got to do with you? I been wondering what you're doing on Breaksea. Now I find out Mrs. Hygate is faking a pregnancy, and you know all about it. How come?"

I'm at a loss. Joseph has always been uninterested in me. Now he's turned private detective. Spotting one of those fake bellies would do that to you, though.

"I'm family," I say weakly.

"So I heard. When did that happen? When they changed your name, Miss Sylvester-I-mean-Hygate? 'Parently you're gonna be the nanny, too."

"News travels fast."

"Weird how you spend all that time sewing baby clothes. I've heard your sewing machine buzzing away all hours of the night. You're pretty devoted."

I gape. So, Joseph's heard my sewing machine, but how does he know I'm making baby clothes? Did he see the fabric in my shopping bags, or has he been in the summerhouse when I wasn't there? He let himself in that first day to replace the light bulbs. He must have a key. What if he's seen my pregnancy book?

"Question is, sweetheart, how're you gonna nanny a fake baby?" Joseph's eyes travel down my torso. He stares at my abdomen. The generous folds of fabric in my dress conceal my figure, but still, I suck in my belly till it feels like it's touching my spine. I take a step backward and nearly knock over a music stand. "There's gotta be a baby, right? If the missus can't have one . . . Rumor is she lost her baby a while back. She kept the nursery ready like she wanted another one, but nothing happened. Then you turn up all silent and mysterious. I knew something was up."

Joseph's eyes are narrowed. Why is he so invested?

"I'm sorry I didn't confide in you." I try to sound casual. "It's nothing personal. The Hygates employ people who respect their privacy, right?"

"Just coz I keep my mouth shut doesn't mean I like what's going on. She deserves better. The boss is rich, but that doesn't mean a woman has to put up with this bullshit."

"You mean Julia? I'm not sure what you think she's putting up with."

"At first, I was sort of relieved to hear you're the boss's cousin. Now I bloody well hope you're not."

"What do you mean?"

"I always thought the boss was on the straight and narrow, but we all have our flaws. I guess he likes little girls like you. You can stop acting innocent. I've figured it out. You're Hygate's whore, and he's gone and knocked you up."

A rap at the door. Chris's voice reverberates through the wood. "Open up!"

Joseph opens the door, and the three of us look awkwardly at each other.

"Joseph knows I'm pregnant," I blurt out. "He walked in on Julia wearing the belly."

Margareta's voice rings out. "Eve!"

I dart into the hallway. Margareta approaches, still in her robe.

Will this woman ever stop wandering around half-dressed? I'd have thought a lady who owns a castle would be more dignified, especially with a grifter like Joseph lurking about the place.

"I'll distract her," I mutter to Christopher.

It seems Joseph is protective of Julia. The last thing I need is him accusing Chris of "knocking me up" in front of Margareta. I whisper in Chris's ear, "We need to keep them apart."

Chris nods and slips into the room. He grips Joseph's arm, his face stern.

"Hey, what are you—" Joseph's words are cut off as Chris shuts the door.

I usher Margareta back to her room with a fake smile. "I've found the brooch. Let's get you dressed." I wish I could stay to hear what Christopher says to Joseph. Will he admit the truth? Will he bribe Joseph to stay quiet?

I have to trust Chris will handle things. He's a clever man, and he's Joseph's boss. The priority is to keep Margareta away. It's bad enough that Joseph knows about the fake pregnancy, but if Margareta finds out, it's game over. I'll be homeless, and once I'm visibly pregnant, it will be virtually impossible to get a job.

I help Margareta into her dress, fasten the brooch to her bodice, and pin up her hair, hoping she won't notice my trembling hands.

Margareta takes so long to finish her makeup that I can hear guests arriving. I'm desperate to find out what has happened with Joseph, but she won't let me leave the room.

A knock at the door. It's Julia. She's wearing a floor-length dress of ravishing pink satin—a color I'd never dare wear as a redhead, yet she looks gorgeous. Her baby bump is pronounced.

"Time to join the party, ladies! You both look lovely, but,

Granny, you haven't got your shoes on! Oh well, come down when you're ready. It's going to be such a fun evening!"

Julia looks so relaxed that my stress levels drop to something approaching normal. She glides away, while I help Margareta into her glittery shoes. Moments later, Margareta and I descend the staircase arm in arm. We're greeted with a sparkling scene thronging with men in tuxedos and women in evening gowns.

Zelde is standing at the foot of the stairs. "Good evening, ma'am," she says to Margareta. She turns to me. "Mrs. Hygate, that gown is exquisite."

"Wha— It's Eve," I say, my eyes wide with astonishment. I know Julia and I have similar features and coloring, and the difference in our height is less obvious when I'm standing on stairs, but I would never have thought anybody could get us mixed up.

Looking flustered, Zelde turns away and picks up a flute of champagne, which she hands to me. "Especially for you, *Miss* Hygate," she says with a pointed look.

"Goodness, it's terribly hot," Margareta complains.

I find Margareta a chair near the open doors. I gasp at the sight of the lawn lit up like a fairyland. The pools, transformed by underwater lights into otherworldly lagoons, are surrounded by more champagne-sipping guests.

Margareta and I sit and admire the scene. Meringue-pink clouds float in the twilight sky, and the moon hovers above the ocean like a giant topaz, spilling a pathway of light across the water. The clink of glasses and the merry chatter of guests mingle with the lively music playing over the high-tech sound system. This is the life.

Margareta falls into conversation with an elderly couple. I slip away to look for Julia and Chris, hoping to find out about Joseph. Has he agreed to stay quiet?

They're at the far side of the room, surrounded by guests. They look the perfect couple. Christopher's strong frame is accentuated by his tailored tuxedo. Julia, close at his side, looks radiant. Her hair is swept up in a profusion of russet curls, and her diamond necklace shimmers.

Chris holds a champagne flute, but Julia's clutching a can of soft drink. It's out of keeping with the style of the party that her drink hasn't been served in a glass. I guess she wants everyone to realize there's no rum in that Coke.

Chris catches sight of Margareta. He calls for silence, and the hubbub of voices dies away.

"Ladies and gentlemen," he begins, "most of you know that I don't need an excuse to throw a party."

A murmur of laughter goes around the room.

"However, I'm pleased to say I have two excellent reasons for tonight's festivities. The first is to welcome my wife's grand-mother, Margareta, to our home. It's always a pleasure to spend time with you, Granny Meg."

People applaud. Heads turn toward Margareta, and she stands to perform a deep curtsey. In her purple gown and lavish tiara, she looks like a queen.

"Now to the second reason. I'm delighted to announce that my beautiful wife and I are expecting a baby."

The crowd erupts with cheers—although nobody sounds sur-prised. Julia's bump has already given the game away.

"A toast to Julia!" someone calls. Julia raises her Coke can with a rueful grin.

"Nine months with no Chardonnay!" a man cries in a jovial tone. "Can it be done, Julia?"

I hold my glass to my mouth and pretend to sip. I presume Zelde has given me fake champagne for appearance's sake. It smells like grape juice.

When the speeches end, people rush to congratulate Chris and Julia. I should hang back and wait for a quiet moment, but I'm too anxious to know how things stand with Joseph. I won't be able to get the lowdown, but a word or two from Chris would set my mind at ease.

The Hygates' social circle is impressive. The way the guests are dressed, I doubt they're from the village, which is the sort of place where locals wear work boots to the pub. No, these people have come all the way to the island to attend this party. Their wealth is evident in their clothes, their confident voices, the way they carry themselves.

I approach the throng surrounding Chris and Julia. Two women, both heavily pregnant, are showering Julia with hugs and kisses. They drip with jewels. It takes me a beat to realize the older men with them are their husbands.

"The Supreme Court doesn't offer paternity leave to judges," one of the women says in a plaintive tone. She has glitter in her hair and fake nails and keeps tottering on her high heels, as if thrown off-balance by her baby bump.

"Never mind, Ming." The gray-bearded man pats her belly, which bulges beneath her red A-line dress. "I told you I'll take a sabbatical when Olly arrives."

"Oops! Cat's out of the bag," Ming gushes. "We're having a boy. I hope you have a boy, too, Julia! They'll be best mates!"

The other pregnant woman, whose bottle tan and bleached hair make her look like a photographic negative, pipes up. "I wish Spencer could take a sabbatical. When you're the CEO of a blue-chip company, it's difficult to get away." She twirls her bejeweled bracelet around her wrist with an air of self-satisfaction.

The balding, rotund man beside her, presumably Spencer, laughs. "Thank goodness for that. The last thing you'll want when the baby comes, Emma, is me hanging around the house getting on your nerves."

"It would be like having two children to look after," Ming remarks with a friendly wink.

More fabulous people press forward with congratulations, and I'm forced away. I circle the party, looking for someone to talk to, but I can't think how to start a conversation. Some of the guests aren't much older than me, but they seem like they were born middle-aged. I catch snippets of conversation about "median house prices" and "too many private schools going coed."

Margareta gives me a friendly smile as I pass, but I don't stop to chat. I've lied to her enough for one day.

This evening is so luxurious—soft lighting, sumptuous food, sophisticated clothes—but I'm too tangled up in deceit to savor it. The music cranks up, and Julia and Chris take to the dance floor. Clearly, I won't get them alone tonight. I slip outside and skirt the pool, but rather than heading to the summerhouse, I turn toward the marina. It's probably stupid to try to find out what happened from Joseph, but if I happen to see him, he might volunteer something.

Footsteps behind me. I turn. A male figure is silhouetted against the party lights.

"Where are you going, Eve?"

"Chris! I wanted to talk to you. What's happened with Joseph?"

Chris steps forward, and a shaft of light falls across his face, but I can't interpret his expression. "Why do you ask?"

I speak softly. "I'm thinking we can't get away with this. Julia's not a natural liar. The Coke can was too obvious, and the belly was too big. A few days ago she wasn't wearing any belly at all."

Chris is cool and collected. "Isn't it too late for misgivings?"

"Maybe not. Margareta doesn't seem like a judgmental person. She loves Julia and has no other family. Would she really be so unforgiving?"

"Are you suggesting we tell Margareta we've lied to her? Perhaps I should grab a microphone. Ladies and gentlemen, my earlier announcement was slightly inaccurate. My wife's not pregnant, but this young lady is. Apologies for the confusion."

"That's not what I meant." I shake my head. "It was a mistake for me to be here tonight. I should have hidden properly from the start. Not in the summerhouse. Somewhere far away and secluded. Now Joseph knows—"

"That's because you told him."

"I only confirmed what he suspected—"

"I wonder what else you plan to tell him." He nods toward the marina. "You're on your way to see him."

"Only to find out . . . I wanted to make sure he'd keep quiet."

"You don't need to worry about Joseph. He's not the weak link in this chain. I'm about to make arrangements with him myself. You go to bed. Late nights aren't good for the baby."

I have no choice but to head to the summerhouse. I skulk away like a naughty child sent to her room. Still, it's a relief to hear Chris has everything in hand.

In bed, my body aches with fatigue, but my brain is buzzing. It's bad enough that I'm deceiving all these people. Worse that our scheme seems likely to be uncovered, but this isn't the worst of it.

The worst is what Joseph called me. *Hygate's whore.*

Has Chris told Joseph he's not the father? I can't bear anyone thinking my baby is the product of a dirty affair. As I drift off, the same thought echoes around my head. Xander's name is being buried by lies, and I'm letting it happen.

"Oy! Wake up!"

I'm roused from sleep into pitch-black. A movement. Someone's at the foot of my bed.

"Where's the bloody light switch, Eve?" It's Joseph.

I leap out of bed. "What are you doing in my room!" I glance at the clock. It's 4:30 a.m.

"Calm down, missy. I'm not interested in the boss's tail. Don't know what he sees in you, to be honest. Would you turn the bleeding light on?"

My fingers fumble for the switch above my bed. Light floods the room, revealing Joseph dressed in his uniform and holding a suitcase.

"You're to get up and pack," he says. "Get all yer gear. Here's an extra suitcase for all the rubbish you bought since you moved in. You're to be gone by daybreak."

CHAPTER 18

The room is spinning. I can't process Joseph's words. Is this what Chris meant last night by making arrangements? They're sending me away?

They don't want my baby anymore. My heart is falling out of my body.

At times last night, I questioned whether I wanted that snobby life for my baby, but as the Hygates' daughter, she could have whatever life she wanted. What kind of life can I offer her?

"Get a move on, would ya? You're going on *Torrent*."

"Joseph, I can't leave without talking to the Hygates."

"I'm to keep you away from the house."

"Do they think I'm going to tell someone about Julia? I would never do that. I want our plan to go ahead."

Joseph narrows his eyes. Is he disgusted with me? He must still believe I slept with Chris. I'm desperate to correct his mistake, but I can't risk making things worse. Whatever Joseph thinks, he's still carrying out Chris's orders.

Joseph nods. "You'll be happy, then. Boss isn't firing you, but he thinks you're too fat for people to see you anymore. I'm to take you away. Boss tells everyone you caught an early flight. After the guests leave, you double back to the island, stay outta sight properly this time."

The air feels lighter. I've been holding my breath. Now I want to squeal. I could almost hug Joseph.

"Pack everything," he says. "No more half-arsed pretending. You wanna fool people, you gotta go the whole hog. I'll be waiting outside. You have ten minutes."

I throw on warm clothes and start stuffing my belongings into my backpack and the two suitcases. My heart's still pounding from the shock of believing the Hygates were canceling. Did Joseph give me that impression on purpose? He seems to dislike me. Maybe he enjoyed watching me panic.

I'm zipping up the cases when Joseph reappears. "Time to go. Leave the door unlocked. Maids are gonna clean." He grabs my luggage.

As we head to the marina, I glance toward the mansion with its darkened windows, wishing Chris or Julia would appear. I have an uneasy feeling about this sudden departure. Chris believes I blabbed to Joseph. Maybe he thinks I planned to tell Margareta. I wish I could reassure him.

No one sees us board *Torrent*. Joseph doesn't start the engine. He raises the sails, and the yacht glides out of the bay in perfect silence.

Torrent is skipping along the coastline as dawn breaks. Joseph is at the wheel.

"I could take a turn at the helm if you like," I call from the pilot house. "I know how to steer."

"You stay outta sight," comes the gruff reply.

"How long before the guests leave? Will we wait in Hobart until they're gone?"

"Are you kidding? You can't go gallivanting around Hobart. You people don't know how to pull off a hoax, do you? You think we know nothing about you."

"My God, does anyone else know Julia isn't really pregnant?"

Joseph sneers. "The way you're all carrying on, it won't take long. You get below before you're spotted and I have to make up more lies to cover your arse."

I retreat down the ladder. Despite everything, the motion of the yacht lulls me into a daydream. I lie on the saloon sofa, close my eyes, and imagine my daughter fully grown, living in her castle. I live with her—secretly she knows I'm her mother. She attends parties far grander than last night, parties where everyone's too classy to talk about money. She inherits the family jewels and wears Margareta's tiara on special occasions. Ming's and Emma's children wish they could be her friends, but she's far too wealthy and fabulous . . .

I know I'm being ridiculous, but I need to imagine some reward for all these shenanigans.

I'm almost asleep when I hear Joseph's voice. He must be talking on the radio. "We left an hour ago. Nah, she can't hear me. She's asleep below."

My ears prick up.

"Yeah, it'd be good night nurse if Silas found out, but I'm keeping track of him." Joseph pauses. I can discern a male voice on the other end of the call, but I can't make out any words. "Nah, I don't reckon you're overreacting. It's serious. I don't wanna think about what kind of creative revenge Silas'd take if he got wind of . . . But he's not even in Tassie. No chance of him showing his ugly, scarred face around here anytime soon. We're safe. Anyway, I gotta jibe." I hear him hang up the radio headset.

My brain is buzzing. I keep my eyes shut, feigning sleep, but as Joseph jibes the yacht, it heels violently to port, and I just about fall across the saloon. I grip the table to steady myself.

What on earth was Joseph talking about? Who the heck is this Silas guy who can't find something out or it's "good night nurse"? It sounded as though Joseph was talking about him finding out about the adoption scheme, but that can't be right. The people we're worried about finding out are Julia's family, and the only living member of Julia's family is Margareta.

Joseph's conversation probably has nothing to do with me. I doubt he was talking to Chris. He's probably doing some sketchy deal that the Hygates know nothing about. Maybe selling drugs.

A flash of red in the porthole. We're close to land. The lighthouse is right outside the window.

I bound up on deck. Joseph has brought *Torrent* into Lighthouse Cove. He's at the bow wrestling with the anchor.

"What are we doing here?" I ask.

"Following orders." Joseph throws the anchor overboard. The chain clatters as it rolls out.

"Are we staying here till the guests have gone?"

We've been towing a dinghy. Hopefully, there's time to row ashore. I'll finally get to visit a lighthouse.

Joseph brushes past me and returns to the wheel. He shunts the engine into reverse. "Gotta dig the anchor in."

I wait as Joseph revs the engine to confirm the anchor is holding. He shuts it off, and the silence of the cove settles around us.

I look around. The quiet sweep of water is surrounded by white cliffs, as though nature built an open-air cathedral in her own honor. Barely a puff of wind invades the scene, and the sea is dreamy blue. The bush is so green it almost throbs.

"How long before we go back to Paradise Bay?"

Joseph begins coiling ropes.

Much as I wanted to see the lighthouse, I'm getting a bad feeling. "How long are we here for? Tell me!"

Joseph scowls. "Don't you start ordering me round, girlie. Just coz the boss pretended you were family in front of those fools. Nobody's around to playact for now. I know what you really are."

"You don't know anything! I'm not—" I stop. I want to say that I'm not "Hygate's whore," but it might be better not to. Joseph wouldn't dare let harm come to what he thinks is Chris's baby. I swallow my outrage. "I didn't mean to order you around. It's just that you didn't tell me we were stopping here."

Joseph guffaws. "Course nobody mentioned it. Boss didn't want you making a fuss, but you shoulda figured it out by now. 'Parently it was your idea in the first place to go somewhere remote."

"Tell me straight. What's going on?"

"Might as well. Too late for you to complain. Boss doesn't want anyone to know you're still around, so you've got new digs."

He points behind me, and I turn to face it. The thing I yearned to visit, but I sure didn't want to live here.

Breaksea Lighthouse.

CHAPTER 19

Joseph is loading my luggage into the dinghy.

"I can't live in the lighthouse," I say. "Is there electricity? Is there a bathroom?"

"You'll survive," says Joseph. "It's a roof over your head. No one's charging you rent. Stop complaining. We've got a shit ton of stuff to haul to shore. Must be a week of food here."

"I'm staying for a week?"

"That's up to the boss. And you. You need to convince him you'll behave." He jerks his head toward the dinghy. "Get in."

I hesitate. Getting in that dinghy is the last thing I want to do. Once I'm in, I'll have no hope of making it back on board *Torrent* and returning to Paradise Bay. Joseph is about as open to negotiation as a tidal wave. But if I kick up a fuss, what will Joseph do? Wait me out? More likely he'll take matters into his own hands and force me ashore.

I'm already a prisoner. My best chance is to cooperate. As Joseph said, I need to convince Christopher I'll "behave."

I climb into the dinghy.

Onshore, we lumber up a rough path to the lighthouse. Joseph unlocks the door, and it swings open with a horror-movie creak, revealing a dim, musty room with a rudimentary kitchen.

I head up the spiral staircase. At the top is a circular room with windows offering wraparound ocean views. The room is dominated by the great light, which is encased in a glass sphere. This all-seeing eye resembles that of a giant insect and stands in the middle of the room. I can't help admiring it, but where am I meant to sleep?

Joseph appears with a camping mattress and drops it on the floor. "Bedding's in the green crate," he mutters.

He stacks the food crates in the storeroom beside the light-house. He explains that the roof collects rainwater and supports solar panels. The toilet is in a separate outhouse. Everything is functional but old and decrepit. Whoever lived here left a long time ago.

As I set about tidying the place, I watch Joseph. I'm acting like I'm cool with being here. I'm not sure whether I'm hoping he'll drop his guard or simply avoiding the humiliation of acknowledging I'm in his power. Either way, I can't overdo my act. There isn't a lot to praise.

"Thank goodness there's a kitchen," I chirp. "The place will look quite nice once it's had a good scrub."

Joseph grunts. His expression gives me no clue whether he buys my cheery façade, but the whole time we're unpacking, he doesn't turn his back on me. He never lets me get closer to *Torrent* than he is. He doesn't give me a single chance to make a run for it.

He shows me how to check the water level in the tank and monitor the solar panels so I don't run low on electricity. Now we head back down to the beach.

"Listen up," he says as he pushes the dinghy into the water. "Keep the door locked. Don't leave anything lying around outside that'll tip someone off that you're here. If a boat comes into the cove, you stay inside. The type that come, trust me, you don't wanna meet."

Is he for real? If Joseph knows the people who sail these waters, and he of all people thinks they're sketchy, I'd rather steer clear of them. I nod.

"I'm off." He reaches into his pocket and chucks me a piece of black cloth—an eye mask. "You'll need this to sleep when the light's on."

"Wait! I can't stay here alone. I'm pregnant. What if something goes wrong with the baby?"

"Old Finch is gonna come and stay with ya. She'll have a phone for emergencies."

I gape as the implications sink in. I'm to stay here with Zelde? This is bad. If the plan were to leave me here alone, it would obviously be short-term. Julia and Chris wouldn't risk the pregnancy, but with Zelde here . . .

Joseph isn't offering to give *me* a phone. They're not letting me call for rescue.

Before I can say more, Joseph is rowing out to the yacht. I guess the sooner he's gone, the sooner he'll be back with Zelde. It's about an hour's sail each way. She should be here by lunchtime.

I return to the light room to watch *Torrent* chug out of the bay. Here I am standing inside a lighthouse at last. I never imagined it would be under such circumstances.

I stay at the window for a long time, gazing out at the blue circle of sea and the dome of halcyon sky. A lone albatross soars above the waves. Fatigue hits me, and I lie on the flimsy mattress and promptly fall asleep.

When I wake, it's afternoon, and I'm starving. I make an egg salad in the kitchen, checking outside every few minutes.

Half past five, and Zelde still hasn't arrived. I climb back upstairs to await *Torrent*'s return. I watch until the setting sun daubs the sky with her rosy fingers, turning my world pink. The scene is glorious, but I don't feel joy. Where is Zelde?

I'm alone on this rocky outcrop, stripped of any ability to contact another human being, dependent on a surly jailbird to be returned to civilization. If anything happens to my baby, how can I get help?

Darkness descends, and the great light fires up. When viewed from afar, it seemed to pulse on and off, but in fact it's a continuous light, revolving at high speed.

It's bright. Surface-of-the-sun bright.

At least the track is well-oiled. The light rotates in silence, but apart from that, I might as well be in a nightclub with a supercharged strobe. I could spend the evening in the kitchen, but it's windowless and there's nowhere comfortable to sit. In the end, I lie on the mattress and don the eye mask. Obviously, Zelde isn't coming till tomorrow.

I'm almost asleep when a thought strikes me. I sit bolt upright.

What if Chris and Julia don't know where I am?

Last night, Chris said he was "making arrangements" with Joseph. When Joseph came to collect me, I assumed he was carrying out Chris's orders. What if he wasn't?

That radio call Joseph made on the way here—I have no reason to think he was speaking to Chris. He mentioned a guy called Silas with ugly scars who would take "creative revenge," which doesn't sound like something Chris would be involved in.

Am I being paranoid? The obvious reason for a man to take a woman prisoner doesn't seem to apply to Joseph. He wouldn't be interested in me if I were the last woman on earth.

I take off my mask and let the light dazzle my eyes as I revisit last night's events. What if Joseph has kidnapped me? He might believe Chris would pay millions to ensure the baby's safety.

Joseph said Zelde was coming, but maybe that was just to placate me.

How could I escape? I can't cross the ravine between the rock and the island. I'd have to climb down the sheer cliff, and if by some miracle I made it to the bottom, waves would dash me against the rocks.

Next morning, I'm up early, hoping against hope to find a route across the ravine that doesn't require mountaineering skills. No luck. I can't believe how narrow the gap is between where I stand now and the bluff known as Lighthouse Lookout. It seems only yesterday I stood on the other side, yet the gap might as well be a thousand miles wide.

I head away from the lighthouse toward the far end of the rock. En route, picking my way through long grass, I stumble upon the ruined foundations of a cottage, complete with fireplace.

Now I understand why the lighthouse is so basic. When this light was manned, nobody lived inside. No wonder there's barely room for a bed. How presumptuous of Chris to expect me to stay here—*if* it was his idea.

I reach the point furthest from the lighthouse, where clumps of scrubby bushes are doing their best to cling to the clifftop despite the exposure to wind and waves. Looking for somewhere to sit, I catch sight of a sunken gray square.

The weather-worn headstone is marked simply with the word *Angel.* It's the grave of Chris and Julia's baby.

I sink to my knees with a sigh. The forlorn appearance of this headstone seems to draw my breath out of my body. I understand the Hygates wanted to be private about their loss, but how sad to bury a baby on a lonely clifftop. My gaze is drawn to the horizon. I hope Angel's spirit is free to soar over the vast blue desert of the Tasman Sea.

I clear weeds from the neglected grave. When I lift a rock, a lizard skitters out. I'm afraid it will bite me, but it disappears into the undergrowth. It's the same type of lizard I saw the day I walked to Lighthouse Lookout. Its scales form a harlequin pattern: forest-green diamond shapes on a background of coral pink. It's the prettiest creature.

I make my way back toward the lighthouse. The sun is warm once I'm out of the wind, and the cove's blue water is enticing.

I can't spend every minute waiting for Zelde to materialize. I haven't swum since the tropics. Who cares if it's cold? I want to remember how I felt when Xander was alive.

I drop my clothes on the sand and wade in. The water is cold but soothing against my skin. I glide beneath the surface.

I'd forgotten how peaceful the sea can be. I've been wary of the wild ocean since I arrived in Tasmania, but summer will tame it. Storms will be less powerful. The water is growing warmer each day. If Joseph doesn't return, maybe I *could* swim back.

I roll onto my back, closing my eyes against the sunshine. I've gained enough weight in my hips that I don't need to kick to stay afloat. I lie still, enjoying the cleansing sharpness of the salt water.

A fluttering inside me. I gasp. Did I imagine that?

The movement is faint but real.

My baby is kicking.

She's alive. She has life and motion and a will of her own.

And now it hits me: there are two prisoners on this rock. If I try to escape with some harebrained swim, I'll endanger my baby.

I emerge from the water shivering and hurry to dress. I return to the lighthouse, lie on my mattress, and stare at the ceiling.

I'm imprisoned here, not only by unpassable cliffs and hostile ocean but by love for my child.

CHAPTER 20

As dawn breaks the next morning, I'm on the beach, searching the shoreline. It's unlikely anyone left a rowboat hidden in the bushes, but I have nothing else to do.

I'm at the far end of the beach when I hear the chug of an engine. I remember Joseph saying I should hide in the lighthouse if anyone visited the cove.

I crouch among the shrubs. The boat enters the cove. I recognize her bowsprit and canoe stern. It's *Torrent*.

I peer at the approaching yacht. Who's on board? If Zelde has come, that means Joseph isn't holding me for ransom. If Joseph's alone, that's not good, but at least he's checking on me. Maybe Chris has paid the ransom and Joseph has come to collect me.

A male figure runs to the bow and throws the anchor overboard. Joseph. No sign of anyone else. Maybe Zelde's below deck.

I wait. Joseph returns to the cockpit. He cuts the engine. I wait for him to call Zelde up on deck, but he doesn't. He loads some crates into the dinghy.

He's bringing more food.

My heart sinks. This can only mean one thing. Joseph's not planning to collect me today. I'm still hoping Zelde will appear, but now Joseph steps into the dinghy and begins rowing ashore.

That's it. He's alone.

A wave of nausea hits me as Joseph pauses rowing and scans

the shoreline. I shrink back into the foliage as his gaze passes over me, unseeing.

When Joseph brought me here, he watched me the whole time. I couldn't evade him and get to the yacht. But today, he doesn't know where I am. He has no reason to guess I'm out and about early in the morning. He'll assume I'm asleep.

This is my chance.

The dinghy reaches the shallows. Joseph leaps out and drags it up the beach. He leaves it at the high-tide mark and lopes up the path toward the lighthouse, carrying a crate.

My breath comes fast and shallow. As soon as he goes inside, I have to make a break.

The problem is Joseph has left the dinghy right beneath the lighthouse. It's closer to him than to me. If he comes outside as I'm dragging the dinghy down the beach, he'll be on me in no time.

Joseph knocks on the lighthouse door, opens it, and disappears inside.

Wait. I could swim for it.

No time to waste. I need to go now.

I leap up and sprint to the water.

I'm up to my thighs. My chest heaves with panicked breaths. I take one huge gasp and dive.

My skin feels electric as I hit the cold water. I plunge downward, swimming close to the bottom.

Joseph must have discovered that I'm not in the lighthouse, but if he looks out the window, he'll see the dinghy where he left it. With luck, the ripple where I entered the water will be disguised by the wavelets whipped up by the breeze. He'll think I'm up on the cliff somewhere.

I open my eyes. Through clear water, I see pale seabed, the blurry shapes of rocks scattered among the sand. Ahead, the shadow of *Torrent*'s hull is a dark silhouette on the ocean floor.

I'm near the yacht. My lungs burn. Blackness appears at the edges of my vision, but I can't give up. I can't come up till I'm behind the yacht.

My head bangs into the swimming ladder. I grab it and surface as my lungs force me to inhale. Hidden behind *Torrent*, I take noisy gulps of air.

What if Joseph's rushing back already? I mightn't even have time to pull up the anchor.

I'll cut the rope. The breeze is offshore. *Torrent* will drift seaward. I'll run to the stern and start the engine. I'll be home free. No way can Joseph row faster than the yacht can motor away.

I scale the ladder and tumble into the cockpit. I scramble to my feet.

"Who's that?" A female voice.

I freeze. Julia?

Sure enough, Julia emerges from the cabin, eyes wide. "Eve? What in Heaven's name are you doing?" She's dressed in sporty maternity wear with the fake belly in place.

Some wild part of me wants to push her overboard and carry on with my escape, but how stupid would that be? If Julia's here, Joseph hasn't kidnapped me. But why has he brought more food?

"I could ask you the same thing," I say. "Take me back to Paradise Bay."

"Oh, honey, of course! I'm sorry Joe had to bring you to this godforsaken place. Are you all right? I haven't slept a wink knowing you were here." She gestures at the lighthouse as if it's to blame for what's happened.

"Why didn't you come and get me?"

"Let me find you a towel," Julia says. "You rest."

I sit, and Julia fetches a towel. While I dry off, she steps up on deck and waves to Joseph, who has reappeared on the beach.

"Eve's here!" Julia calls. "She swam to the boat." She makes it sound normal, like I just fancied a morning dip and ended up on board.

"Why did Joseph bring me here?" I ask.

"Eve, I don't know how to tell you this news." Julia sits opposite me and takes my hand. "Chris has cold feet. With Joseph finding out, it's a shambles, and Chris has lost faith in you. He's convinced you were going to tell Margareta the truth. The night of the party, he decided we had to give up the adoption. He told Joseph to take you to Hobart and put you on a plane back to Sydney, but I managed to intervene. Joseph brought you here—that was his idea—and I've been, well, negotiating with my husband. Plus, Granny fell ill yesterday. That's why Zelde and I couldn't come. Zelde was the only person nearby with medical knowledge."

I knew Chris misinterpreted my intentions. "Can I talk to Chris? I'm sure I could persuade him to trust me."

She waves her hand. "You don't need to. I've convinced him to carry on with the adoption—on one condition. He . . . he wants you to stay here."

I gape at her, eyes wide.

Julia bows her head. "I'll understand if you want to pull out, Eve. It's been one disaster after another. But we can't risk anyone seeing you again. I mean, you are looking . . ."

She glances at my belly. In my soaking T-shirt and shorts, I'm looking a lot rounder than I was even a couple of days ago.

I gaze at the water. What do I want? A minute ago, I was planning to steal this yacht and sail to Hobart. I thought I needed to escape a kidnapper. But I was never kidnapped. I'm free to leave. I just need to say the word.

I thought I hated it here, but perhaps what I hated was the sense of being imprisoned. The rock's lonely, but it's idyllic. I have more freedom than at the summerhouse. I can go outside during the day. I can swim whenever I like.

But to live on an uninhabited islet for six months? Surely that would be too hard. I shake my head. "I can't."

"The thing is, if you come back today, Chris has said that's the end. Could you stay for a little while? At least take some time to think about it?" Julia squeezes my hand. "You can change your mind anytime, and I'll simply pretend to have a miscarriage . . ." Her voice quavers. "It's up to you."

Her words tug at my heart. She's trying not to show how devastated she'll be if the plan falls through. I feel bad for her. She's not great at deception, but nor is she to blame for the bad luck we've had.

"Okay," I say with a certainty I don't feel. "I'll stay."

"Oh, thank you, Eve. You're a fabulous girl. Just say the word if there's anything you need. Zelde can stay with you. She's here. I asked her to wait below while I spoke with you. She's in the cabin setting up the portable ultrasound. Joseph went ashore to fetch you so we could check on Baby. I didn't realize you'd swim to us. Were you already having a dip when we arrived? Why did you swim in your clothes?"

"I was so keen to see you," I mumble, "and I don't own a maternity swimsuit."

"We'll fix that right away." Julia envelops me in a perfumed embrace.

As she leads me below deck, I glance at Joseph, who's smoking a cigarette on the beach. Thank goodness I haven't had to confess my embarrassing suspicions about him. I can't believe I entertained thoughts about swimming to safety. I might have risked my life—and my baby's—for no reason.

We pass through *Torrent*'s blue-and-white saloon and into the for'ard cabin where Zelde is waiting. She's dressed in her gray suit, her hair in its bun, as though she's in a city office instead of the cabin of a yacht. She greets me with her usual scowl and tells me to lie on the bunk. The machine she has set up is a weird plastic contraption.

"Can you really scan me with that little thing?" I ask.

"It doesn't produce as clear an image as the big machine, but it's still useful." Zelde runs the probe over my skin, and a blurry image appears on-screen.

Julia gasps. This is the first time she's seen the baby.

"Baby's growing well," says Zelde. "Would you like to know the gender?"

"Yes!" cries Julia, at the same time as I say, "No, thanks."

Julia frowns. "You don't want to know?"

I can't explain my feelings. I turn to Zelde. "Isn't it too early to tell? You said we'd find out in December. That's still a month away. I can't see anything on the screen."

Zelde gives a tight-lipped smile. "It takes practice to interpret radiographic images, but at fifteen weeks I can certainly discern the sex."

Her eyesight must be better than I thought.

"I don't see anything that looks like boy bits," I say, "so I guess my hunch is right."

Zelde speaks tersely. "If you choose not to know, I recommend you consider whether you'll adjust if the child isn't what you expect."

Julia twirls on the spot—a difficult feat in the cramped cabin. "It's a boy! I knew it! How fabulous!" She wraps me in an exhilarated hug. "Eve, you want a son, don't you?"

Zelde looks confused. Didn't she realize her words made it obvious I was mistaken about the gender? My uncertainty about her crystallizes into dislike. She should have known better than to reveal something her patient preferred not to know.

Xander, you're going to have a son.

"What's wrong, Eve?" Julia asks. "Aren't you happy?"

"I'm over the moon," I lie.

PART II

Five Months Later

CHAPTER 21

It's a sunny April morning, and I'm standing at the lighthouse window cradling my huge belly and watching as Joseph rows Julia and Zelde to shore.

I've grown to love it here. I can go outside whenever I like, instead of keeping quiet inside the summerhouse, afraid to turn on a light. The rock has a stark beauty, and being in the wilderness has helped me grieve. Zelde visits regularly to check on my pregnancy, and Julia often accompanies her, but the stretches of solitude don't bother me. With no one around, I feel closer to Xander.

I rise with the sun each morning for a walk and a swim. I know the rock like the back of my hand, but it's different every day—the weather and the sea state are always changing. The place teems with birds and sea creatures. I love it when I see an unusual species—a mollymawk soaring above the cliffs or a pod of dolphins cavorting in the lively seas outside the cove. On land, I often spot the pink-and-green lizards. Occasionally, if I find a pretty shell on the beach, I take it to Angel's grave and lay it on the headstone.

Indoors, I pass the time sewing or crocheting baby clothes and reading books. I linger over meal preparation, enjoying the array of ingredients Joseph delivers. Xander taught me to fish when we were crossing the Pacific, so I asked Joseph for a rod. In the heat of summer, the water teems with trevally and salmon. I fish off the rocks in the late afternoons and never come away empty-handed. In the evenings, I watch the sunset from the light room as I eat my freshly caught supper.

Christmas was followed by a sultry January in which I seemed to spend as much time in the water as out of it. I couldn't imagine being stuck inside in such weather. Now, as autumn steals the heat from summer and I'm forced by my growing girth to do everything a little more slowly, I find myself resisting the idea that it might be time to leave. My pregnancy has been uneventful. It's hard to imagine anything could go wrong.

Joseph pulls the dinghy up the beach, sits on a rock, and lights a cigarette. The women ascend the path to the lighthouse. Julia's practically running, and Zelde's having a hard time keeping up. I head downstairs to let them in.

"You need to take this more seriously." Zelde's voice, snappier than usual, penetrates the closed door.

"Nobody's around for miles." Julia's tone is petulant. "I accept I should wear the belly till we get here. We never know when another yacht might pass by, but nobody's going to sail into the cove. At least loosen the horrid thing."

I open the door. Julia has thrown up the back of her maternity blouse, revealing the straps of the fake belly.

"You need to act like a pregnant woman." Zelde tugs Julia's blouse back down, like a mother dressing a young child—a mother nearing the end of her patience. "Real pregnant women can't take a break. They can't remove their bellies and roll in the grass or sprint up a hill. Your movements need to be automatic—your walk, the way you get in and out of chairs. You ought to sleep in the thing."

"I think I'm doing a great job." Julia turns to me. "Hello, Eve. I'm getting used to wearing the biggest belly now. Would you like to see my pregnancy walk?"

"Go ahead," I say, beckoning her and Zelde inside.

Julia places a hand on the small of her back and mounts the stairs with an exaggerated waddle. "Convincing, right? And can you tell I've gained weight to make myself look fuller around the face? It's great having an excuse to eat cinnamon buns."

"You still don't look pregnant to me," Zelde mutters as we follow Julia upstairs, "although maybe that's because I know you're not."

"I agree with Zelde," I say. "You should keep up the act. If you stop and start, you might mess up one time."

"How's your shawl progressing?" Julia asks in a bright voice. Clearly, Julia's casual attitude toward her fake pregnancy is a sore point between her and Zelde, and she's keen to change the subject.

I pull the shawl I've been crocheting for the baby from my craft bag. Nanna taught me to crochet lace, but I never had the patience for it till now. Living on this rock, anything that takes up time is a blessing.

I created a circular design based on the stained-glass window in Xander's apartment. Like the window, the shawl is many shades of blue, from light eggshell to deep sapphire. Petals radiate from a central point, capturing the elegance of a stylized rose.

Julia holds the shawl up to the light. "Wow. It's as fine as gossamer. This must have taken forever. Why is there a big hole here?"

"I'll make the baby's name later and graft it in place."

In truth, I've already made the squares that spell out my daughter's name, but I've hidden them under the bed Joseph delivered a few months ago. I don't want to admit to Julia that I still believe my baby is a girl. Zelde said it was difficult to interpret those images. I'm convinced she made a mistake.

It was odd how elated Julia was by the gender reveal. Despite her reassurances that they "just want a baby," I'm still suspicious that she might have some special reason for preferring a son.

"Why don't you finish the shawl now?" Julia asks. "You'll be busy after he's born."

"Um, I haven't decided on the name," I lie.

"Huh? You were so clear about wanting to name him. I've been dying to know the name, but I was sticking to your plan to tell us after he's born."

"Um, I . . . I need to make sure he suits his name once he's born." I stuff the shawl back in its bag and change the subject before Julia can ask any more questions.

Soon, she stands to leave. Her belly looks out of place.

"You're wearing the belly too low," I say.

Zelde gives Julia an absolute death stare, and Julia titters nervously.

"Heavens, I'm over this." She flicks her abdomen. "I didn't want to bring it up since it made Zelde so mad, but I had a close call the other day. I woke from a nap and wandered downstairs in a daze, not realizing the belly had shifted. Sarah commented that Baby had 'dropped.' That's what they call it when the baby's head engages and your bump gets lower shortly before the birth, apparently. It was a shock to realize how closely I was being observed. Since then, I've had to wear the belly low every day. Once a baby has dropped, he stays dropped."

"You're lucky the belly was too low," I say. "Imagine it had been too high or off-center. That would've been harder to explain."

"Precisely," says Zelde. "You must pay more attention to details, Julia."

"I do! Ever since then, Chris helps me position the belly in the dropped position every morning. The rest of the day, I hardly dare touch it in case it shifts."

I open my mouth to speak but close it again. If Julia's so afraid of the belly shifting, why did she ask Zelde to loosen it when she arrived here? She mightn't be able to make it look the same when she reties it. It bothers me that Julia still, after all these months, isn't treating the plan with the seriousness it deserves when the whole shebang relies on her not slipping up even once.

"I might have to fire Sarah," says Julia. "She asked me the name of my obstetrician. I pretended it had slipped my mind."

She sounds so offhand. I overheard some other servants talking about Sarah while preparing for Margareta's party. A mother of three, she was struggling to make ends meet after her husband left her. Her youngest is only a year old.

"Surely that's not necessary?" I ask. "We're almost at the finish line. You only need to get through another three weeks."

"I warned you it was risky to keep a maid who's had a baby herself," says Zelde, "and the next few weeks will be the riskiest."

"Maybe I'll send Sarah on a little holiday," says Julia.

We head down to the beach, and Joseph rows us out to the yacht, where Zelde performs a checkup in the cabin. After measuring my belly, she looks me up and down with her habitual frown and calls Julia in.

"We'll induce labor in the next few days," she announces. "Baby is large for his dates. Eve, you'll probably need a ventouse delivery. We'll put you on an oxytocin drip."

I sit up on the narrow bunk. "Is that necessary? I'd like to try for a natural labor." I turn to Julia, hoping she'll support me, but she doesn't meet my gaze.

"Your Bishop score is zero," says Zelde. "You won't go into labor naturally for weeks. The Hygates didn't hire me to sit around twiddling my thumbs while you put their baby at risk with hippie nonsense. This is a big baby." She looks at Julia. "We should move Eve back to the summerhouse tomorrow morning."

Julia nods. "Thank you, Zelde."

"Is it okay to have the baby early?" I ask.

"Baby's ready."

I open my mouth to argue and shut it again. Zelde must know best.

CHAPTER 22

All afternoon I'm antsy. I don't want to leave the lighthouse tomorrow. It feels like home.

I spend the afternoon cleaning, even though I doubt anybody will care whether I leave the place tidy. I go a little crazy over it, getting down on my hands and knees to scrub the stairs.

Over the last few weeks, I've had a few "practice contractions" most evenings, particularly if I've had an active day. According to my manual, real contractions are more regular and more painful. I realize I've overdone the cleaning when my practice contractions arrive earlier than usual. Around three o'clock, I abandon the scrubbing and settle into my chair to finish the shawl.

As the sun wears its way across the sky, I work around the edge of the shawl, and the elaborate lace border gradually appears.

"Maybe Zelde was right about us going back tomorrow, bubs," I tell the wriggling being inside me as another spasm radiates across my belly. When it passes, I cast off the final few stitches and stretch the shawl over my bed. In the soft light of late afternoon, the shawl's colors are vibrant. I can't help feeling I've made something magical, like a garment in a fairy tale that keeps the wearer safe no matter how dangerous the world.

I fetch the squares that spell out my baby's name and graft them in place. The shawl is perfect. As I finish, another contraction hits, so intense that I fall onto the bed.

What if I'm in labor? Zelde isn't coming until tomorrow.

I don't need to panic. Real labor isn't like in the movies. It takes hours. Usually, when I have a run of contractions like this, I go to bed and they fade away.

I curl up on the bed now and draw the shawl over myself.

I'm woken by the world splitting into pieces. The pain is white hot. My bed's soaked. I only slept a short time—it's still daylight—but everything's changed.

My waters have broken.

I have to get off this rock.

When the contraction eases, I feel completely normal. It would be easy to pretend nothing's happening, but I have to use this time. The baby's coming.

I don't even have a phone. Joseph brought one, but there was no reception, so I gave it back. I have no way to summon help.

I make my way downstairs, gripping the banister for dear life, and open the door. Outside, the sun is touching the horizon, blasting spectacular rays of orange and gold across the sky. The sight is as sudden and dazzling as my pain.

I gaze across the ocean, willing a yacht to appear. If only some sailor would come into the cove. *I could ask him to take me to hospital in Hobart. I could keep you. I wouldn't have to share you with them.*

Another contraction hits, taking my breath away. Daggers pierce my spine. The pain yanks me from my daydream.

I'm not going to be rescued by a stranger. The whole time I've been here, I haven't seen a single ship.

I shut the door and turn to the kitchen. I'll have to give birth to this baby on my own. In the Pacific, I met mothers living in remote villages. They gave birth without medical aid. I don't need those procedures Zelde talked about. I'm young, and this is a natural process. My body will do its thing as long as I'm in a safe place.

I take a deep breath as I'm hit with another contraction. When it passes, I force myself to concentrate. I need supplies. Water to drink. A clean knife to cut the cord. A towel to wrap the baby in. I grab the items and head back upstairs.

By the time I reach the light room, I can't walk. I crawl to my bed. I'm meant to time my contractions, but I can't keep track. I had two—or was it three?—coming up the stairs.

The faster they come, the sooner she'll be born. I'll be alone with her. I'll have a few hours of being truly her mother.

Another wave hits. This time I ride with it. I'm on the sea. The pain is the crest of a wave, and after it passes, there's a trough, and I can catch my breath.

Each contraction brings the baby closer, as every wave in a storm brings a ship closer to shore. I can do this.

I'm on my hands and knees on the bed. I pick up the shawl and cling to it, my eyes closed. There's nothing in my world but the soft smell of wool amid darkness and pain.

I couldn't get help if I tried, but I don't want to anymore. I'd rather be alone. Women have given birth alone since the dawn of time.

Women have buried their babies since the dawn of time, too.

The words spring into my head as though someone is speaking to me. I open my eyes, and a flash of light almost blinds me. The light has come on.

Every fiber in my body tells me to push. But the most important thing is that my baby lives. She's three weeks premature. She needs every chance. I must get help.

I drag myself to my feet. Another contraction grips me. Leaning against the table, I wait, breathing through the pain until it subsides. Now I lift a chair, raise it high above my head, and smash it into the light.

DON'T PUSH.

Each contraction is a tsunami of pain. I gasp for air.

I'm in total darkness.

Shards of glass must be all over the floor. I can't move from my bed. The only thing anchoring me to this world is the soft smell of wool in my arms.

A thrumming sound. Helicopter blades or blood rushing through my ears? Now boots are stomping on the stairs. Light flashes around.

"Found 'er!" It's Joseph.

"The baby's coming," I pant. "Oh my God, it hurts!"

More footsteps, and now a strong arm grips me. Christopher?

"I'm here, Eve." Yes, it's Chris. "We're going to get you out of here."

"Watch out for the glass," I mumble. "Is Zelde here?"

"We'll get some pain relief into you," says Chris.

"No," I say.

I can't explain. The pain is bringing my baby to me. The pain is my body doing this right. I need the pain.

A sharp jab in my leg. Everything blurs.

I'M ON AN island with palm trees and warm sand. I'm in ultramarine seas. I'm floating with you, Xander.

In some other world, a woman is having a baby.

I open my eyes.

Chris's face hovers above mine. "You're awake."

I'm flat on my back, and this isn't the lighthouse. I'm in the birthing room at the summerhouse. The light is dim. Why am I giving birth in this gloom? Did I pass out?

"Is my baby okay?" I try to lift my head to look. *Is my baby still inside me?* I want to see what's happening, but I feel paralyzed.

"Everything's fine," Chris says. "You're doing great. Baby's nearly out."

A contraction hits. I push, and pain ravishes me. I cry out—

My daughter leaves my body. I feel her slip out into the world.

"Ten minutes past midnight," says Chris. "Zelde's just clearing Baby's airways."

"What's happening?" I ask. "Is she breathing?"

Silence. A chill passes through me. Is she all right? I try to move but my limbs refuse to obey. Damn that pain medication.

Still no sound. *Where is she? Why isn't she crying?*

I try to sit up, but Chris places his hand on my shoulder. "Stay still. Everything's fine."

Now the most beautiful sound fills my ears. The cry of a newborn. The light flicks on, and Zelde appears holding a bundle. The wriggling, perfect, alive creature is placed on my abdomen, wrapped in a white blanket. I cradle her in my arms.

She's big and warm and has a shock of reddish-blond hair. Wide awake, she gazes at me with bright blue-green eyes.

"Xander," I murmur.

She smells so good, so right. She smells like Xander.

"She's glorious," I say. "Is she okay?"

"You're both perfectly well," says Zelde, wrapping a second blanket around us both. "You're sensitive to opiates, so you were a bit dozy there for a while, but don't worry, it didn't affect Baby.

It was a straightforward delivery. I've never seen such a bonny baby boy."

CHRIS IS HOLDING the baby. The boy. He stands above me as I settle into my regular bed in the summerhouse. Zelde is in the birthing suite tidying up.

"You don't remember the helicopter trip?" Chris asks. "It was a hairy take-off from the beach."

"I remember hearing the helicopter arrive," I say. "You and Joseph were there. I don't remember Zelde being there."

"She was. Who else do you think gave you the pain medication?"

"Right. I remember that. I felt a jab in my leg. I thought it was you."

Chris chortles. "What on earth could have kept Zelde away? We've paid her salary for months for the sole purpose of having her deliver your baby. I certainly wasn't qualified to do anything other than fly the chopper, although Joseph and I came in handy getting you downstairs. When Joseph told me the lighthouse was dark, I knew at once something was wrong. Thank God we got you here in time. The only pity is Julia missed the whole thing. This was meant to be her last trip to Hobart before the birth."

I remember now that I asked for Julia to come to my labor. I'd barely noticed her absence. I was really out of it.

"Now what happens? Julia has to pretend to go into labor."

Chris nods. "She's on the late ferry. Once she's home, we'll stage a birth scene. Zelde will make our bedroom look as though Julia had a baby in there. Now that I've witnessed a birth, I can coach Julia on the details."

"Would anyone have heard the helicopter?"

"No. The staff had left for the day. Everything's worked out. Eve, he's perfect. *My son.* I can't believe I'm a father. We waited so long. Do you want to hold him again?"

"You hold him for now."

"You've barely looked at him. Julia told me you had to look at him when he was born to decide if he suited his name."

His name. How can I tell Chris I don't have a name for a boy? I didn't spend a single minute of my pregnancy choosing a boy's name. He'll realize I've been in denial, fantasizing about a daughter.

"I heard you call him Xander," says Chris.

I can't speak. I wasn't calling him Xander.

"It's a great name!" Chris exclaims. "Julia was hoping you'd chosen to name our baby after your fiancé. We love Alexander."

I try to smile.

"Alexander Hygate," says Chris. "Do you want to call him Xander for short?"

"No."

Chris looks at me quizzically.

I can't call the baby Xander. I can't be reminded of Xander every time I hear my son's name. That's the very thing I wanted to avoid, the reason I convinced myself he was a girl the whole way through my pregnancy.

The name Alexander is so long you can split it in half and make two names: Alec-Zander.

"Could we call him Alec?" I ask.

"Alec? Yes, it's perfect. I have to return to the house. Hold Alec for a few minutes first. You won't see him for a while. You need to stay in the summerhouse until you no longer look like you've had a baby."

"I don't need to hold him. You take him."

Chris tries to argue with me, but I remain firm.

He leaves with Alec. Zelde departs shortly afterward.

I lie alone.

I remember calling the baby "she" straight after the birth. Chris must have heard. He'll think I didn't want to hold the baby because I didn't want a boy.

It's hard to believe I don't have a daughter, but that isn't the reason I refused to hold my baby. I refused because I knew, if he were placed in my arms at that moment, I could never, never, never let him go.

CHAPTER 23

Zelde wakes me the next morning, clattering up the stairs before seven. "Could you get up," she says. It isn't a question.

I struggle out of bed. My body aches, and I'm still sleepy from the medication injected into my thigh. That must have been one strong painkiller.

"Quick smart," says Zelde. "The staff don't come back till tomorrow, so I have to run the whole household single-handed today." She hands me a box of pills. "These will stop your milk supply."

"Are you sure I'll need them?"

"Believe me, if you don't take these, you'll regret it. Your breasts will be engorged with milk. It hurts like heck."

"These are paracetamol tablets."

"Didn't you hear what I just said? It hurts like heck. You'll need pain relief. And here's cabergoline, which will dry up your milk."

Typical Zelde to double down when she makes a mistake, acting like she meant to do it. The woman obviously needs glasses.

"My pregnancy manual says breast milk is good for babies. Perhaps I could express milk for—"

She turns an outraged glare on me. "Don't let the Hygates hear you talk such nonsense. The idea is disgraceful. This isn't your baby. Get used to it."

My cheeks grow hot. Zelde is so rude to me. The Hygates are

paying her salary, but I'm her patient, along with Alec. Isn't she meant to treat us respectfully? I hope she's kinder to Alec than she is to me.

"Even if he weren't my baby, there's nothing disgraceful about donating milk."

"The Hygates have made it clear they prefer formula."

I wonder whether Zelde's being truthful. It seems doubtful that she and the Hygates discussed the prospect of my donating milk, given she thinks the idea is "disgraceful." But what's the point of arguing? I'm not going to change her mind.

Zelde finishes my checkup and hurries off to the house.

I climb into bed, but I can't get back to sleep. *My baby. They took him away.*

The hours drag by. This feels like the longest day of my life, but if I were trying to raise Alec alone, I'd have to leave him in childcare for hours every day. Instead, I'm going to spend most of the day with him throughout his early years. He's going to have a better life than I could have given him. He's going to have a father.

And yet, my world is sorrow. I'm haunted by half-forgotten dreams of Alec and Xander disappearing into blackness, but the real world is darker. I feel as though I've lost both of them.

In the evening, nobody brings my dinner. By half past seven, I'm starving. Perhaps I should go over to the kitchen and get it myself. That way, I might see Alec.

Christopher told me I needed to stay in the summerhouse until my post-baby belly was gone, but I don't see why. The staff aren't here.

I shower and pull on sweatpants and a hoodie. I check my appearance in the mirror. If anyone saw me, I'd pass for someone who'd gained a few kilos and liked dressing casually.

Outside, I head toward the mansion. My ears strain for the sound of a baby crying. If Alec's awake, surely I'll be allowed to see him. Hungry as I am, I'm more interested in seeing my baby than in eating.

I'm on the beach when I hear a newborn wail. My heart surges, and I speed up, pulled toward the sound as if by magnetism—but I'm not heading toward the mansion. The crying isn't coming from the mansion. It's coming from further along the beach.

Is it the acoustics of the bay? Some kind of echo? I continue toward the marina. The cry gets louder. My blood seems to fizz in response. In a moment, I'm approaching the office, nearly tripping over the dozen or so glass cages stacked by the door. The crying is coming from inside.

I yank the door, but it's locked. I knock.

No answer.

"Julia!" I cry. "It's me."

I wait. She must have heard me.

My eyes fall on the empty cages. Terrariums, I remember they're called. People keep reptiles in them. In fact, I can see a molted lizard skin inside the top cage. It's barely longer than my finger and almost translucent, but I can make out faint diamond shapes like the pattern on the lizards I saw living on Lighthouse Rock.

I rattle the door. "Julia! Let me in!"

"What the bloody hell are you doing here?" Joseph's accusing voice comes from behind me.

I turn.

He approaches along the pier. "You were told to stay in the summerhouse," he growls. He's holding a portable VHF radio.

My eyes roam over the marina. Has a new boat come in? No, nothing looks different.

"Nobody brought my dinner, so I thought I'd collect it myself."

"From the marina?" His tone is sarcastic.

"I heard Alec crying. What did you expect me to do, ignore him? Let me in. It sounds as though nobody's holding him. What's he doing here, anyway?"

"Babies cry."

"I'm asking why he's in your office and not in the house."

Joseph takes me by the arm and leads me away from the door. "You ask too many questions. You were told to stay in the summerhouse. The servants might not be here, but other people are. You can't be seen." He takes the hood of my sweatshirt and tugs it up over my hair.

"I just want to hold my baby."

"If you want to keep being Alec's nanny and not have bad stuff happen, then you'll listen to me for once, missy. Go back to the summerhouse and stay there till you're told otherwise. Stay quiet and don't make a fuss. Don't tell anyone you came here tonight. *Ever.*"

"Surely—" I begin, and then I stop. I was going to say *surely Julia heard me.* The only way Julia—or Christopher or Zelde—could have *not* heard me is if none of them is in the office.

Why would they leave Alec alone?

They must have left him with Joseph. Maybe they're busy preparing for the staff to return—although Joseph's the last person I'd ask to babysit. Maybe Alec was asleep and Joseph thought he could nip down to one of the yachts, and then Alec woke and started crying. Joseph told me not to mention it because he doesn't want to get into trouble.

Maybe. But as Joseph escorts me back to the summerhouse, I notice something else. The biggest berth in the marina is empty, as always, but ropes are set out—thick mooring lines in great coils on the pier. Joseph is preparing for a yacht to come in.

Something's happening, and I have a feeling it has to do with the terrariums I saw. Joseph doesn't seem the kind of guy who would keep reptiles as pets, and there were too many cages for it to be someone's hobby.

I try to act as though I haven't noticed anything, as though I'm too distracted by my baby. I *am* distracted by my baby. But if Alec is going to grow up with this lowlife hanging around, I want to know what he's up to.

I loved the animals I saw on the rock, especially the pretty lizards. If Joseph is catching and selling them, I guarantee he isn't doing it legally. He isn't the type to bother with the permits and paperwork you'd need to trade in wildlife. Maybe this was the secret I overheard him talking about on the ship's radio—not drug-dealing but wildlife smuggling.

"I won't say anything," I tell him as I reenter the summerhouse.

I need time to figure out what's going on. Could Joseph's dealings place Alec in harm's way? I've never found out how Chris and Julia handled Joseph's discovery of my pregnancy. The one time I asked Julia, she gave evasive answers, and the grim set to her mouth suggested I should ask no further questions. I'm sure they had to pay Joseph off.

Half an hour later, Zelde comes to the summerhouse with a casserole. Stacked outside the door are my suitcases and backpack.

"Joseph sailed to the lighthouse this morning and collected your belongings," she says. "Here's your dinner. Oh, and I thought you might want to see these photos."

She hands me her phone. I swipe hungrily through dozens of photos of my beautiful son. He looks content and well cared for, held by Julia or Chris. I can see the yellow walls of the nursery in the background.

"The Hygates believe it's better for you not to see Alec for a few days so you get used to being apart from him, but I knew you'd find it hard. I thought these photos might be a comfort. He's absolutely thriving."

"Thank you," I say, trying not to sound surprised by her change in attitude since this morning. It's almost as though Zelde knows something has unnerved me, but given that Joseph swore me to secrecy, he wouldn't have told her that I heard Alec at the marina. I want to ask Zelde why Alec was there, but something stops me. I've sensed distrust between Joseph and Zelde. I don't want to be the one to stir up trouble between them.

After she leaves, I carry my meal onto the balcony and eat in the fading light. For the next hour, I watch the ocean.

Paradise Bay is veiled in darkness. I'd never have seen it if I hadn't been watching for it. A big red schooner glides silently into the harbor and heads for the marina. I can tell from the life raft lashed to the deck and the wind generator mounted at the stern that it's an oceangoing yacht. Despite the gloom, its navigation lights are off. It disappears from view behind the trees, but over the next half hour, I hear a few muffled thuds. Cargo is being loaded on or off the yacht. After less than an hour, the yacht departs, still with its lights off.

Joseph is definitely doing something shady. Nobody sails at night with the nav lights off unless they have something to hide.

Has the schooner brought in lizards? That would explain the stack of empty cages. They've obviously held lizards before.

Breaksea would be the perfect place to smuggle goods. When Xander and I sailed into Sydney, he told me Australia's border security is focused on the north, where international shipping passes within a few miles of the land and boat people attempt to enter from Southeast Asia. Tasmania is thousands of stormy miles away from anywhere. New Zealand, the nearest country, is a week's sail away and isn't exactly teeming with drug smugglers or asylum seekers. Tasmania's borders aren't seen as requiring surveillance.

The one thing I can't figure out is why an oceangoing yacht would be involved in this business, given that the lizards live on the rock. Joseph could collect them himself. Zelde said he sailed to the rock earlier today. It's possible Joseph is smuggling the lizards *out* of Australia, but the cages were empty before the yacht arrived.

I always knew Joseph was some kind of crook. What I can't understand is how he expects to get away with this right under the Hygates' noses.

When I wake the next morning, Joseph's pickup truck is gone from its usual spot near the summerhouse. It doesn't return until late afternoon. I'd bet good money he was taking the lizards to the next point on their journey.

On the third day after Alec's birth, Zelde tells me I look "nice and slim" and suggests I try on my regular clothes. I struggle into a pair of trousers. They're a tight fit, but the sooner I can pass as a childless woman, the sooner I can see Alec.

"Can you breathe in there?" Zelde asks as I fasten the waist-band.

"Totally," I say, trying to sound relaxed.

"Fine. Tomorrow, you can 'arrive' and start nannying. After all, they've paid you for months, and you haven't had to lift a finger."

I'm too excited at the prospect of seeing Alec to point out that pushing a baby out of your body is more work than lifting a finger.

I need to prepare to act normal. I can't stare at him. I can't smell him. I can't kiss him. I must act as though looking after him is just a job.

CHAPTER 24

Joseph and I leave for Hobart on *Torrent* before dawn. I'm determined not to mention the reptile cages or the mysterious red yacht, but if I don't say something about Alec, it will seem strange.

I wait till Joseph has set the sails and we're clear of the island. "About the other day, I didn't mean to be critical. I know babies cry, and you can't always pick them up right away. I was just surprised that you were in charge of Alec." I try to sound as though that's all I noticed.

"It won't happen again," says Joseph. "I've told them I'm not their babysitter. Just you keep quiet about it."

"Deal." I guess my theory that the Hygates and Zelde were busy that day is correct. Maybe Alec kept Chris and Julia up all night and they gave him to Joseph so they could have a nap while Zelde was "running the whole household single-handed."

In Hobart, I buy a cellphone, the first I've owned since I lost my phone overboard back in Fiji. Reception is terrible on Breaksea, but an intercom and Wi-Fi were recently installed in the summerhouse. I'm not sure whether the Hygates did this for my benefit or because they want to be able to summon me without coming over and knocking on my door.

I consider reconnecting with people from my past on social media, but I'm not sure how the Hygates would feel about this.

In any case, I can't bring myself to do it. The one thing I'd want to tell them all is the one thing I can never say. *I just had a baby! I'm a mother! He's the most adorable little boy with red-gold hair . . .*

So, when the guy at the phone shop asks me if I want to reclaim an old number, I shake my head. It's time to make a new start. Now that I'm out of hiding, I'll make real-life friends who live nearby.

I catch an afternoon ferry back to Breaksea to make it appear I'm fresh from the airport. This is the last time I'll secretly leave or pretend-arrive. The lies are ending or at least getting easier. I no longer have to hide a pregnancy, and Julia no longer has to fake one. From now on, I get to spend every day with my son.

When I step off the ferry, a newly hired vineyard worker picks me up in the minivan and we head along the bush-lined road toward Paradise Bay.

"We've all been busy moving into the servants' quarters," he says. "Apparently the staff moved out only a few months back. Everyone said the bosses wouldn't last long with no overnight help."

Chris appears on the terrace as the minivan pulls up.

This is my cousin Chris, I remind myself. *My cousin whom I haven't seen for six months and whose wife just had a baby. I've been nannying in Melbourne. I'm excited to be back, nannying my cousin's baby.*

I haven't set foot inside the mansion since the night of Margareta's party. It looks even grander than I remembered. I hurry up the path while the driver takes my luggage to the summerhouse. Despite the hot summer we had, the lawn is as verdant as ever, and autumn blooms flourish in the flower beds.

Chris ushers me into the violet room, where Julia is waiting. The place is thronging with servants. I haven't seen Julia since her last visit to the lighthouse, just before the birth. She's wearing a linen shift and looks believably postpartum. I suspect she's wearing the smallest belly, which is a good move. She seems to have got better at deceiving people at last.

"How lovely to have you back on Breaksea, Eve. I'm so glad you're going to be our nanny." Julia kisses me, takes a bundle from Zelde, who's standing behind her, and passes it to me. "Meet Alec. Isn't he handsome?"

I've mentally rehearsed this moment, yet I can't stop my eyes from filling with tears.

"Hello, little cousin," I say in a bright, false voice. I direct my gaze at the ground, but it's no use. My eyes are drawn to my baby's face, and next thing I'm kissing him and breathing in his beautiful scent.

"You're perfect," I murmur.

The shawl is ready on top of my handbag. I've altered it so it spells his name. I wrap it around him. "I made this for him."

"How thoughtful of you." Julia's taking him back already. "We have a busy few days ahead. We'll christen Alec tomorrow. We're throwing a party fit for a prince! Come up to the nursery."

I follow Julia upstairs, where voices are drifting out from the yellow room. I step inside to find two women sitting on the sofa with infants in their arms. Both are breastfeeding their babies, who are double or triple Alec's size.

"You remember Eve? She's going to be our nanny," says Julia.

It's Ming and Emma from the party.

"How lovely to see you both and to meet your—" I begin.

"Smart to get your nanny on board right away," Ming says to Julia. "I struggled for a week trying to do the earth-mother thing before Philip put his foot down. He hired a night nanny so we could get some decent sleep, and we've never looked back. The next day, I hired a day nanny and reclaimed my life."

I set to work folding a pile of laundry, trying to keep my head from swiveling toward my son. He's awake, making gorgeous murmuring noises, and yet Julia isn't looking at him. Her smiles are directed at her friends.

I need to get over myself. She's clearly delighted with my baby—*her baby*. If I start judging her parenting, I'll drive myself crazy.

"You should definitely hire a second nanny," says Emma.

How many people do these women think it takes to look after one baby? Surely with two nannies, you'd barely see your child.

"You both should have advertised for a nanny-housekeeper," says Ming. "Then she can't complain when you ask her to cook or clean. Speaking of cleaning, Julia, from here I can see a thick layer of dust." She points at the floor under Alec's crib.

I bend down. It looks as though nobody's cleaned under there for months.

"The staff are too busy to dust today," says Julia.

"I'll do it." I don't want Alec developing asthma because people were busy with hors d'oeuvres and champagne fountains. I fetch a duster, get down on my hands and knees and dust under the crib. My trousers cut painfully into my post-birth belly.

"Hello, what's this? The milking shed?" says a jolly male voice.

I turn as Emma's husband, Spencer, enters the room, carrying two bulky canvas bags. His gaze passes over me without recognition.

"Spencer!" cries Emma. "That's an insensitive comment when you know poor Julia can't breastfeed!"

"I don't mind," says Julia. "I've known for a long time I wouldn't be able to breastfeed because of a medical issue. Chris is warming a bottle." She perches on the edge of the toy chest. "Are those the porta-cribs, Spencer? You can set them up in the corner."

"Toot-toot, milk delivery!" Christopher enters, a baby bottle in one hand, his phone held high in the other, recording video footage. "Daddy's here, little man. Daddy's made your bottle, and he has to prove to Mummy he can get it right. How's this, Julia?" He points his phone at the other women. "Look, here are Ming and Emma and babies Olly and Molly. Shit, is it poor form to film while you're breastfeeding?"

Ming laughs. "No, Chris, but it's poor form to swear in front of children."

"My bad! Sorry, babies."

I can't believe the transformation. Christopher Hygate, powerful businessman, is cooing and fussing. He's apologizing to babies.

Meanwhile, Spencer spreads out pieces of the portable cribs in the corner. He's muttering to himself and making no progress. He's muddled the two cribs up, even though one is blue and the other is pink.

More people crowd into the room. I overhear comments about what great hosts the Hygates are, inviting everybody for the weekend.

"We'll all be too hungover to make it to the christening," one man chortles.

"Nanny, Spencer needs a hand with the porta-cribs," says Julia. "Be a good girl, won't you?"

I turn away before she catches my expression. *Nanny?* Do I not have a name anymore? And doesn't she realize that I have no idea how to assemble a crib?

Here goes nothing. Spencer seems to have given up on the cribs, so I pick up the biggest piece of the pink crib and pull the rails apart, and the porta-crib springs into shape. I place it on the floor and pick up the only other pink thing in the room, a foam mattress, and place it inside the crib.

"Ta-da!" I say. The whole operation took ten seconds.

"Ah, it takes a woman to do this sort of thing," says Spencer.

I remember Spencer talking endlessly about fixing his cars. I guess he just can't fix things if they're pink.

Now Ming starts talking about whom Alec resembles more: Julia or Chris. It's lucky Chris hired a detective to find out what Xander looked like. Several people comment that Alec's red-blond hair "obviously" comes from Chris.

"I'm so clucky," says a matronly brunette. "Can't I hold him?" Julia passes Alec to her.

"Gawd, I don't know how to hold a baby!" The woman's voice is megaphone loud. She's handling Alec as though he's a poisonous and very slippery snake.

Alec lets out a cry. I'm desperate to march over and snatch him out of this incompetent woman's arms, but I can't move. Despite the medication, my breasts are responding to my baby's cry. The milk is trying to escape.

I'm wearing nursing pads, so the milk won't soak through, but instinctively I fold my arms across my chest.

Another woman grabs Alec. "He's so heavy!" she says. "What a whopper! How on earth did you manage a home birth?"

I tense up. I hope Chris has coached Julia on childbirth.

"I'm trying to forget about the birth." Julia screws up her face. "Now, ladies and gentlemen, will you join me downstairs for a drink?" She stands, casting a mock-pitying glance at Ming and

Emma. "I might as well enjoy the benefits of bottle-feeding. This will be my first Chardonnay in nine months! Ladies, let Nanny know what your babies need."

She takes Alec from the woman, places him in my arms, and leaves the nursery.

As the guests file out, all I can do is gaze at my son and smell him. His scent the night he was born reminded me of Xander, and while he smells a little different this afternoon, his beauty and his rightness are astonishing. They stop my brain.

"Did you hear what I said?" Emma is staring at me. She rolls her eyes. "I don't have time to say everything twice. I'm sure you know what you're doing. Babies are all the same. See you in the morning."

I'M ALONE WITH three babies, and I have no idea what I'm doing. Over the past few hours, I've somehow managed to feed them, change them, and tuck them all into their cribs, but here my luck runs out. How on earth do you settle three babies simultaneously? Alec has nodded off, but Olly and Molly seem to have no idea that sleep is expected of them. Poor Molly flails in her pink crib like a fish hooked on a line, and Olly's cry is loud enough to raise the dead.

Something about the noise reaches into my soul and twists. I need to take a breather. I step outside onto the balcony and slide the door closed.

I inhale sweet night air. The sound of waves lapping and the soft gleam of the ocean calm my jangled nerves. I might not be a nanny, but I'm a mother. Any half-sensible adult must be able to look after babies, or the human race would never have survived.

I step back inside. To my relief, the babies are quietening down. Olly and Molly are settling into sleep. Now Alec awakens, but he's calm. His big eyes look at the world like it's something surprising.

Finally, we're alone. I lift him out of his crib and sink onto the sofa. "Let's get to know each other, beautiful."

For two hours, I hold my baby. He drifts contentedly between wakefulness and sleep while I marvel at his round head, his satisfying heaviness, his ten perfect fingers with their nails like shells. His red-blond hair and blue-green eyes are the perfect mix of Xander's and my genes.

Music pulses up from downstairs. I hope Julia isn't partying hard—that she realizes a brand-new mum wouldn't take to the dance floor.

Around nine, Alec becomes unsettled. I don't want him to wake the other babies, so I take him into the hall and pace up and down.

Philip emerges from the bathroom. "Hungry little beggar," he observes as he heads downstairs.

I'm startled. My baby's hungry, and I didn't realize.

"Excuse me, um, Your Honor," I call after him, remembering he's some kind of judge. "Could you please ask the kitchen to send Alec's bottle up?"

"I'll tell a maid," Philip replies.

Soon, Zelde comes upstairs. She's not holding a bottle.

"Didn't you get my message?" I ask. "Alec's hungry."

"His next bottle isn't till ten. It's your job to settle him. Teach him his schedule. Newborns don't know night from day."

"It would help me to settle him if I could feed him."

She points at the nursery door. "Put him in his crib and teach him who's boss."

"But—"

"Don't argue with me, young lady. I'm the professional. Put him down, switch off the light, and let him exercise his lungs."

"Is Sarah around?" I ask. Sarah, a mother herself, would be the ideal person to help me with the babies, and surely Julia doesn't need her personal maid midparty.

"Sarah was let go."

"What? Why?"

Zelde shakes her head at me, as if to say I should know better than to ask. She turns and marches back downstairs.

I gape at her retreating back. Is she for real? I can't believe Julia would want her baby to go to bed hungry, but I also doubt she'd welcome me appearing in the middle of her party to tell tales on Zelde. This afternoon it was made clear I'm just Nanny.

Clearly the Hygates are not loyal to their employees, even a good worker who was a single mum. I'm sad for Sarah. I'd hoped we might become friends.

It's stupid to put a crying baby in the same room as two sleeping ones, but Zelde might return to check whether her orders have been obeyed. I return to the nursery and close the door. Through the tall windows, the crescent moon rises above a silver ocean. By its light, I find my way to the sofa.

Maybe Zelde's right. Maybe babies need to learn schedules. Maybe crying's good for their lungs. But my baby is so little and so new. Life has many sorrows, but he doesn't need to learn that just yet.

What he needs to learn is love. I want him to learn someone

loves him enough to hold him close in the dark. To comfort him when he cries.

I rock him and whisper to him, but his hunger grows. When it pierces his sleep, his grizzling turns to a sharp cry, and my body reacts. The milk flows.

He's my son, and he's hungry. I know it's wrong, but I have to do it.

I feed my baby.

CHAPTER 25

When I wake the next morning, having slept on the nursery sofa, a christening robe is hanging on the wardrobe door. Wrought in ivory silk trimmed with handmade lace, it looks like a precious heirloom. Perhaps Margareta brought it from Romania.

All morning, I'm busy with the babies as guests bustle around getting ready. Women clip about in high heels, and the scent of hairspray and perfume wafts into the nursery. I'm still in casual clothes, and I smell of regurgitated formula.

Is it possible I'm not invited?

I can't miss my son's christening. I don't care if they've decided to call me Nanny and order me about. I'm going to find a way to be there.

Perhaps I could ask Margareta to put in a word for me. Even though I've met her only once before, she feels like a friend. I'm looking forward to seeing her grand clothing and hearing her booming voice.

At eleven o'clock, I decide to chance it. Soon, everyone will leave for the church. I deposit Olly and Molly in their cribs and hurry along the hall to the red room with Alec in my arms. I knock on the door, ready to plead my case with Margareta.

The door opens, but it's not Margareta. It's Ming, dressed in a slinky black number with a thigh-high split. She's holding a lipstick.

"What's up?" she asks. "Is Olly okay?"

"He's fine," I mumble. "Sorry, wrong room."

I scuttle back to the nursery, but I'm too late. Julia's standing in the center of the room, looking radiant in a high-necked white dress, disapproval flashing in her eyes.

"Where have you been?" she asks.

"I wanted to speak to Margareta."

"Granny's not coming. She fell ill again and had to cancel her flight."

My heart sinks. "She's going to miss her only great-grandchild's christening?"

"Eve, this is terrible. Nobody's watching the children."

Just my luck to leave the babies alone for ten seconds and get caught. It looks as though I've been swanning around the house all morning.

Julia glances at her watch and tuts. "Zelde was meant to take over an hour ago. You need to put on a nice dress. You'd better run. I'll dress Alec. Didn't Chris tell you? We want you to be Alec's godmother."

Soon afterward, we leave for the church. I ride in the limousine with the Hygates and with Philip and Spencer, who will be Alec's godfathers.

I've barely had time to shower and dress. I should be annoyed at Julia for being so last-minute, but I'm too pleased by her request. I'm to be Alec's godmother. It's such a thoughtful gesture on Chris and Julia's part. As Alec's godmother, I can shower him with gifts and take him on special outings, and our relationship can be lifelong.

We arrive at the quaint stone church in the village, which is soon filled to capacity with the glitterati in their incongruously snazzy clothes. Julia gives my arm a reassuring squeeze as we make our way to the altar. "All you have to do is say yes whenever the priest speaks to you."

Chris, Julia, Spencer, Philip, and I stand beside a marble font brimming with clear water. The priest reads aloud from the Bible in a foreign language, presumably Romanian. The ceremony is in the Eastern Orthodox tradition, which must have been planned for Margareta's benefit, since I don't think Julia and Chris are churchgoers. I can't help picturing Margareta lying at home, sick and alone, and wondering why the Hygates didn't reschedule.

"Eve Hygate!"

The priest's words pierce my daydream. Chris places a hand between my shoulder blades and pushes me forward.

I must get this right for Alec.

"Yes," I say.

"Do you acknowledge that this child, Alexander, is the son of Christopher and Julia and will be raised by them as a member of the Christian church?"

I pause. I wish the question were worded differently. I don't want to lie in a church, but what else can I do? "Yes." My voice is tremulous.

"Do you wish to be appointed godmother of this child?"

"Yes."

"Do you promise that, if Christopher and Julia cannot perform their sworn duty to raise Alexander as a member of the church, you will perform the duty in their place?"

Why didn't Chris and Julia warn me I would be asked this? Of course I'd raise Alec if something happened to them, but I'm not a member of the Orthodox church. I know nothing about what I'm committing to.

A murmur goes around the church. Everybody's staring at me. I feel a sharp jab in my back.

"Yes."

BACK AT THE house, Alec is the center of attention. Passed from guest to guest, he's gushed over by men and women alike.

Julia is every inch the proud mama. However unhappy I feel at the Hygates' overcrowded social schedule, they're doing it for Alec's sake. His godfathers are influential men, and Olly and Molly are his future friends, picked from good families. I couldn't have given him any of this.

Yet I leave the party. Zelde will suspect I'm disappearing before I'm saddled with more childcare, but it isn't that. It's Angel.

Angel was the baby for whom these festivities were intended, the rightful heir or heiress. I feel as though even Julia has forgotten her lost child. Still in my formal dress and Mary Jane shoes, I find myself walking south through the bush toward Lighthouse Lookout. I can't reach Angel's grave, but I want to be close to it.

Tasmanian bush doesn't produce many flowers, but as I walk, I collect some pretty foliage. The sun is high in the sky when I emerge onto the bluff. The walk here takes only forty minutes. It's surprisingly quick, considering it takes an hour to sail to the rock, because a yacht must detour several miles offshore to avoid the outlying reefs.

The lighthouse where I lived for months looms across the ravine. I stand at the cliff edge, close enough to spot a pink-and-green lizard basking in the sun. It seems I'm always on the wrong side.

I kiss my makeshift bouquet and prepare to fling it toward Lighthouse Rock. "For Angel," I say.

Angel never drew breath. Angel never saw the ocean or the sky. Angel is so lost and forgotten that nobody visits his or her grave.

The wind whips my hair into my face, and my eyes sting with tears, but it isn't Angel I'm crying for. I'm crying for my baby. He's surrounded by well-wishers, yet he's also lost. He doesn't even know he's lost. He doesn't know he's in the wrong family. By the time Chris and Julia tell him he's had somebody else's childhood, it will be too late.

Perhaps I've been hoping Alec would sense the truth about me, but now I see that's impossible. How could a child ever find his true parents when he doesn't know he needs to look for them?

I throw the bouquet, and it flies up into the sky, whirls around, and scatters into the boiling ocean. As it disappears into the maelstrom, I see the truth.

I can't do this anymore.

I have to take back my son.

CHAPTER 26

The following afternoon, the guests finally leave, and the mansion is quiet once more. I return to the summerhouse exhausted from nannying three babies, but I can't rest until I've broken the news to the Hygates.

I've told them I need to speak with them as soon as possible. In the meantime, there's something I've been intending to do ever since I saw that lizard yesterday.

I connect to the Wi-Fi and search *Tasmanian lizards*. I learn that eighteen species of lizard are found in Tasmania. I look at images of each of them. None looks anything like the lizards on Lighthouse Rock. Are they an unknown species? It seems unlikely given lighthouse keepers used to live on the rock. The lizards sure are noticeable.

Perhaps the lizards were recently brought to the rock from another country. Perhaps that's the red schooner's role in the smuggling operation—if that's what Joseph's doing. Joseph might usually meet the yacht at the rock. It's a suitably remote place— and Joseph did warn me that bad people visited there. If he's been smuggling lizards for a while, perhaps a few have escaped and started breeding.

The schooner came into Paradise Bay on a night when it was unlikely anyone would see it. The Hygates and Zelde were busy, the staff were off-site, and I'd been told to stay in the summerhouse.

How do you search for something when you don't know its name? I enter *diamond lizards* in the search bar, but all I get is a bunch of lizard-shaped jewelry. I try *colorful lizards* and *beautiful lizards* and then *endangered lizards*. Finally, a familiar sight appears on the screen. My little pink-and-green friends.

I read the text: *The harlequin gecko is found only on New Zealand's southernmost island, Rakiura. The gecko's striking patterned coat causes it to be prized by wildlife collectors, but trade in these endangered creatures is strictly forbidden worldwide, and New Zealand's remote location and stringent airport security make them almost impossible to obtain on the international black market. Several European nationals have recently been jailed after attempting to board planes leaving New Zealand with contraband geckos concealed on their bodies. The lack of supply of these reptiles has caused their price to skyrocket.*

I'm staring at the screen. It all makes sense. A yacht is such an easy way to smuggle goods—if you can sail. Customs often don't bother to visit a yacht before clearing it to leave port. They merely require the skipper to report to their offices with the paperwork. On my Pacific voyage with Xander, the few times customs officials did step on board *Joy*, it felt like a social visit. They didn't search the yacht. Anything could have been hidden under floorboards or behind wall panels.

Surely the Hygates aren't involved in Joseph's dubious dealings. They're already rich and don't need to get mixed up in smuggling. But they're afraid of Joseph. They don't trust him, yet for some reason, they're stuck with him. He had some power over them even before he found out about the adoption. Now, presumably, his power has grown. He knows their secret.

Somehow, the Hygates have kept Joseph from revealing the truth about Alec. Julia was so worried about Joseph finding out, but Chris seemed to resolve the problem the night of Margareta's party. I hate to think how much money he must have handed over.

My phone rings. I almost jump out of my skin. I'd forgotten I gave Zelde my new number. It must be her. "Hello?"

"I believe you asked Mr. and Mrs. Hygate for a private word." Zelde's tone suggests she considers this the height of impudence. "They're on their way over to you. Don't keep them too long, will you? They've left Alec with me, and I don't have time to spare on childcare this evening. I need to do the payroll."

I hurry off the phone and look through the window. Chris and Julia are approaching through the blackwood trees.

Forget about Joseph and the geckos. I need to focus on Alec. This conversation is going to be intense.

The summerhouse is a bombsite. The last thing I need is to look disorganized and lazy. I quickly shove the worst mess under my bed. I'm hiding my stupid mountain of baby-girl clothes as Chris and Julia come up the stairs.

"Oh, Eve," says Julia, flopping onto the couch, "we're so embarrassed that you were asked to babysit Olly and Molly. What a fiasco! I'd told my friends you were an experienced nanny, and then I couldn't think how to refuse them your services. I sent Zelde to help you, though. She's become such a mainstay. Did I tell you she's agreed to carry on here as our secretary? Thank Heaven!"

"Zelde was no help." I sit at the table, hoping it will conceal my trembling hands. "She only came when I sent for her, and she refused to bring Alec's bottle when he was hungry. She seems to think she's in charge of Alec."

"I can see you and Zelde don't get along," says Julia.

"It's not a case of our not getting along. I'm the nanny. The nanny should make the decisions when the parents aren't around. Speaking of people not being around, was Zelde even at the birth?"

Chris is leaning against the balustrade at the top of the stairs. "Eve, this must be some delusion caused by the medication. I don't see how you could know who was or wasn't present. You were too sozzled on painkillers to remember the helicopter ride. You'll just have to trust me that Zelde attended to you diligently throughout your labor."

I can't escape the feeling that something strange is going on in Paradise Bay. People are never where they're meant to be. Zelde was absent from my labor—I'm sure of it despite Chris's denial. Margareta was absent from the christening, even though the Romanian ceremony seemed to be designed to please her. And Alec was left at the marina with a sketchy sailor the day after he was born, despite having *three* parents and a live-in midwife.

"Getting back to your main point," says Julia, "I understand things are complicated with you and Zelde because she has qualifications and you don't. I don't want my baby to go hungry, but Zelde must know what she's doing. However, we hired *you* as nanny, not her. I'll tell her to comply with your wishes in future."

Christopher nods his agreement.

That's it?

Julia's taken the wind out of my sails. I thought she would defend Zelde. But this isn't about making Alec wait for his bottle or landing me with other people's kids. Even when Alec was happy, being celebrated by Chris and Julia's friends, things didn't feel right. That was when they felt worst.

"It doesn't matter about Zelde," I say. "My problem isn't with her."

"Who is your problem with?" asks Chris.

I'm holding my breath. There's no easy way to say this.

"I've made a decision. You're wonderful parents, and you've been so kind to me, but it's too painful to watch Alec being raised as somebody else's child. I can't do it. I'm sorry, but I can't carry on."

The silence seems to last forever. Chris gazes at the wall, his expression unreadable. Julia stares at me, her eyes wide. Tears start flowing down her cheeks.

"This is terrible news." She leaps up and starts pacing the room. "I can't believe you feel like that. Surely we can do something about it. Please don't go, Eve. There must be another way. Say the word, and Zelde's gone."

I sit on my hands. "It's not Zelde. The plan was wrong from the beginning. You remember I said no at first. I wish I'd stuck with my instinct. I'm sorry to have put you through this, but it's wrong, and I can't fix it."

"We were so happy to have a nanny who loved Alec so dearly." Julia wipes her cheeks with her hands. "Where will we find another one?"

Her words hang in the air.

"Where will you find another *what*?" I ask.

"Another nanny for Alec. I don't think I'll try. No nanny could love him as much as you and I do, Eve. I'll give up my charity work and raise Alec myself. I don't want him to experience the trauma of a change in caregiver."

I gape at her. I thought I'd said the hard part, but she didn't hear me. I need to say it again. "Julia."

She looks at me with her limpid eyes.

"I'm not proposing to leave Alec with you. I'm sorry, but Alec's my son. He's coming with me."

Silence again. This time, it's thick and heavy.

Chris says, "It's too late for that."

"What do you—"

He holds up his hand. "Eve, stop. The more you say, the harder it will be for you later. You see, you've committed a crime."

Time stops. The room seems to grow darker. I wait for him to explain. I could almost believe he's joking, but his jaw is set firmly. His eyes are stony.

"What are you talking about?" I ask at last.

"Child trafficking," says Chris.

The color drains from the room. Chris's expression is cold. He looks at me as if we're strangers.

"How can I traffic my own child?" I ask. "I'm allowed to take him."

"I don't mean it's a crime for you to take him. The crime is what you've already done. You sold Alec to us. You accepted payment throughout the pregnancy, and you did nothing in return but give us a baby. The law regards that as trafficking. A child must never be bought or sold."

"If what we did was wrong, surely I'm making it right by canceling?"

"If only the law worked that way. Bank robbers could return the money. Drug dealers could hand over their products to the police. Unfortunately, criminal law is concerned with what you've already done. Things have gone too far. If you'd changed your mind earlier, perhaps we could have pretended Julia had suffered another miscarriage. Now dozens of people have seen Julia's

living baby. At the christening, all three of us stood up and confirmed he's Julia's and my son. You made a vow to that effect in
the presence of witnesses including a Supreme Court judge. The
law is severe. Selling a child is slavery."

I'm reeling. I was so excited to be godmother I barely paused
to consider that I was making a false vow. The act that I thought
guaranteed me a close relationship with Alec is the act that sealed
my doom. "You make it sound as though I did this on my own!"

Christopher shakes his head. "Julia and I are culpable, too. We
bought Alec from you. If word got out—which it would if Julia
and I suddenly *didn't* have a child—we'd all go to prison, unless
we found an exceptional lawyer who could sway a judge." Chris
has a menacing gleam in his eye as he speaks these words. "Even
if we avoided prison, child welfare authorities wouldn't allow any
of us to retain custody of Alec. Since Margareta is too old to care
for him and you have no family, Alec would end up in foster care."

My head sinks into my hands. Why didn't I realize it wouldn't
be straightforward to reclaim my son? What did I think the Hygates would tell their friends?

"You told me I could take him back!" I cry. "You said everything depended on my goodwill!"

I can see the Hygates don't want the police involved. Julia's
eyes are wide with fear. Yet if it came to it, I'd be worse off than
them. They'd have a great lawyer. I wouldn't.

"You misunderstood me," says Chris. "We do depend on your
goodwill. If you don't like the way we're raising Alec, you can
blow the whistle. Alec will be removed from our care and will be
safe, but he won't be given to you."

Julia whirls around to face her husband. "Oh, Chris, please
stop. I wish we weren't having this conversation. Eve, I think of

you as family. Can't we back up a little? Please reconsider. Don't leave your son."

I can't handle what Chris has said, but Julia's words shock me more. She understands nothing about me if she thinks I would leave, now that I know I can't take Alec.

I'd do anything to avoid Alec being put in foster care, being passed around from place to place by those vultures with fake-happy voices and saccharine smiles. This is why I left school and went to live with roommates when Nanna died. No way was I letting the vultures into my life again. No way will they be part of Alec's childhood.

All my thoughts about Alec being in the wrong family seem stupid. Any family is better than none.

"Don't women have hormonal issues after childbirth?" asks Chris. "I'm sure that's all this is. No offense, but you'd have to be a little out of whack to think Alec would be better off being raised by a homeless single mum than growing up at Paradise Bay, heir to Margareta's fortune."

"Christopher!" exclaims Julia. "That came across as rude. I'm not saying you're wrong—Zelde mentioned mood swings—but there's no need to be so blunt."

"This is our fault for overtiring Eve." Chris sits opposite me. His tone softens, but it still has a sinister edge. "Our guests have gone. We don't need to keep up appearances. Eve, you'll stay in the summerhouse and rest. Alec will be taken off your hands. We'll tell the staff you have a cold. In a week, I'll come and see whether you've thought better of this foolish idea."

"I'm sure a day or two will be plenty for Eve to see her mistake—"

"Julia, I've made up my mind. Come. Alec's due for his feed.

You need to get him onto that schedule. It's never too early for him to learn self-discipline."

With that, he and Julia are gone.

I sit frozen in place. How deluded I was. Chris was jollying me along, letting me believe I pulled the strings, like a parent who lets a child believe he's choosing to go to school—until the day he wants to stay home.

Chris is not who I thought he was. I saw him as a kind father, but he's a businessman, ruthlessly protective of what belongs to him. I should have known when I learned Sarah was fired. The Hygates aren't some charity devoted to helping single mothers. The Hygates are devoted to helping the Hygates.

Even when Chris made his voice sound friendly, there was no true friendship beneath. What did he mean by a lawyer who could sway a judge? Would the lawyer persuade the judge with brilliant legal arguments or with bribes?

It hardly matters. I can't let the adoption become known to the authorities. I no longer want Chris to be Alec's father, but the alternatives are worse. I could try to run away with Alec, but the police would hunt me down. I'd be charged with kidnapping. If I said that Alec was my baby, I'd be charged with trafficking.

Julia also isn't who I thought she was. Since Alec was born, I've seen another side to her. She's preoccupied with appearances and easily influenced by her husband and his rich friends. I already don't like her parenting style.

But Julia isn't a bad person. She loves Alec. Despite our awkward conversation, the Hygates are willing for me to stay on. They've fired a warning shot, but as long as I comply with their wishes, they're prepared to give me another chance.

True to his word, Chris doesn't return to the summerhouse for a week, and I don't dare visit the mansion, but it doesn't take me a week to make up my mind. It's not even a case of making up my mind. I simply have no other option. I must keep Alec in my life.

I'll swallow my pride, beg for forgiveness, keep my opinions to myself like all the other staff. I'll become what Christopher calls a bootlicker, because, no matter what he's said in the past, that's what he actually wants.

I'll do whatever it takes to keep my job. I'll do anything to stay with my baby.

PART III

Six Years Later

CHAPTER 27

Alec is sitting on the bench in the summerhouse kitchenette, reading to me while I bake.

"The king was delighted to see the glittering gold the maiden had spun." Alec looks up from the book, flicking his blond hair out of his gorgeous turquoise eyes. "Why do people in stories always want gold? I'd rather get cake."

"That's lucky, since cake's coming your way soon." I hand him the spatula. "Have a taste."

Alec's eyes bug at the sight of the creamy mixture. "Am I allowed? Mummy says it's greedy."

"We only had a light lunch. Besides, it's hard to get the batter off without a dishwasher." I wink. "You'll be helping me."

Alec closes his book with a happy grin and tucks in. I watch with a mix of pride and sadness. He's a lovely kid, but thanks to Chris's rigidity, his life is so full of rules that he's afraid to enjoy himself. Even an offer to taste cake batter requires a fraught decision.

For six years, I've raised my son in accordance with the Hygates' decrees. Since Alec was barely out of the cradle, he's been expected to behave like an adult. He isn't allowed to eat between mealtimes, leave toys on the floor, or get dirt on his clothes. If he misbehaves, punishment is swift. He's sent to his room, his playdates are canceled, or he's kept home from soccer practice.

It's been hard watching my son be raised this way, but every time I consider the alternatives, I conclude things are best left as they are. I worry about Joseph living nearby, too, but he pays no attention to Alec. I haven't seen the red schooner or any other sign that Joseph is smuggling geckos since that night when Alec was a baby. Presumably, Joseph has gone clean.

Things began to change at Paradise Bay around a year ago. First the gardeners were let go, then the maids, one by one, until the only hired help left living on the property were Zelde and me. The Hygates don't say anything, but it's obvious they've suffered a serious financial setback. Without a team of people to keep it spick and span, the property at Paradise Bay is becoming neglected, inside and out.

I was afraid the Hygates would fire me, too. Instead, over the past few months, they've got their money's worth out of me by leaving Alec in my care twenty-four-seven while they disappear on frequent business trips. I have no idea where they go—they never tell me anything—but I suspect they've started a new venture that they hope will solve their financial woes. In the past, they were seldom gone for long, since Chris's business meetings were usually in Hobart and Julia dropped her charity work years ago. I'm pretty sure Julia used to accompany Chris to Hobart purely for the chance to go shopping, but now their trips seem more focused. She doesn't return with shopping bags anymore. The lavish parties the Hygates used to host are also a thing of the past.

This summer has been bliss. The Hygates have been away for a month, and with no one to countermand me, I've given Alec all the experiences his parents withhold. I've let him splash in puddles during summer storms, climb trees heavy with ripe pears, and stay up past his bedtime to watch for shooting stars. Today, we're having cake, even though Alec isn't supposed to eat sugary food on weekdays. After all, it's my birthday.

"What do you want for a present?" Alec asks. "Thirty is a big birthday, like turning ten for the third time. I didn't get you anything."

Poor Alec. I wouldn't expect a six-year-old to have organized a trip to the village to buy me a present.

"I don't want anything." I wipe a splotch of batter off his nose. "When you reach my age, you'd rather do things than get things."

"What would you like to do, then?"

"I'd like to eat cake with you."

"Grown-ups always say what they *are* doing. I mean if you could do anything in the world. If you could fly to the moon or ride a T. rex."

I slide the cake into the oven, lean against the bench, and close my eyes. "I'd like to be on a yacht in the middle of the ocean with no land around. Nothing but blue. I'd lie on the deck in the sunshine, and a pod of dolphins would come and keep me company." In fact, I got Joseph's permission to take *Torrent* out for a solo-sail today, but Alec's playdate fell through, so I couldn't go.

"Only dolphins, no people?" asks Alec. "Wouldn't you be lonely?"

"You'd be there."

Alec jumps down from the bench and approaches me. "Evie, why don't you have your own little boy?"

The question jolts me. Of course, I imagined Alec would be with me, but to him, it must seem a strange assumption. I try to brush him off. "I don't need one. I have you."

"But, Evie, when you get married, your husband will want his own little boy."

"Maybe I'll never get married. I'm not likely to meet anyone on this island. All the men are already spoken for, or else they're a bit peculiar."

I try to sound offhand. I don't want Alec to sense that I dream of a life beyond Breaksea for us—a life in which I've found a man, someone who's a good stepfather to Alec. I'd like to rekindle my designing career, too, but the fashion industry is all about connections, and I can't make any while living in such a remote place.

Alec runs outside to play while the cake bakes. As I tidy the kitchenette, I count the short days before the Hygates return and school starts. It's nearly the end of January. I'll see so little of Alec this year. He no longer needs me to drive him to school now that he can ride a bike. The Hygates promised I could stay until Alec was grown, but I'm beginning to feel like the proverbial fifth wheel. If I were Alec's mother, I could return to paid work, move to a bigger town, and find new friends. As his nanny, I can't. I'd never leave him, but I can't help feeling my son and I are living the wrong life.

When the cake's ready, I call Alec inside. He appears at the door with a shy smile.

"Happy birthday." He holds out a posy of hand-picked forget-me-nots, slightly squished in his little fist. "I got blue flowers because blue's your favorite color."

My heart swells. "What a fabulous present! Thank you. I'll put them in water."

We ice the cake, and I carry it to the table. As Alec is placing the candles, he asks, "Are you going to wish for a husband?"

I laugh. "I think the usual procedure is to find a boyfriend first and then see if he turns into a husband."

Alec pauses, candle in hand. "Did you ever have a boyfriend?"

"A few."

"Why didn't any of them turn into a husband?"

"Mostly, we were too young. And then one of them I wanted to marry, but . . ."

"What?"

It must be my self-pitying mood, but I can't bring myself to lie to my son about his father. "He died in a car accident. I loved him very much, and I was sad for a long time. I moved here and started looking after you, and time passed, and now I'm not sad anymore."

Alec climbs out of his chair and wraps his arms around me. His turquoise eyes gaze into mine. "Then why are you crying?"

As I'm WASHING up, my thoughts turn to where I might be today if I'd never met the Hygates. When I was pregnant, I thought I couldn't manage as a single mother with my migraines, my grief, and my lack of means. By the time I got up the courage to give it a shot, the Hygates had trapped me with their false promises.

The irony is I haven't had a migraine in years. I probably could have made it work.

I gaze out the kitchen window at the blackwood trees. Things have turned out so different from what I hoped. Over the years, I've made friends with a number of servants, only for them to be "let go." I thought Margareta would be a fabulous great-grandmother and a friend for me, too, but she died when Alec was a baby without ever returning to Breaksea. The Hygates didn't invite me to her funeral. As for the castle, there's no sign of it. I was given to understand that when Margareta died, the castle would pass to Julia to be held in trust for Alec. At the time, the Hygates lived so lavishly that an increase in their wealth would have been difficult to notice, but now that they're in financial strife, I'd expect them to try to turn a profit on such a valuable asset—by renting it out perhaps. Yet they never speak of it. I wonder whether they have somehow lost ownership of the castle, or perhaps Margareta *was* just a batty old lady who made up a story. Is that why Julia was embarrassed about the castle—because it never existed?

It makes no difference. I don't care how rich or poor Alec might be. I only care that I'm living a lie.

"I can tell you're still sad," says Alec, coming into the kitchen. "You shouldn't have cried on your birthday. Daddy says if you cry on your birthday, you'll cry every day for a year."

I'm always careful not to contradict Christopher. "Crying because you loved someone is worth it. It's important to remember your love."

"What was his name?" asks Alec. "If you tell me about him, I can help you remember."

"Well, you're named after—I mean, uh, you have the same name as him."

"His name was Alec?"

"It was Alexander, but I called him Xander. I'm glad you're called Alec because it helps me remember Xander, without being too similar."

"What do you mean?" Alec looks pensive.

"It can be confusing when two people have the same name, especially when they're both tall young men with blond hair and blue eyes like you and Xander. You look quite alike." I'm treading dangerous ground. "What a sunny day. Shall we go to the beach?"

"Evie, why didn't you go sailing for your birthday?"

Man, Alec is full of awkward questions today.

"I'd rather be with you, matey," I say.

"Why don't you ever take me sailing?"

"I'm not allowed to take you off the island, remember?"

This is another of Christopher's rules.

"But you took me to Hobart."

"Your parents gave me permission that one time."

Allowing me to take Alec off the island a few weeks ago as a new year's treat was an unusual move on the Hygates' part.

Alec screws up his face. "They only sent us away so they could sneak back here without seeing me."

I place the last dish on the drying rack and turn to him. "No, honey. Is that what you thought? Your parents would never do that. They miss you."

"I smelled Mummy when we got back from Hobart. Her room smelled like that flower that grows on the fence at school."

"Like her jasmine perfume? That doesn't mean Mummy was there. Zelde must have brought some jasmines into the house."

Alec shrugs. "Anyway, we could sail to another part of the island. How long would it take to sail to the lighthouse?" He jiggles on his tiptoes with excitement.

We wander onto the balcony. The sheltered waters within Paradise Bay are calm, but beyond the headland, whitecaps ruffle the surface—the sign of a perfect sea breeze. It's early in the afternoon, and the sail to the lighthouse would only take an hour—a beam reach in both directions—but it's out of the question. "I don't have a life jacket for you."

Alec points to the yachts, each of which appears, in the glassy water, to have an upside-down twin. "My life jacket's at the marina. Come on, I'm allowed to go to the lighthouse. I know I am because Daddy flew me there once, only it was too rough to land."

"It's not that simple, Alec. I don't have your parents' permission to take you sailing."

"They didn't say you *couldn't*?" Alec tilts his head.

"No."

"I won't tell. Joseph's gone to the village, and Miss Finch thinks I'm at Leo's. She never cares where I am, as long as I turn up on time for dinner and don't traipse sand all over the floor."

Alec has a point. Zelde doesn't know his playdate was canceled. I told Joseph I wouldn't be sailing *Torrent* today after all, but presumably he wouldn't care if I did.

"Just because no one will know isn't an excuse for doing something wrong."

Alec sighs. "Grown-ups always think anything fun is wrong. You're just like Mummy and Daddy. When I grow up, I'm going to remember to have fun."

I turn back toward the ocean. It's so glorious out there.

CHAPTER 28

The breeze ruffles my hair as *Torrent* cuts through the sparkling waters. The weather is as wonderful as it looked from the summerhouse. Our wake ripples across the ocean behind us in a satisfying V. The only sign we've been here vanishes in minutes. Xander used to call it the trackless sea.

I watch the mansion disappear behind the headland. I lean into the cabin and cry, "All clear!"

Alec steps into the sunshine, a wide grin on his face. His life jacket is fastened tightly.

"Here are the rules," I say, remembering my first sailing lesson from Xander. "Number one, don't fall off the boat. Number two, don't fall off the boat. Number three . . ."

"Don't fall off the boat!" Alec finishes, laughing.

"You're a fast learner. Come and hold the tiller. It's like a steering wheel, but it goes in the opposite direction. Push it to starboard and the boat turns to port. Push it to port and the boat turns to starboard."

"Which is which?"

"That's the next lesson. We'll make a sailor of you in no time."

Alec takes the tiller. I grab a pen from the nav station and draw a star on his right hand. "As long as you're facing the bow, this is starboard. Your left hand is port." I draw a circle on his left hand to represent a porthole.

I keep my hand on his as I show him the telltales on the sail and explain how they "tell the tale" of the wind, warning him of gusts and lulls.

"It's confusing," he says.

"Don't think about it. Feel it. The tiller's joined to the rudder, which pokes out under the yacht like an oar. The ocean is humming to you through the wood. Remember, wood used to be a tree, so it's still kind of alive. Notice the breeze on your face and watch it dancing across the water. Soon, you'll feel the sea's music, the way they say deaf people feel a song. You'll steer without knowing you're doing it. See the lighthouse? Keep it straight ahead."

Alec goes quiet, as though in a trance. As I loosen my hold on his hand, I feel him take over. At first, we're wobbly. Our wake becomes "snake wake." But Alec steadies up. *Torrent* is a small craft, and he's a big boy for his age. He's a natural.

He was right that sometimes adults refuse to do things *because* they're fun, as though having fun is wrong. As though we don't deserve happiness. Even if I don't deserve happiness, Alec does. It's my job to give him freedom and enlarge his world. One day, I fear, he'll rebel against his upbringing—or maybe that's what I hope.

Alec stays at the helm for almost an hour while I make sure we navigate clear of the reefs. I take over in order to maneuver *Torrent* into Lighthouse Cove. We didn't tow a dinghy, so we anchor close to the beach and swim ashore. Soon, we're standing on the white sand in our bathers, dripping and smiling. Above us, the red-and-white tower pierces the sky.

I can't believe I've brought Alec back here. I feel he was meant to be born here. I wanted to give birth to him in the lighthouse. Even though it was the sensible decision to seek help, it felt wrong.

Yet I've got what is most important to me. My child is happy, and we're together.

Alec sets off running up the bank. It's cool how interested he is in the lighthouse, as though he has some memory of it from his time in the womb.

"Wait!" I cry, hurrying up the path. When I reach the clearing at the top, Alec is nowhere in sight. I try the door to the lighthouse, but it's locked. He must have gone into the bush.

"Alec!"

No answer.

I don't want to walk through the bush barefoot, but I can't let Alec wander off alone. The wind's chilly up here.

"Alec! Where are you?" I head into the bush. "Come on, honey! Let's look for seashells on the beach!"

I'm picking my way through vines. Alec is nowhere to be found. I would have thought this rock wasn't big enough to get lost on.

I'm close to the cliff when he shouts.

"Look what I found!"

I follow the sound through thick undergrowth.

"Watch out," he says, appearing beside me. "You're nearly standing on it."

I stop short. At my feet is Angel's headstone.

"Why is there a grave here?" Alec asks. "Someone must have been shipwrecked. Someone called Angel."

I've already blurted out too many secrets today. Angel's story is not for me to share. "Time to head back. No arguments, please.

My teeth are chattering. It's not so easy to get through this bush. It's way more overgrown than it used to be."

Alec looks puzzled. "I thought you'd never been here."

Oops. I've always given Alec the impression I haven't visited the rock, since otherwise I knew he'd ask endless questions, and I didn't want to give away that I'd lived here. "It's way more overgrown than the bush on Breaksea, I mean. Come on, Alec. Why did you run off?"

"I saw a weird-looking lizard—a pink one with green patches."

"Hmm." I try to sound uninterested. I never got to the bottom of how endangered New Zealand geckos ended up on this rock. So, they're still here. Does this mean Joseph is still smuggling them, or are they breeding here of their own accord? Either way, I hope Alec doesn't mention them to anyone.

We swim out to *Torrent* and climb the ladder. On board, we change into warm clothes, but Alec is still shivering.

"Perhaps we'll delay half an hour," I say. "I'll see if I can make us something hot to eat or drink."

I descend the ladder into the saloon. The combined kitchen-dining-living area is compact, but the blue-and-white furnishings are so neat and nautical that it doesn't feel cramped. A sofa is built into the starboard wall, curving with the shape of the hull, while the port wall features a built-in stove and benchtop.

I flick on the stove, but it won't light. I go back on deck and find the gas tank in an exterior locker. Gas tanks are kept outside a boat's hull to prevent a build-up of gas in the event of a leak, but Joseph has been extra cautious, disconnecting the tank from the hose. I reconnect it, return to the saloon, and put the kettle on, but I can't find any food or drink. I've taken out the

Hygates' yachts a few times over the years, and they're usually well-stocked, but *Torrent*'s lockers are bare.

I duck through the doorway into the for'ard cabin, which I haven't entered in years. It's strange to see the bunk where I used to lie while Zelde performed my antenatal exams. All the kitchen supplies have been stashed in the cabin's lockers. Joseph must be in the middle of rejigging the galley. I find soup sachets, and soon, Alec and I are sitting at the fold-out saloon table enjoying delicious hot soup.

"This is the life," I say. "The best part of a swim is warming up afterward."

"This is the best birthday," says Alec.

After we've cleaned up, I tell Alec to take the helm while I pull up the anchor. I don't need him to steer, but it keeps him safe in the cockpit. He does so well that I let him steer out of the cove into open water.

Alec turns *Torrent* toward home, leaving me free to trim the sails. We're a good team. He's growing up to be like Xander, and I should feel proud, but the flip side of celebrating his maturity is having to say farewell to his babyhood. Every accomplishment of Alec's brings him closer to the day he won't need me anymore.

I'm so wrapped up in my thoughts, gazing at the glimmering horizon, I barely notice the wind has picked up. I'm chilled to the bone. Alec must be even colder.

I glance at him. He's focused on helming, alert yet relaxed, but his fingers are blue.

"You'd better go below deck and warm up. Keep your life jacket on. I'll take over." I place my hand on the tiller, and our fingers touch.

"You're cold, too, Evie."

"I'm a grown-up. I can handle it. Go on, get out of the wind."

Alec heads down the ladder. A moment later, he reappears with the blue shawl I made when I was pregnant, which he must have packed in his backpack. "This will warm you up."

When Alec was small, I used to say the shawl was magic because it felt warm despite its light, lacy weave. His faith in the shawl's special powers is touching.

"Thanks, but I don't want to get salt spray on it. I'll have to suffer." I smile tightly.

Alec disappears below deck, and it doesn't occur to me that he might make another plan to warm me up. It doesn't occur to me to ask what he's doing down there. I carry on sailing.

The wind has veered. Maybe I should ease the main. We've steered clear of the reefs extending from the island's southern cliffs. It's safer to stay a couple of miles offshore, but we could—

A blast. I'm jolted against the rails. Heat. Flames. My ears ring. Something has exploded in the saloon.

Xander, I'm coming.

Fire and smoke billow out of the hatch. I stagger forward.

My baby is down there.

This can't be happening. The person I love is trapped in a fire. Again. I look wildly around for a fire extinguisher. Nothing.

No time to think. I have to get him out.

I grab our wet towels and throw one over my head. I take a deep breath, rush to the ladder and leap down into the saloon.

It's dark with smoke. Through the towel, I feel heat powerful as an animal on the hunt. My eyes sting. I don't dare breathe.

Don't let him be dead.

I crash forward. Burning pain. My body screams at me to go back.

The explosion has blown everything to pieces. The floor is littered with debris. I reach the far end of the saloon, groping for Alec as I stumble forward. No sign of him.

I drop to my knees and feel my way through the doorway to the cabin. "Alec!" I rasp.

Wool. A wriggling bundle on the floor. Alec is huddled inside the shawl.

He's alive.

"I'm scared, Evie."

"Stay low, honey."

I glance back. Through thick black smoke, I glimpse leaping flames. The saloon has become an inferno. We can't get out that way.

I wrap the other towel around Alec. "Breathe through this. I'll get us out of here." I reach for the overhead hatch.

Wait. Letting oxygen into this cabin could be a serious mistake.

The door between the cabin and the burning saloon is hooked open. I need to close it before opening the hatch, but I'll have to step back into the saloon to unhook it. If I breathe much more of this smoke, I'll die. I'm holding my breath. My life is as short as the air in my lungs.

I leap into the saloon, wrestle the hook free, dart back into the cabin, yank the door shut. Smoke billows through the cracks. I haul the quilt off the bunk and jam it into the gap under the door, but the cabin's already half full of smoke. I clamber onto the bunk and push against the hatch.

Nothing. The hatch doesn't move.

I slam my hands against it with all my might. Still nothing.

Alec is silent. I hope he can breathe down there.

Push.

The hatch doesn't budge. Is something on top of it? What could be blocking it? I try to picture how it looks from the deck.

I'm an idiot. The hatch doesn't swing open. It slides. I slide with both hands and sky appears. Fresh air.

If I pass out, I can't save Alec. I lift my chin high and suck in one sweet breath.

Now I drop back into hell.

CHAPTER 29

I crouch and shout into Alec's ear. "Get up! Climb on the bunk!"
I haven't lifted him in years. He's big for a six-year-old, and I'm small. He scrambles onto the bunk, the shawl and towel still around him.

I'm directly under the hatch. "Stand on my shoulders."

I hold back a scream as his full weight lands on my singed flesh. His hands grab at my hair. He reaches for the hatch and lifts off me like an angel taking flight. He's gone.

Alec is safe.

He's not, though. He's standing on the deck of a burning yacht miles from land. If he's going to live, I need to get out of here.

I leap onto the bunk and push my face through the hatch. I pant, hungry for oxygen. The fire will burn through the door soon. I have to be quick.

"Evie, you're burnt!"

I grip the edges of the hatch and try to pull myself up, but the angle's too awkward. I can't lift my body weight.

"Evie, climb up! Get out!"

"I'm not strong enough!"

"Just climb! It's easy!"

He doesn't understand. My body was a ladder for him to climb. There's no one to do the same for me.

"I don't have anything to climb."

"I'll pull you!" Alec leans into the hole and grabs me by my shoulders. He's straining to lift me.

I grasp the edges of the hatch and pull. I'm rising. If I could get my shoulder up . . . I'm too weak. I can't do it. I'm slipping.

I fall back onto the bunk. "Try again!" I shout.

"No! The fire's coming." He disappears from sight.

"Alec!" I scream. "Come back!"

He can't help me, but I can't bear that he's gone. I'm going to die down here.

A loop of rope falls through the hatch. It drops to waist height. I reach for it.

"Don't grab it yet." My son's voice is calm. "I'm wrapping it round a post. Wait. Okay. Now."

"You can't pull me, Alec. I'm too heavy."

"I'm not pulling. Put your foot in the loop. It's like a step."

I can hardly get my foot high enough, but when I do, I instantly feel stronger. With my foot in the loop, I grab the rope, and in one great heave, hoist myself up. My head and shoulders rise above the hatch. I flop onto the deck like a fish and wriggle free.

Flames rush through the space behind me. The door has burned through. *Torrent* has become a stove, her hatches chimneys. Fire leaps skyward, setting the mainsail ablaze. A rush of heat. I push Alec toward the bow.

"I'm sorry, Evie! I tried to make you a hot drink. I was looking for the cocoa."

"It's not your fault. There must have been a leak in the hose." *That's* why Joseph disconnected the tank.

Beneath our feet, the deck is growing hotter. The fuel tank. What will happen when the fire reaches it?

Alec's wearing his life jacket. If help arrives fast enough, he could survive. It's late summer. The water's as warm as it ever gets around here. We have a few hours of daylight left. I can't radio for help—the radio will be turned to ash—but if someone onshore notices the blaze, they could rescue us.

I don't have time to weigh options. If the fuel tank explodes, we're finished.

I pick up the shawl from the deck and adjust Alec's life jacket to secure the shawl in place. I grab the hatch cover. It's so hot it hurts my hands, but we need something that floats. I yank, and it comes off its sliders. I look around for anything else buoyant, but I'm out of luck.

"Alec, we have to jump in the water."

"No!"

"I don't want to either, but the boat could explode. We must get away."

"I can't jump, Evie."

"It's okay, baby." I gather him up in my arms. "Hold on tight and close your eyes."

I stand at my full height. Alec clings to me as tightly as a baby monkey. I climb over the railing.

For a moment, I'm standing on the bowsprit in the searing heat, an arm wrapped around Alec, my other hand gripping the hatch cover.

Now we're falling into the blue oblivion of the ocean.

NIGHT IS CLOSING in. *Torrent* is gone. Her fuel tank didn't explode. She burnt to the waterline and sank, leaving us alone in the gathering dusk.

Alec is mostly out of the water, supported by the hatch cover and a cockpit squab that escaped the flames. All the same, he's cold. His flesh feels rubbery. His face is gray.

My son and I float alone in the vast indigo sea.

At first, I kicked toward land, although I'm not sure I made any headway. As I've grown colder, my legs have become dead-weights. Now I can't command them to move.

"Evie, what if nobody comes?"

"Someone will come. It's past dinnertime. Miss Finch will be looking for you." Even when he spends the night in the summer-house playroom—the room that used to be the birthing suite—Zelde expects Alec to turn up for dinner.

"Miss Finch doesn't know we went sailing."

"Joseph will notice *Torrent*'s gone."

"Joseph isn't there, remember?"

Alec's words send a chill through my already frozen frame. He's right.

"Miss Finch will phone Leo's mummy, and when she hears the playdate was canceled, she'll know something's wrong. She'll know we've been missing for hours."

I try to keep my uncertainty out of my voice. Did Zelde pay attention to where Alec was supposed to go for his playdate? Would she bother to find out why he hadn't returned? When he didn't turn up for dinner, she might have assumed he was on a sleepover. If she goes to the summerhouse and finds it empty, she might think I've gone to the village pub for dinner, something I'd do if Alec was away.

This is all my fault.

My one hope is the wind. We must be drifting toward the shore, although the land doesn't seem to be getting any closer. The problem is the sea breeze is dying as the sun sets, as often happens in summer. If a night breeze springs up, it will blow in the opposite direction.

Immersed in the water with only my life jacket to keep me afloat, I'm colder than Alec. If only we could reach shore. We weren't wrecked at the southernmost part of the island, which is bound by cliffs. Here, the shoreline is a series of shingle beaches. The landing might be dicey, but sea breezes don't make for dangerous surf. We would make it through.

"If you get to shore, Alec, you must hold on to the hatch and the squab. You might get caught in a wave, but if you take a big breath and hold on tight, you'll end up on the beach. Then you must stand up and start walking, no matter how tired you are. Go up the slope till you find the track and then turn right and walk along the track. Right is your writing hand, remember."

"My starboard hand," says Alec.

"Yes. When you get to the house, ring the doorbell over and over. Bang on the door and shout."

"But, Evie, you'll be there. You won't let go of me, will you?"

"I'll never let go of you, Alec. I love you more than anything. You're my world. But you might need to let go of me."

"Stop it, Evie. Don't say scary things."

I wish I didn't have to scare Alec, but he's going to last longer than me. He has a good chance of making it. "I have to, honey. If you love me, you'll do as I say. Hold on as long as . . . as long as I keep talking to you, but if I go to sleep and you can't wake me up, promise me you'll do this. You'll unclip my life jacket. See here where it clips? Lift it over my head and clip it onto your own body. Two life jackets are better than one. Then you must let me go. Do you promise?"

"I promise, but please don't go to sleep. Don't die."

We hold each other tighter. I hope my body is providing some warmth to him.

"I'm trying not to, baby, but if I do, remember my spirit will stay with you, watching over you and making you strong."

"I don't want you to." Alec starts to cry. "Don't go away from me."

"I'll never leave you, not really. My love will stay with you forever, because love is stronger than anything. Stronger than death."

Alec, I'm your mother.

I can't tell him. It's not fair to him. If he does survive, he'll know his real parents are both dead. He'll be alone in the world with two people who have lied to him, to whom he does not truly belong.

THERE IS NO darkness as absolute as the night ocean. No moon has risen. Clouds have gathered overhead, and no starlight shines through.

Someone exhales behind me. I turn with radiant hope. A rescuer?

There's nothing. Although I can't see, I can tell no boat is nearby.

Another breath. Slow, noisy, huge. I smell sulfur.

"Who's there?" asks Alec.

"It's not a person."

He whimpers. "Is it a shark?"

"It's a whale."

Light appears, a ghostly glimmer in the blackness. The whale's fin has breached the surface. Her movement sets off a dance of phosphorescence. Her shape appears, outlined in gold.

"Why is the whale shiny?" Alec asks.

"She's come to comfort us." As if to prove my words, the whale swims nearer, circling us with graceful ease. "She's come to be a light for us."

Alec shivers against me, but I no longer shiver. This is a bad sign. I'm near the end.

"There's another whale." Alec points below us, underwater. "A littler one. It's golden, too."

Deep in the blackness beneath, a shape appears—immense, but smaller than the first whale. This whale rises to the surface, too, and exhales, so close that spray lands on my face. The sea surface lights up, sparkling gold.

"Two of them, just like there are two of us," I say. "A mother and a baby."

"Can they rescue us?"

"No, honey. They belong to their own world. They're here to show us that the world is good. That everything will be okay." I squeeze him gently. "You'll always remember your Eve. Remember me in all the magical places on this earth. Remember me wherever there is blue sky and sunshine. Remember me where the ocean shimmers."

"Alec?"

"What is it?"

He's nearly asleep. I want to let him escape this horror into his dreams, but I'm scared he won't wake up.

"You remember I said I didn't want a little boy of my own?"

"Yes."

"There's one thing I do want. Nobody has ever called me Mummy. Do you think you could say it, just once?"

"But you're not my mummy."

My heart feels ready to stop at the blank finality of his answer.

"I know, honey. I just thought we could pretend."

"I wish you were my mummy."

When my son says the words I've yearned to hear for so long, all I can think is that they are probably the last words he will ever say to me.

He wraps his cold arms around me and whispers in my ear. "I love you, Mummy."

PART IV

Past and Present

The Past (Eight Years Earlier)

CHAPTER 30

Julia

Julia stood on the flagstones of a rustic hall, her face warmed by the blaze of the open fire. Great wooden beams supported the high ceiling. A stag's head was mounted above a door.

She handed the terrarium to Paul. A tubby guy with a weak chin, he seemed younger than he'd sounded on the phone. All the same, he exuded a sense of quiet menace. Julia had been so confident on the two-hour drive inland from Sydney, but now that she was here, the farmhouse felt isolated. Night was never this dark in the city. This was the real outback.

Paul placed the terrarium on a table and lifted out a reptile. Its pink scales were adorned with diamond-shaped patches of green, like a creature designed by God during his LSD years.

"Harlequin lizards," he muttered.

Julia corrected him. "Harlequin geckos."

"I thought they'd be bigger." Paul held the creature close to the hearth. Its reptilian eyes gleamed with reflected fire.

Julia suppressed a sigh of exasperation. "I told you they're babies. Fully grown geckos would be twice the price—at least fifty thousand each."

"Humph." Paul returned the gecko to the terrarium. Now he reached into his bag and produced a radio scanner, running it over the glass. A red light appeared on the scanner. "What's this?"

Julia shrugged. "I have no idea."

Paul reached his meaty hand into the terrarium and shoved rocks aside. He pulled out a small black device. "A GPS tracker? You planning to sell me these lizards and then steal them back?"

"I didn't know that thing was there." Julia said casually. She couldn't be in trouble for something she hadn't done. Surely Paul would realize that.

But now she swallowed hard. She hadn't planted the tracker, so who had?

Silas.

Julia couldn't bear the thought. Not Silas. Not her boss—the very person she was trying to escape from.

It must have been Silas. And there was only one reason he would track his own product.

He knows I'm stealing from him.

Julia raked her hands through her hair. "Listen, Paul, Silas doesn't know about this deal. He told me not to sell to you."

"I don't care what your boss knows. I care that you wanted to track me."

"Don't you see? *Silas* planted the tracker. That means he suspects me. I've got to get out of here. He might be on his way here."

Julia glanced around the farmhouse. The windows looked like black eyes, watching her. In the sublime darkness of the outback, anybody could be lying in wait. Surely no one had followed her? She'd checked her rearview mirror constantly and hadn't seen any headlights. But with a GPS tracker, Silas could have hung back out of sight.

Julia began to shake.

"I'm done with your shit." Paul pulled something from his jacket. A flash of silver. Was that a pistol?

The blow came from nowhere, knocking her to the floor. Her chin smacked into the flagstones. A jolt of pain. She was sprawled, helpless, face down.

Paul straddled her body. A cold, hard object pressed against her spine. It *was* a pistol. This was it. She was going to die.

Bang!

The blast shattered the peaceful night. Julia couldn't move. She was dead, or fatally injured—she must be. She was stuck, pinned to the ground.

Shards of glass lay everywhere. A window had smashed.

I'm alive. I'm still breathing.

Footsteps. Somebody was climbing in through the broken window. Someone was in the room. Not Paul. Paul was lying motionless on top of her.

"Get up."

No, don't let it be him.

Julia turned her head. Standing above her, a shotgun in his hand, was Silas. With his scarred face and hulking physique, he looked like a man Satan would gleefully welcome into hell.

He had followed her and he had brought a gun. But he hadn't shot her. He'd shot Paul. Julia felt blood trickling onto her neck. She was lying beneath a corpse.

"Get up," Silas repeated.

Julia didn't think she could move, but she had to obey. Her heart pounding, she struggled out from under Paul's weight, trying not to look at what Silas's shotgun had done to his head. The man was very dead.

Silas grabbed her ponytail and shone his flashlight in her face. "I should never have got someone as pretty as you involved in my trade." His voice was gravelly. "Men understand they will receive no mercy, so they obey me, but a girl like you thinks she's an exception."

"Please don't hurt me." Julia stifled a sob. "I'll do anything."

Silas grinned as though her begging amused him. "Do you dye your hair?"

"Huh?" Why was he asking this? Could it be that he had some plan for her other than killing her? "No," she said truthfully, hoping it was the right answer.

"Have you ever been fingerprinted?"

"No."

"Make sure you never are." Silas removed the unused cartridge from the shotgun and handed Julia the weapon. "Put your finger on the trigger."

Julia dared not argue. She might have hoped he had shot Paul in order to rescue her, but she knew better. She'd heard about Silas's *penalties*, as some of his other employees called them. The rumor was he had sliced the ear off one of his henchmen for not listening. Julia had been inclined to disbelieve the stories. Until now.

"Come and put your fingers on the windowsill."

He was framing Julia for the murder he'd just committed, but he'd checked that the police didn't have her fingerprints. This was hopeful. Perhaps he *was* showing mercy. As long as she lived the rest of her life without being fingerprinted, she could get away with it. Whatever his plan, it didn't seem to involve leaving her corpse on the farmhouse floor with Paul.

Julia took care to place her hands in the right position. Silas would see that she was reliable. Apart from this one mistake, she was a valuable employee.

But Silas sneered at her meek compliance. "You think this is some scared-straight program for nice girls, don't you? You should know me better than that, Julia. I don't cut anybody slack."

Of course there was a catch. She couldn't bring herself to speak. She sensed that what Silas was about to say would change everything.

"I'm sparing your life because I want something from you, Julia. Something more valuable than your freedom. More valuable than your life. I want the one thing you'll find harder to give up."

CHAPTER 31

Julia sat at the bar twiddling the straw of her cosmopolitan, trying to look nonchalant. The inner-city pub was crawling with men this evening, but one in particular had attracted her interest. She crossed her legs and flicked a glossy auburn curl over her shoulder, risking a glance behind her, where a well-dressed man sat alone at a table.

Julia had arrived in Hobart only this afternoon, and here she was, already tipsy. It was stress. She couldn't believe how much her life had changed since last week, when the gecko she was minding for Silas had unexpectedly given birth to four live offspring. Julia had thought she'd hit the jackpot. She had thought she could outwit Silas, sell the baby geckos on the side, and make enough money to get out of the trade and away from Silas forever.

Silas. The thought of her boss made Julia break out in a cold sweat. He'd always made her nervous, but since last night, when he'd killed Paul in cold blood, she was petrified of him. Then Silas had told her what she had to do. Her "assignment." It was ghastly. Julia could hardly bear to think about it.

At least Silas had given her enough money to last until the job was done. He'd told her to leave Sydney, which was one part of the assignment Julia had been happy to comply with. Sydney was big enough that she'd managed not to cross paths with her violent, boozing parents in over a decade, but she was always aware her luck could change. *Tasmania.* It was not a long flight, but it would surely be a different world from mainland Australia. This morning, Julia had packed her things and caught a flight to Hobart, where she checked into a cheap hotel and came out in search of a stiff drink.

Now Julia glanced again at the stranger. Tall, with strawberry-blond hair and ice-blue eyes, he was definitely interested in her. He was outright staring. Despite—or perhaps because of—her sky-high anxiety, Julia felt a surge of desire. In this man's company, was it possible she could forget about Silas for a few hours? She had never approached a man in a bar, but if there was a time to change that, it was tonight. She needed whatever solace she could find to get through the *assignment.*

Julia knocked back her drink, slipped off the barstool, and straightened her tight, short dress. How should she start the conversation? Should she think of a clever opener or just say hi? Smile from a distance or boldly sit down beside him? This was not easy.

A voice behind her. "Can I buy you another?"

Julia turned. It was the man with strawberry-blond hair. He was even more handsome than she'd realized. And *he* had come to *her.* It was destiny.

"Hi," he said. "I'm Christopher."

He invited her to his table, and with his suave manner and the soothing effect of the cocktails that followed, Julia began to relax. After several hours, they ditched the bar in favor of an upmarket bistro where they ate steak washed down with Shiraz. Christopher insisted on paying for everything and politely overlooked Julia's growing inebriation. When the bistro closed, they strolled through the city streets, enjoying the fresh night air, hand in hand.

Julia's blood pulsed in her veins, setting her on fire. She had never met a man like this. Christopher was so polished. His conversation was attentive and genuine. He exuded charm, power, wealth. Her body felt drunk, but her mind was oddly lucid.

She wanted this man. Her desire was so intense she felt as though anybody, even a casual passerby, could see it on her face. She was aching for Christopher to take her in his arms. She almost wished he would pull her into an alley and have his way with her against a wall.

A familiar building loomed ahead.

"Oh," said Julia. "This is my hotel."

Christopher glanced at his Rolex. "It's nearly midnight. Time has flown. I suppose I should say good night. It's been a wonderful evening."

Julia's heart sank. He wasn't interested in sex. Perhaps he didn't even want to see her again.

But now he kissed her, and Julia felt as though her heart was floating away. The kiss was burning yet tender. He was holding back, restraining his passion.

"Can I see you tomorrow?" he asked, taking a step away.

"Uh . . ." He was leaving? He didn't want to spend the night? But she could ask him.

She gazed into his eyes. *Come up to my room.* But what if those words destroyed the evening, destroyed everything? He wanted to see her tomorrow. What was one day?

It would be better to hold back. Tomorrow, surely, Christopher would want her as much as she wanted him. Tomorrow, it wouldn't be a one-night stand. There would be romance, a spark of magic. Julia needed something magical to get through the months ahead.

"Tomorrow it is," she said. The assignment could wait.

JULIA STOOD BEFORE the hotel room mirror and wriggled, letting the sleeves of her gold dress slide off her shoulders. Six weeks had passed since she'd met Christopher—the best six weeks of her life. He'd taken her out almost every night. Each date was more wonderful than the last.

She was particularly pleased with her appearance tonight. The dress's low neckline showcased the flawless alabaster of her throat. Her auburn curls tumbled to her waist. Her makeup accentuated her aqua eyes, and her brand-new bottle of jasmine perfume, a gift from Christopher, smelled divine.

But perhaps the off-the-shoulder look was a little too obvious. The last thing Julia wanted was to look cheap. Christopher was so refined. He came from a different world. He'd told her about his upbringing—nannies, private schools, overseas holidays. It was guaranteed *he* had never woken up to find his dad passed out drunk and his mother beaten black and blue, as Julia had many times throughout her miserable childhood.

Julia was desperate to measure up. Christopher had fortunately never realized that she had been looking for casual sex that first night, and on the dates that followed, Julia had quickly transformed into the elegant lady he seemed to desire. She hadn't exactly lied. She'd admitted to growing up in an "ordinary" suburb of Sydney, leaving home "rather young," and supporting herself with "poorly paid jobs" ever since. But she omitted the animal trafficking. She omitted Silas.

She pulled her sleeves back up over her shoulders. That was

better—seductive but tasteful. The amount she'd spent on this dress was eye-watering. She was burning through the money Silas had given her.

And that was the problem. Julia had made no progress with her assignment. Her romance with Christopher had become a distraction. A boyfriend was the last thing she needed. To have a boyfriend while completing the assignment was not only absurd, it was dangerous.

Yesterday, Julia had been on the point of telling Christopher it was over, but the words were so hard to say. Then Christopher announced his plan for this weekend. He'd booked a restaurant for tonight, and after dinner he would take Julia on his private yacht to his island home.

"This weekend will be unforgettable," he'd promised. Clearly, he wanted to make love to her at last.

Julia had swallowed her words. Three more days.

Now she slid her feet into her stilettos and grabbed her purse. She took the elevator to the ground floor and strutted out into the night, crossing a secluded park. A stranger lounging on a bench beneath a lone streetlight regarded her hungrily.

"How 'bout it, babe?" he called, taking a swig from a bottle of beer.

Julia's gaze swept over him. The man was rough round the edges, but in his trim jeans and plaid shirt, he was not unattractive. He had a strong jaw, a clear complexion. He fit the bill.

It wasn't too late to bail on Christopher. If it was so hard to break it off with him, why not simply not show up? Julia could take this man home instead, consoling herself for leaving the man of her dreams by throwing herself into meaningless sex with an unwashed stranger.

But Julia kept walking. She knew she was making things complicated. She had let herself get involved when she needed to stay aloof, but she couldn't bear not to see Christopher tonight. Christopher with his broad shoulders and his deep voice. Christopher with his way of looking at her as though she were "the one." Christopher with his yacht and his island.

She'd give herself the weekend. Three days of lovemaking ensconced in his mansion, and then she would never see him again.

Several hours later, Christopher and Julia were sitting in a private room in the best restaurant in Hobart. Candles illuminated the gilt furnishings, and a night breeze wafted through the open window. Julia was glad she had opted against the off-the-shoulder look. This was a classy evening. Christopher, in a blazer with a crisp white shirt, looked so good it was almost intimidating.

The man on the park bench was forgotten.

The waiter had brought out so many delicious courses that Julia's dress was beginning to feel tight. Now the conversation dipped. Dessert was late, and Chris was getting cranky.

"I told the maître d' we need to leave at ten," he muttered. "They're ruining everything."

"Does it matter what time we get to the island?" Julia asked. "We have all weekend."

"If we sail against the tide, the journey takes twice as long."

Julia shrugged. "Then let's skip dessert."

"We can't skip dessert," he growled. "I'm going to let them have it." He stood.

Julia fell silent. Chris had a short fuse? She should be pleased he wasn't flawless. It might make leaving him less painful.

The maître d' came hurrying over. "Sir, your dessert is moments away. The chef is ensuring that it's absolutely perfect."

The man spoke with an odd tone. A look passed between him and Christopher. Christopher resumed his seat.

Seconds later, the waiter arrived at their table, carrying a dish covered with a silver lid. He set it before Julia.

Julia touched the lid. It was cold. "They've mixed up our desserts. I ordered the hot cocoa soufflé."

"I'm afraid I overruled your selection by advance arrangement." A smile played on Christopher's lips.

Julia felt a shiver down her spine—a glorious shiver. Was this what she thought it was? Could it really be happening? Could a man like Christopher feel so strongly about her?

But the timing was terrible. If only she'd met Christopher earlier. If only she'd never met Silas.

"Darling," Christopher said, "I know we haven't known each other long, but . . ." He knelt. He lifted the silver lid. Beneath was a red velvet box. "Will you be my wife?"

Julia gaped at Christopher. This changed everything.

She knew she was in trouble. She could never leave Christopher. She could never complete the assignment. How was she going to deal with Silas? She had no idea. But she loved Christopher. She had to accept him.

"Yes!" she exclaimed.

Christopher picked up the box. "Open it."

The diamond was enormous.

As Christopher slid the ring onto her finger, an idea struck Julia.

Christopher's island was so remote. Silas didn't even know Julia was in Tasmania. He'd told her to go somewhere nobody knew her, and Julia had chosen Hobart. He'd said not to get in touch until she had news, and Julia had obeyed.

Julia would marry Christopher, take his name, and move to his island. She would live a quiet but luxurious life, the stay-at-home wife of a rich man. She wouldn't have to complete the assignment or do anything unpleasant ever again.

Silas would never find her.

The problem was she would have to persuade Christopher to marry her quietly and quickly. Not that most men wanted a big wedding, but he'd have questions about her need for secrecy and speed. She needed a story that would arouse his gallantry. *A bad man wants to hurt me.* Would it be too much to say she was being forced into prostitution or drug dealing? *Rescue me, my white knight.*

Christopher got to his feet and swept Julia into his arms. Their lips met. Julia put her heart and soul into their kiss.

She would tell him in the morning. Tonight, in his bed, she would give the performance of her life. If Christopher thought he was in love with her now, wait till they'd slept together. She would make sure she had him. He was her ticket out of Silas's world.

CHAPTER 32

Eve

I'm swimming in a sea of nightmares. Xander is dead, and I don't know where Alec is. I'm alone in the dark, hot and cold, burning and freezing, in fire and in water. Fighting to keep the person I love alive. Doomed to fail again.

Save my son. Save my son.

"Do you mean Alec?"

The female voice is matter-of-fact, almost impatient, but it makes my heart leap with hope. *I'm alive. We've been rescued.*

Where am I?

I try to remember being pulled from the water. I remember lights. Joseph's voice. The looming hull of a yacht. I was so cold.

I open my eyes. A woman in a blue uniform is leaning over me. A nurse. I'm in hospital.

"Where's Alec?" I try to sit up. A jolt of pain passes through me.

"Lie still. I'm trying to change your dressing. You have a burn on your neck." The nurse, a young woman with a buzz cut and heavy black studs in her ears, dabs my raw flesh with ointment. "You've asked the same question about a hundred times.

They've taken you off the meds now, so hopefully this time you'll remember."

"Remember what?" I stare at the nurse's name tag: *Frankie*.

"Remember when I tell you Alec's fine. He's already been discharged. I don't know why you keep calling him your son. His parents collected him on Monday."

Frankie disappears, and I lie in the early morning sunshine, listening to the clatter of the breakfast trolley making its way around the ward.

Everything's fine. Alec is alive. I keep reminding myself of Frankie's reassurances, but I can't quell my anxiety. I need to see Alec for myself. When the doctor, a spry woman with close-cropped gray curls, arrives on her ward round, I ask her to discharge me.

"You've only been in hospital five days," she says. "You should stay a little longer. The burn on your neck is healing well, but the skin hasn't yet formed a seal. Blood will seep through the wound for a few more days."

"Please, I promise I'll take it easy. I just want to lie in my own bed."

The time since I was rescued is a jumble of confused images. I was awake at times, but I didn't know I was in hospital. At one stage I remember blabbering senselessly at a tall, quietly spoken man—another doctor, I guess.

"How did I get to hospital?" I ask now.

"A man called Joseph Jones found you in the water," the doctor says, adjusting her glasses to reread her notes. "Luckily, he knew the correct first aid. Death after rescue is common in cases of severe hypothermia. You were airlifted from Paradise Bay. When you arrived in the emergency department here in Hobart, you were unconscious and had to be rewarmed slowly using intravenous fluids. You were in the intensive care unit for two days."

It's hard to imagine Joseph caring for me, and yet he saved my life—and Alec's. We both came so close to death.

Alec. I know he's all right, but I need to see him.

"I'd really like to go home if that's okay."

"You're a free woman," the doctor says, throwing up her hands. "Make sure you rest, and whatever you do, don't get the burn wet. Sponge wash rather than showering. Make an appointment with your family doctor in two days' time for a dressing change."

She walks away looking as though she regrets giving in.

Frankie offers me a hand mirror so I can see my injuries. The burn on my neck follows the line of the merino shirt I was wearing, which protected me from more extensive burns, while the wet towel protected my face and head. The ends of my hair, sticking out beneath the towel, were burnt off. In the mirror, the skin on my neck is pink, raw, mottled with blood. A ghoulish woman with dark circles under her eyes stares back at me through the glass, her hair a mess of singed ends.

"Can you help me cut my hair, Frankie?" I ask when she has re-dressed the wound.

She gestures at her own shorn head. "My clippers are in my bag." She smiles. "I dare you."

"Why not?"

Frankie disappears and returns with clippers. She accompanies me into the bathroom.

"Has anybody visited me?" I ask as she guides the clippers over my head. Disheveled auburn locks fall to the floor.

"Only Officer Maxwell."

"Officer Maxwell? A policeman?"

"Don't sound so worried," Frankie says. "I'm sure it was just routine. You don't remember? Tall guy with dark hair and a moustache."

"The quiet guy? I thought he was a doctor."

"You were kind of confused at the time, thanks to the meds. Doesn't that look great?" Frankie dusts stray hairs off my neck.

I gaze in the bathroom mirror. I've lost the long hair that Xander loved. I look like a boy—a tired, sad boy. But somehow, the haircut suits my mood. "I like it."

Soon afterward, I step out the door of the hospital. The clothes I was wearing during the shipwreck were ruined, so I'm wearing a red T-shirt, capri pants, and sandals that Frankie found me from some clothing pool.

I could phone the Hygates and ask for help getting home, but something stops me. According to Frankie, the Hygates didn't visit me when they collected Alec from hospital. Maybe they've tried to call my cellphone. I left it behind when I took Alec sailing, because there's no reception out on the water. Wouldn't they have realized I didn't have it with me? They could have phoned the hospital to get in touch, but it seems they didn't.

I hope they're not angry with me. Surely it wasn't unforgivable for me to take Alec sailing when he was left in my care for the entire summer. I was told never to take Alec off Breaksea, but it wasn't clear whether a sailing expedition to another part of the island was prohibited. And surely Joseph's explained about the gas leak. The accident wasn't my fault.

In the afternoon heat, I walk through central Hobart to the

bank. My burnt neck hurts, but I feel energized from being outside in the sunshine after lying in bed for days.

Despite never receiving overtime or a raise, I've saved money over the years. One of the tellers has been helping me invest my nest egg. Now he issues me a new bank card, even though I have no ID, on the basis of a signature match.

I withdraw cash and catch a bus to the ferry terminal, where I buy a ticket for the three o'clock sailing to Breaksea.

After a smooth sail, I step off the ferry at Breaksea Village and walk along the street, looking for a familiar face. At this time of year, the village is thick with tourists, but if I'm lucky, I'll see someone I know who might give me a lift to Paradise Bay.

I'm almost at the end of the street when I spot the guy. Tall and lean, with black hair and solemn dark eyes, he looks about my age. He's dressed in khaki pants and a T-shirt.

"Hi," I say. "Don't I know you from somewhere?"

"I'm Officer George Maxwell. I came to see you in the hospital." His voice is quiet and steady.

A pang of anxiety passes through me. The policeman. "Sorry, I don't remember."

"It's fine," he says, adjusting his baseball cap against the blazing sunshine. "I came to interview you, but I realized you were medicated, so I left. Perhaps you could step into my office for a few minutes? I'm off duty, but it would be good to clear things up." He doesn't sound as though he thinks I'm a criminal.

"Okay."

We walk down the road. He lets us into the police station and directs me to his office. We pass a sign pointing to jail cells downstairs. Nobody else is here—it's a one-man operation.

My chest feels tight as I enter a drab room with barred windows. Maxwell is polite, but there's something unusual about his manner. He seems to be scrutinizing me.

"Take a seat." He opens a folder and leafs through it. "Originally, I came to see you to investigate the boating accident." He pauses.

"Did you speak to anyone else about it?" I ask.

"Like who?"

"Like Joseph Jones, the marina manager."

"The guy who rescued you? Yes. I've also spoken with Alec Hygate."

"So, you'll know there was a mix-up," I say. "Joseph told me I could take the yacht out, but then I canceled, so he didn't tell me there was a gas leak—"

"I know," Maxwell interrupts. "It was an unfortunate chain of events, but it appears nobody was to blame. The maritime authority will conduct its own investigation, but my role was to establish whether an immediate arrest should be made. Clearly, that isn't the case."

I wait. I should feel relieved at his words, but I don't. He shifts in his seat.

Maxwell has more to say. He didn't call me into his office off duty to tell me everything was fine.

He clears his throat. "You're known on the island as Eve Hygate, but the hospital records show your legal name is Sylvester. Why do you use the name Hygate?"

"Uh . . ." What should I say? I've always stuck to Christopher's story that I'm a distant cousin, but I can't lie to a policeman. "You see, the Hygates wanted me to take their name. They wanted me to be seen as family. I'm Alec's godmother as well as his nanny."

"But you're not family?"

"N—no."

"I never heard of a godmother being expected to change her surname."

I shrug. The comment hangs in the air. Maxwell shuffles some papers.

"Miss Sylvester, it's important you answer my questions truthfully. I'm investigating a serious matter. You made an allegation regarding Mr. and Mrs. Hygate."

A prickling sensation at my temples. "I did?"

"You don't remember?" He raises an eyebrow.

"What did I say?"

"You told the medical staff that Alec Hygate is your son."

The room feels airless. I can't speak.

Maxwell's eyes are boring into mine. "When I visited, you repeated the claim."

"I don't remember saying that."

Damn it. Frankie told me I had called Alec my son, but I didn't realize she wasn't the only person I'd said it to—or that anyone was paying attention.

I want to tell the truth to this man, but I remember what Christopher told me. His words from all those years ago echo inside my head. *Child trafficking. The law is severe.*

"As you say, I was medicated," I mumble. "I was disturbed by the accident. I thought I was going to die out there."

"Concerns were raised about Alec's welfare. Mr. and Mrs. Hygate left him in your care for an unusual length of time. We decided to conduct a DNA test on the Hygates and Alec."

The walls seem to close in. This policeman knows everything. He knows Alec isn't Chris and Julia's son. He knows Alec wasn't legally adopted.

I swallow hard. "Officer, please, I don't want Alec to go into foster care."

Maybe I'm too late. Maybe Chris and Julia have already been arrested. Where is Alec now? Has he been taken away by social workers? Part of me wants to bolt from the room. Those jail cells downstairs—am I going to end up in them?

I raise my palms. "I was very young when I was pregnant with Alec. I agreed to let Chris and Julia adopt him, and yes, they paid me. I didn't realize I was breaking the law."

"Well, *you* wouldn't be prosecuted." Maxwell sounds offhand, as though this conversation is theoretical.

Is he trying to lull me into a false sense of security? "Sir, I know I committed a crime. When I tried to take Alec back shortly after he was born, Chris said it was too late, that the illegal adoption would be found out and we'd all be imprisoned."

I stop. I'm gabbling, leaping ahead. I've just admitted everything. I'm buzzing with fear, but I'm also strangely relieved. I've finally told the truth.

Maxwell shakes his head. "You sure are convincing. This is why I took your claims seriously even though you were medicated. What you said seemed credible. These cases come up from time to time. People arrange a private adoption, hiding it from authorities, usually because there's some problem with citizenship. Just so you know, birth mothers are never prosecuted. Birth mothers are treated as victims, not perpetrators."

I leap to my feet. "Really? Are you sure?"

He nods. "I checked with the legal department."

"Oh my God! This is unbelievable!"

My head is in a whirl. I'm not a criminal? That means I could have told the truth when Alec was a baby. I wouldn't have gone to prison. Alec was never in danger of being taken into foster care.

Sobs come in a rush. *Christopher lied to me.* I should have known. I've suffered for six long years, hiding the truth from Alec, missing him whenever the Hygates took him to their house, saddened whenever they were severe and unloving toward him. All for nothing. He could have been mine. He could have grown up calling me Mummy.

But this is amazing news. I'm free to claim him. Nothing can happen to me.

"I'm taking him!" I exclaim through my tears. "I'm taking him now! He's my son."

"Sit down." Maxwell's tone brooks no argument. His expression is somber.

I sit.

"Miss Sylvester, I've concluded my investigation. Christopher and Julia Hygate volunteered to have a DNA test. I'm satisfied beyond doubt that they are Alec's biological parents."

CHAPTER 33

Julia

Julia stood on the third-floor balcony in her wedding dress. She gazed down at the beach, where a gazebo festooned with roses arched over the sand, and breathed a deep sigh of pleasure. This was it. Her troubles were over. This island would be her safe haven.

She still couldn't believe her luck in finding Christopher. Having recently turned forty, Chris felt new urgency in his search for a bride. Spencer and Philip, two business associates whom he was eager to impress, had both married in the past year, and their wives were now pregnant. Chris was keen to follow suit. He'd even invited Spencer and Philip to be his witnesses today. Chris's matter-of-fact approach might have put off some women, but it suited Julia. *When you know you've found the one, why wait?* The wedding had been arranged with efficient haste.

Footsteps. Someone was in the master bedroom. The door closed softly, and the lock clicked. Who would lock the door? Surely Christopher hadn't come to see her on the wedding morning. He knew it was bad luck.

"Where's the product?"

Julia froze. *No, not his voice. Not Silas.*

She lurched against the railing, grasping it to steady herself. *Please don't let it be him.*

Uttering a silent prayer, she turned.

Silas stood in the middle of her bedroom, holding a revolver. His scarred face was twisted into a sneer. "Paradise Bay, huh? What a piece of heaven you've sunk your claws into, Julia. Tell me, what are you doing out there? Enjoying the serenity of the summer ocean or feasting your greedy eyes on your land?"

Julia stepped inside. "Silas, you're here?" She spoke softly. She couldn't risk a servant overhearing. "What the— How?"

She should have known he'd find her. Silas had contacts everywhere. When he first gave her the assignment, Julia had known she couldn't run from him. Then, when Chris proposed, she had deluded herself into thinking she had found a way to escape. What a fool she was.

"I guess my invitation got lost in the post," said Silas. "I thought I'd come and watch you tie the knot. Hard to imagine you mouthing a bunch of sweet promises, a little skank like you. Everything's a bit quiet, though. You don't seem to have invited many guests. I bet you feel hard done by, getting married on the sly, unable to show your friends how you've come up in the world. All this money, and you can't throw a party on your special day."

"Does my fiancé know you're here?"

"I haven't had the pleasure of meeting him exactly, but I've seen him. Tell me, you found the redheaded man all right, but what happened with the rest of your assignment? Did you forget?" Silas strode to the white sofa and sank into it. He held up the revolver. "Perhaps this is the wrong weapon for the occasion. Is this a shotgun wedding?" He gestured at Julia's waist, cinched tight in her form-fitting dress. "Doesn't look like it."

Julia shrank back against the wall. "How did you find me?"

"Answer my question. It's been months. Where's the product?"

"S-Silas, since our last meeting, everything's changed." Julia's eyes darted between the locked door and the revolver. There was no chance she could escape. She was going to have to talk her way out of this. "Please, let me explain. I tried to carry out the assignment, I really did. But things happened. I met Christopher, and we fell in love. Before I knew it, he was proposing."

"And you thought: new name, new life."

"I admit I thought you wouldn't find me here. I'm sorry." Julia injected remorse into her voice. "I couldn't do it, Silas. I guess you just picked the wrong girl."

Silas let out an ugly laugh. "You should have been an actress, Julia. Nice try, but I know how you think. You're the right girl, not just because of your looks but because you're too much of an ice queen to let sentiment get in the way of finishing the job." Silas settled back in his seat. "You'd do anything for the right price. The only reason you bailed was you got a better offer. Marrying Hygate meant more money for less work."

"I'm not marrying for mon—"

"Nice place you've got even if it's the arse end of nowhere." Silas gestured at the panoramic view. "Big block of land. Sheltered marina. You've landed with your bum in the butter, that's for sure."

A cold sweat broke out on the back of Julia's neck. "I have, and I'm willing to make amends however I can."

Silas stood. "I've been looking for a place like this. Sweet charter business your bloke has going."

"Are you leaving the wildlife trade?" Julia's tone was hopeful. This would be a stroke of luck.

"You'd like that, wouldn't you?" Silas jeered. "We could both go clean. Shake hands and be chums again. But we were never chums, Julia. You're a cheat, and I don't like cheats. I'll tell you what's happening. Customs are asking questions about my Tasman crossings. A charter business would be a good cover."

"That's an excellent idea," Julia said slowly, "although not *here*, of course. Breaksea Charters isn't profitable. The weather's too rough for most people. Christopher runs the marina as a hobby. Sailing's his passion."

"All the better. I wouldn't want tourists getting in the way of my comings and goings."

"Christopher loves his yachts. He'd never sell his marina, but I'm sure I can help find another—"

"He's not going to sell it. He's going to give it to me. You'll persuade him. You're lucky, Julia. This is the second time I've planned to put a bullet in that lying little head of yours, but yet again you turn out to be more useful alive. Here's what's going to happen. What time's the wedding?"

"Midday." Julia glanced at the clock. The ceremony was minutes away.

"At midday, you're going to prance down that posh staircase looking peachy as pie. Marry your fat cat and get that ring on your finger. Once you've got him snagged, you're gonna tell him how it is. Actually, I don't care what you tell him. Just get him to give me the marina."

"You said you'd let me out of the trade," Julia said, her tone rising.

"But you didn't keep your end of the bargain, did you? You're getting off lightly. I don't want you involved in my business anymore. I want you dressing nice, hobnobbing with the rich listers, making everything look legit. I'll bring in my own man to run the marina. Probably Joe. He's out of the clink. I'll keep the boats here, make it look like a real outfit. All you and hubby need to do is keep your mouths shut. Let everyone think you still own the business."

Someone was coming up the stairs. The door handle rattled.

"I'm here to help with your jewelry, ma'am," said a female voice.

Silas pointed the revolver at Julia.

Julia forced her voice to remain steady as she called, "I want to be alone, Sarah. Please wait downstairs. I can put on my jewels myself."

"Did a delivery man come up here?" was the reply.

"No." Wait. Silas was dressed in a courier's uniform. *That* was how he got past the servants. "I mean, yes, but he's gone now."

Retreating footsteps.

"Silas, please, put the gun away," said Julia. "I'll do it. I'll make Christopher give you the marina. I don't know how I'll explain myself without him wanting a divorce, but I'll find a way. Name your price. I can return the other money, too."

"What money?"

"The advance you paid me for the . . . the assignment."

Silas's lip curled into a sneer. He stalked toward Julia. "I don't care about that money, Julia. What do you think is happening right now? I'm not letting you off the assignment. The marina is your penalty for trying to run off, but the job's still on. Where do you think I would find another girl who could deliver what I want? You found Hygate. That was the first step."

Julia nodded vigorously. "Like I say, I tried to do what you asked. But why does it have to be me? Can't I help you find someone else who could do it?"

"I thought you were smart, but you haven't learned the first thing about me. I never back down. And you know what our buyers are like. They pay a premium to get what they want. They're always picky, but these particular clients are next level, and they're getting impatient. They already paid me half. You better get busy."

"Silas, I wish I could. If it were just me, I'd do it, but how can I ask my hus—"

Julia's words were cut off as Silas slapped his revolver across her cheek. Pain exploded in her skull. She stumbled backward through the open door. Silas slammed her against the balcony railing so hard she almost tumbled over it. He grabbed her hair, forcing her chin skyward. She stifled a scream.

Silas pressed the gun to her temple. Julia held her breath. Hot tears ran down her cheeks. As Silas wrenched her back inside the house, she heard her gown tearing.

He shoved her against the wall. "You have one year, Julia, or your husband will find your body. Cheat me a third time, and no fortune on earth will save you. Next time I see you, you'd better be holding a baby."

CHAPTER 34

Eve

There's been some mistake," I tell Officer Maxwell.

He stares at me across the desk. I run my hand nervously over my buzz cut. I have no idea what to think. Everything's topsy-turvy. One minute it seems all my problems are solved, the next, a new obstacle is thrown in my path.

"Both of them showed up as related to Alec?" I ask. "Chris *and* Julia?"

"Well, I haven't got the results back yet," says Maxwell. "The samples were couriered to Hobart, and it seems they went astray. But the outcome is obvious. If Mr. and Mrs. Hygate weren't Alec's parents, they'd have fought tooth and nail against being tested. Instead, they volunteered. It was enough to remove all doubt from my mind."

"They were bluffing. You said the samples have gone missing? I bet they orchestrated that."

Maxwell tilts his head. "I don't see how they could have. How could they know which courier company I'd use or when the samples would be sent? Besides, what would that achieve apart from a small delay? I'm collecting new samples tomorrow."

"I bet they tried to avoid that."

"Not at all. They offered to come in with Alec first thing in the morning." Maxwell flicks his folder shut as if to signify that there's nothing more to say.

What can the Hygates be playing at? They must have some plan to bamboozle their way through the test.

A few minutes ago, I might have been relieved to hear that the Hygates had managed to fend off police suspicions, but everything's changed now that I know I won't be prosecuted. Alec won't end up with strangers. There's no reason for me not to tell the truth.

I lean across the desk. "I don't know what their game is. *I* gave birth to Alec. The Hygates have found a way to switch the samples or something. Next time, take the samples yourself to make sure there's no tampering."

"The samples were collected under my supervision. There's a chain of custody. There's no opportunity for anyone to interfere with the samples."

"Something's not right here. You believed me when I told you Alec was my son. Otherwise, you wouldn't have done this test, would you?"

"We wouldn't normally act on a claim that came out of the blue like this, but there was other evidence."

"What?"

Maxwell narrows his eyes. The silence stretches between us. "A disclosure was made by the child," he says.

I gape. "Alec told you I'm his mother?"

"He told a nurse."

"How did he know? I never . . ." I trail off.

I've been so reckless. I told Alec he looked like Xander. I hinted he was named after Xander. In the water, I asked Alec to call me Mummy. I needed it so badly. I thought I was dying. I thought I could get away with it.

Or maybe, deep down, I wanted Alec to know. If I was going to die, perhaps I wanted to plant the idea in his head, hoping he'd figure it out when he was older. But I underestimated Alec. He's always guessed more than half my thoughts. All his life, I've struggled to conceal the depth of my love for him. Perhaps, even before the shipwreck, he sensed our bond.

"So Alec knows the truth," I say. Reckless joy bubbles up inside me. I want him to know, regardless of consequences. Our time in the water made me realize life is too short for lies.

Maxwell gives me that inscrutable look again. "I admit I gave the claim some credence. Who would run into a fire and then keep a child warm while dying of hypothermia herself? Surely only a mother. But Mr. and Mrs. Hygate were so eager to be tested. When the swabs were taken, they were completely relaxed. I realized I already had my answer."

Maxwell seems genuine, and yet something is seriously amiss. The Hygates would never volunteer to be DNA-tested unless they were sure they could mess with the results.

Years ago, Chris warned me he could find a lawyer who could "sway a judge." He's obviously not above using money and connections to get his way. Has he bribed someone at the DNA lab? Or perhaps Maxwell himself? Maxwell's strange expression might be intended to warn me to back off.

Christopher is an influential man, but his influence must have its limits. If he has bought off the local police, I'll go higher. I don't care if I have to petition the prime minister.

I stand. "Thank you for explaining the legal position, Officer," I say. And I leave.

It's late afternoon when I exit the police station, but the day has lost none of its heat. I've given up on finding a lift to Paradise Bay. My neck hurts, but other than that, I feel okay. I'll make my own way home.

Beyond the village, a single road leads south along a ridge, as though the island is some slender reptile and the road its spine. As I ascend to the highest point of land, I can see ocean on both sides. To the west, the water is sheltered, a soft blue that calms my nerves. To the east, the Tasman Sea is sparkling fury.

I trudge on as the sun slides across the scorching sky like melted butter. I regret not asking a stranger for a ride. I wipe the sweat from my brow as I start up yet another hill.

I don't have a clue what I'm going to do when I arrive. Part of me hopes the Hygates and I can put these events behind us and carry on as before. Me as the doting nanny, Julia and Chris as the parents who always have the final say. *Never mind your little slip of the tongue, we'll cover it up. The gas leak wasn't your fault. All's well that ends well. We'll never get another nanny like you.*

I doubt they'll be so forgiving. I revealed their deepest secret to Alec and to a policeman. They'll probably want me to resign. Perhaps that would be best. I'll go live in the village and start legal proceedings to get Alec back. I'll keep fighting until I win. The truth will out.

Birth mothers are never prosecuted. I need only prove Alec is my son, and he'll be returned to me.

First, I need to see him. Everyone, including me, has lied to Alec for six years. It's time to tell the truth.

CHAPTER 35

My neck is throbbing and painful when I arrive at the mansion. The front door is locked, so I ring the bell. Zelde answers with the same forbidding frown with which she met me all those years ago when I arrived for my job interview.

"What are you doing here?" She looks me up and down. "I wouldn't have thought you'd have the nerve to show your face after what you did."

"What exactly do you think I did? The police have assured me the shipwreck wasn't my fault."

"I don't think the Hygates see it that way." She purses her lips.

"If Chris and Julia have misunderstood events, it's because they haven't bothered to ask me what happened. I'll soon clear up any confusion."

Zelde's eyes bulge. I've never spoken so assertively to her before. I've never spoken so assertively to anyone. Something has changed in me since I was pulled from the water. It's time to stand up for myself.

"Where's Alec?" I ask.

"School went back today, and soccer practice started up this afternoon."

I forgot about school. I felt we had so much summer break left, but time has passed while I was in hospital. I check my watch. It's just after six. "He'll be home soon."

"He has a sleepover tonight."

"On the first day of school?"

"Yes."

I sigh. I don't want to wait another day to see Alec, but perhaps it's better that I speak with the Hygates first. "I need to see Chris and Julia."

"They're not here, either. They left by helicopter this morning. Hence the sleepover."

It's out of character for Julia to allow a sleepover on a school night, but I suppose she and Chris didn't have any choice. Zelde has always declined to babysit Alec, and no doubt they're occupied with their new business.

"I'll be in the summerhouse." I take a few steps away, but now I turn back. I'm so tired of being under everyone's thumb at Paradise Bay. "Zelde, seeing as you're a healthcare professional, perhaps you could show a more caring attitude toward someone who just got out of hospital. I presume you've heard that I saved Alec's life, and remember, if it weren't for me, the Hygates would never have had a child. Would it hurt you to show me a little respect?"

A strange expression passes over Zelde's face. For an instant, I think she's furious, but now, to my surprise, she smiles. "Eve, you're right. Come and wait in the house, and I'll get you a cold drink. Mr. and Mrs. Hygate are due any minute."

"I thought you said—" It doesn't make sense to me that Alec has been sent on a sleepover if Julia and Chris are due back this evening, but something odd about Zelde's manner stops me from asking her to explain.

I follow her inside. She fetches an apple juice from the kitchen and leads me upstairs. I assume she's taking me to the pink room, but she ushers me in the opposite direction, to the very end of the south wing. She shows me into a vacant servant's bedroom that's now used for storage. Dusty boxes are piled in the corner.

"Stay here," she says.

I'm reminded of the first time I entered this house seven years ago. Zelde showed me in and ordered me to stay put. Back then, she seemed so forbidding. Today, she's different. She seems anxious. She hasn't even commented on my buzz cut or my bandaged neck. Something's distracting her.

"No problem." I sit on the bare mattress and sip my juice, acting as though I haven't noticed her nerves.

Zelde's hand trembles as she pulls the door shut behind her. Her footsteps recede.

The last time I snooped around this house behind Zelde's back, it didn't go well, but I've had enough of respecting the privacy of people who keep secrets from me. Something's up. Why would Zelde make me wait in a disused bedroom? Why is she nervous?

Perhaps Alec *is* here. Right now, Zelde might be heading to Alec's room in the north wing to whisk him away before I can tell him that he's right—I *am* his mother.

I turn the handle of the door and inch it open.

The south hallway is empty. I creep to the landing, where I can see along the north hallway, which is set at a slight angle. It's empty, too. At the far end, Alec's bedroom door is shut.

I dart across the landing and pad along the north hallway to Alec's room. I'll be in a power of trouble if Zelde and Alec are in here, but I don't care. I fling the door open.

Empty.

I look behind the door. Alec's schoolbag is not hanging on its hook, and his soccer cleats are missing. Okay, it seems Alec did attend school and soccer today. My heart plummets. I wanted to see him so badly.

A thrumming above me. Helicopter blades.

I feel as though I'm in a time loop. Zelde is about to catch me sneaking around and explode with anger just as she did that first day.

But I need to figure out what's going on. I return along the hall to the pink room and peer out the window. If Alec is anywhere on the property, he'll run to the helipad to greet his parents. Possibly, he's in the helicopter with them. Either way, that would explain why Zelde put me at the far end of the house.

The chopper touches down. Zelde appears from the house. Her skirt is whipped around in the wind, and she holds her hands over her ears.

Chris steps out of the helicopter and turns toward it. I expect him to help Julia down, but instead he takes a bundle from her, something wrapped in a yellow blanket. She leaps down and takes it back, cradling it in her arms.

I can't see the bundle clearly, but the way Julia's holding it, it almost seems she's carrying a baby.

I shake my head. How absurd. My sense of time has got mixed up—I feel as though I'm back in the past when Alec was an infant. The medication must still be affecting me.

I can't let the Hygates know I was spying. I creep-run to the south wing, making it back to the servant's bedroom just before footsteps approach. My heart's hammering. I slug the rest of my juice, sit on the bed, and slouch onto my elbows, trying to look bored.

Christopher walks in. "Eve, I didn't expect to see you."

"Why not? I live here."

"Uh, I thought you'd be in hospital longer. This morning Julia couriered your phone and some personal belongings to your ward." He closes the door.

If Zelde was nervous, Christopher is agitated. He doesn't seem to know where to put his hands, shoving them in his pockets and then taking them back out.

"From what I can gather, you didn't visit me in hospital or check on my condition. What made you think I would stay there longer?"

"How did you get here?" Christopher ignores my question.

"I caught the ferry."

"Who drove you here from the village?"

"I walked."

"Did you tell anyone you were coming here?"

His question strikes me as odd.

"Who would I tell?"

He rubs his jaw. "The police or someone at the hospital."

"No. I don't know why you think I'd need to tell the police I was going home. They have no interest in me. They told me I'm not to blame for the shipwre—"

"Whether you're to blame for sinking the yacht is neither here nor there. We have a more serious problem."

"Listen, Chris, I never told Alec he was my son."

Chris sneers. "You told the police."

"I was sedated. I don't even remember saying it." I try to adopt an assertive tone, but I sound as though I'm pleading for forgiveness. It doesn't help that I'm sitting on the bed while Chris towers over me.

"Yet you remember being told you weren't to blame for the fire."

"I saw Officer Maxwell a second time—earlier today in fact."

"Did you? Presumably you weren't sedated today. I take it you explained to him that you're not, in fact, Alec's mother?"

I'm silent.

"Obviously not," says Chris.

"What does it matter to you what I said? You've *obviously* got some plan to cheat on this DNA test."

"In a sense, you're right," says Chris. "It doesn't matter to me what nonsense claims you make, but it matters to you. You must realize you can't continue as Alec's nanny. You've betrayed our trust. Julia never wants to see you again. It was bad enough that you took Alec sailing, placing him in harm's way, but then you set the police on us. The indignity of having DNA swabs taken—not just from us but from our child."

"I thought you volunteered?"

"What choice did we have?"

A chill runs through me. Something is off about his tone. It feels as though Chris believed he and Julia would pass the DNA test. How crazy is that?

Chris adds, "I promised Julia that if you turned up here, I'd escort you off the property myself."

My cheeks flush. I feel as though I *am* guilty, the way Chris is speaking. But this isn't so different from what I expected. The Hygates don't want me to stay on, and nor do I. I can't keep nannying Alec while seeking custody of him.

"If I could speak with Julia, I could explain. I'd never place Alec in danger . . ." What exactly am I asking for? I no longer care what Julia thinks of me. "Let's compromise. I'm happy to leave, but I need to see Alec first. He needs to know I'm okay. Please. I promise I won't say anything about who I am."

Chris's lip curls. "You must be joking. As if we'd risk that."

I stand. "I'm not leaving until I've seen my son. I'm still employed by you. It's against the law to fire someone without a reason."

"Perhaps you're right, Eve. But you can't insist on staying here. You've never paid rent at the summerhouse. If I tell you to leave and you refuse, you're trespassing. So, I'm only going to say this once. Get off my property."

The world turns red. I can't believe Chris has the nerve to speak to me this way. I've given him the most precious thing in his life, and this is how he repays me. How dare he? Doesn't he understand the power I hold?

No, he doesn't. He doesn't know that Maxwell told me birth mothers aren't prosecuted.

My fists clench. "You might be able to make me leave today, but you haven't heard the last of me. I'm Alec's mother. And it's no use scaring me with talk of criminal charges. The policeman told me birth mothers aren't prosecuted for child trafficking."

"Eve, Julia and I volunteered for a DNA test. You don't seem to have processed the implications."

"Yes, the results were 'lost.' How convenient. Tell me, who did you have to bribe?"

Chris lets out an ugly laugh, then stares at me for a moment before saying, "Have you ever seen a photo of me as a boy?"

His question is so unexpected that it distracts me.

"What's that got to do with anything?" I ask.

"You'll see. Have you?"

Now that I think about it, I haven't. When I first came to Paradise Bay, I noticed there were no family photos on display. I've never seen any albums, either. I shake my head.

"I didn't think so. Julia took care to hide them. Wait here."
Chris opens the door and strides into the hallway. I hear him
shuffling about in another room.

He returns carrying a photo album. He leafs through the
pages. "Here's a good one." He hands me the album.

The full-page photo shows three children dressed in ski gear
and standing on a snowy slope. The youngest is Alec aged about
five, although I don't remember Alec ever having hair that long.
The other two children, a boy and girl a few years older, look
startlingly like him.

The three strawberry-blond children smile at me from a scene
that looks golden and grainy the way old photos do.

"When did Alec ever go skiing?" I ask.

Chris quirks an eyebrow. "You nailed it, Eve. Alec has never
gone skiing. You might also ask, when did Alec have that shaggy
hairstyle? So seventies. When did Alec have an older brother and
sister?"

"It's not Alec," I say. "Who is it?"

"His father," says Chris.

My heart is a cold black stone.

I turn the pages of the album. Photo after photo appears of a
boy so like Alec that I would swear it was him, but the locations,
the hairstyles, the clothing, the other people in the photos are all
wrong.

These are old photos. Seventies photos.

I want to believe these are photos of Xander, but they're not.
They're Chris. I can see Chris's strong build, his wide cheek-
bones. But the boy also looks like Alec. He has the same red-blond
hair. The boy in the photos has ice-blue eyes rather than turquoise, but still the similarity is striking.

"The older children are my brother and sister," says Chris.

"Okay, these are some of your childhood photos, as you said. Big deal."

My voice falters. I'm not convinced that Alec resembles Chris more closely than he does Xander. I still think either man could be Alec's father. I always thought Alec's hair ended up red-blond because he inherited a mix of Xander's blond and my red hair, but I can see why people believe Alec's hair color comes from Chris.

The problem isn't that Alec looks like Chris. That was the plan all along. The problem is that Chris believes that Alec's resemblance to him is an important secret. So important that Chris and Julia have kept their childhood photos hidden from me for six years.

Chris believes he's Alec's real father. *That's* why he's happy to have the DNA test.

How can he believe this? Chris sure didn't get me pregnant, and Julia was never pregnant. I know that for a fact. I was living here when she was pretending to be pregnant. I saw her fake bellies . . .

A thud. The album has fallen at my feet. The room spins. I clutch the pile of boxes for support.

It can't be.

For months, every time I saw Julia, she looked pregnant. I believed she wasn't. She was wearing a fake belly. Wasn't she?

"It's impossible that she was pregnant," I say.

Chris shakes his head as though he's sorry for me.

Does Alec resemble Julia? His turquoise eyes are similar to her aqua ones. I always believed Alec's eye color was a blend of Xander's blue and my green eyes, but . . .

"Why would Julia make me believe she was faking a pregnancy

if she *was* pregnant?" My voice rises. "The whole reason you brought me here was because she couldn't have a baby! She was kicked by a horse in Mongolia!"

A knock at the door. Chris opens it.

Joseph's in the hallway. "The chopper's refueled and ready for you, boss. The, uh, the schooner's coming in at nine."

"Good," says Chris. "Joseph, as I mentioned, you're to take Eve to Hobart on *Squall*. I want you to leave at once."

I step back. "I'm not leaving till you tell me what on earth is going on, Chris."

"Eve, if you don't want to be dragged off my land, I suggest you leave with Joseph. I'll have your belongings shipped to your new address."

"I don't need a ride. I have a ferry ticket."

"I'd rather be sure you've left the island. Alec's on a sleepover in the village. I don't want you near him."

"What's to stop me catching the next ferry back?"

"I've asked Joseph to explain things to you on your way to Hobart. Afterward, I think you'll see everything differently."

I HATE LEAVING Breaksea. I feel as though I'm abandoning Alec—and I need to see what he looks like. Surely I can't have forgotten my son's face after only a few days apart? Yet the photos have got me muddled. I always thought I saw Xander in Alec, but maybe that was only because I wanted to. I wanted to believe some part of Xander was still here with me.

I follow Joseph out of the house. If I go with Joseph, Chris has promised me an explanation. As we walk along the beach to the marina, I glance back. Zelde is watching from an upstairs window.

It's dead calm and hot as hell despite the evening's approach. The ocean is mirrorlike, the sky a uniform vibrant blue.

As I step onto *Squall*, a sister ship to *Torrent* with the same snug cockpit and narrow teak deck, Chris reappears and calls Joseph aside. I strain to hear their conversation, but they keep their voices low. All I catch is Chris's parting remark. "Make sure you're back before Ruby arrives. I leave at eight."

"Got it," says Joseph. He leaps aboard, starts the engine and throws off the lines.

I sit in the cockpit as Joseph chugs out into the open water.

Alec looks like Chris. Chris believes he's Alec's father.

Maxwell told me the samples got lost, and I assumed Chris and Julia had intercepted them. I never for a moment considered that they might not have to. That they might pass the DNA test.

Can it possibly be true that Alec is not my son?

I saw Julia's fake belly the night of Margareta's party when Joseph walked in on her half naked. Later, at the lighthouse, I saw the rear straps of the fake belly when Julia threw her blouse up.

But I never saw Julia take the belly off. I never saw her body beneath. I assumed her own tummy was flat.

I feel seasick. I clap my hand to my mouth as bile rises.

She was pregnant all along. Alec is not my child. Not my child. Not my child.

What about my pregnancy? Is Chris claiming I imagined it?

Joseph's standing at the helm, steering one-handed.

"Joseph, Chris said you would explain."

He casts a sideways glance at me, a glance brimming with sly malice. "You still haven't figured it out? You've had enough clues. You even heard her cry down at the office the day after you had her."

"What? Who is *her*?"

Joseph grins.

I remember Alec as a newborn crying in the marina office. I knocked on the door, but nobody came. Joseph led me away, warned me not to talk about it. I couldn't understand why Joseph wouldn't let me see my baby. Nor could I understand why Alec wasn't tucked up in his crib in the nursery where he belonged.

Now I know. The truth slams into me.

I speak woodenly. "The baby in the office wasn't Alec."

Joseph nods.

"Alec was in the mansion with Julia."

He nods again.

"The baby in the office was . . . was . . ."

I can't say it.

Her.

Joseph says, "The baby in the office was your daughter."

CHAPTER 36

Julia

Julia stepped off the yacht, taking Chris's arm to steady herself. Her belly was so huge she felt off-balance, as if the turbulent afternoon breeze might blow her off the pier. She hated being pregnant—the discomfort, the nausea—all the while having to give Eve the impression that her pregnancy was fake.

On her wedding night, Julia had put on the performance of her life to convince her husband that she was an innocent victim of Silas's criminal schemes, chosen simply for her unusual auburn hair. Still, she'd seen that Chris considered leaving her. That night—the night that should have been the happiest of her life—his eyes had been distant. Julia had thrown everything into keeping her husband. She made sure their lovemaking brought him to new heights of pleasure before she began her sob story about her unfortunate past. Her message was clear: save me from Silas, and you'll have the perfect wife.

But that might not have been enough if Julia hadn't played her trump card. She waited for the question Chris was bound to ask. Finally, it came. "Is it possible you're already pregnant?"

She knew her answer was all-important. "I do have a funny

feeling," she murmured. "It's too early to test, but we'll know in a couple of weeks."

The lie worked. Christopher realized at once that if he left Julia and she was pregnant, his baby would end up in Silas's hands.

And so Christopher had come up with the plan.

By the time Julia revealed to her husband that the test had been negative, the plan was already in motion. Yasmin and Zelde had been hired. Soon, Julia was pregnant for real, and she knew she'd won Chris's loyalty. She was carrying his baby.

The plan had been difficult to carry out, but despite all the setbacks and complications, she and Chris had got through it together.

Now Julia had visited Eve at the lighthouse for the last time. There would be no more pretending to be fake-pregnant, no more worrying that Eve would discover Julia's pregnancy was all too real.

The only remaining hurdle was the birth. A home birth. Julia would much rather have had a Caesarean in a nice private hospital, but with Zelde in charge and Chris by her side, she would cope.

Zelde stepped off the yacht behind Julia, medical kit in hand. "Time to break your waters, Julia." She turned and raised her voice so that Joseph, who was tying up the yacht, could hear. "First, the four of us should go over the plan. The big swap happens tomorrow. We can't afford to make a mistake."

The big swap. Julia felt a thrill of pleasure at the phrase. As soon as it was done, they would be safe.

"No one's around, right?" Joseph asked Chris.

Chris gave a thumbs-up signal. "I've given everyone three days off."

Zelde checked her watch. "It's noon. Julia's labor will probably take eight to twelve hours."

Julia squeezed Chris's arm. "Darling, by midnight, we'll be holding our son." She was keen to get started. She took a few steps toward the summerhouse, hoping Zelde would wrap up this conversation.

Joseph waved in the direction of the lighthouse. "Tomorrow morning, I bring Eve back from the rock to have her baby."

"Correct," said Zelde. "I told Eve her baby was ready to be born, but the truth is her pregnancy would probably continue for another fortnight if we didn't induce contractions. Julia, Eve wants you present for her labor. Chris will have to look after your son while you attend."

"Nice. A few hours of father-son bonding." Chris rubbed his hands together.

"I hope Eve's quick about it," said Julia. It was so unfair that she would have to spend hours away from her baby so soon after his birth. "Trust Eve to want something inconvenient. I'm dreading finding out what trashy name she's chosen for the baby."

"Let's stick to the important topic." Zelde spoke in a clipped tone. "Once Eve is in advanced labor, Julia makes an excuse to leave the birthing suite briefly and fetches Christopher and Joseph. From that moment, both men must stay right outside the door. Christopher, you'll be holding your son, and it's essential you keep him quiet. Eve must not hear a baby crying while she's still in labor. Joseph, no wandering off for a smoke."

"We'll be glued to the spot," said Chris.

Zelde nodded. "The moment Eve's baby is out, I'll say, "I'm clearing the airways." Joseph, when you hear those words, open the door. It will be dark and Eve will be facing away from the door. I'll be holding her baby girl in a blanket. The baby might look weird, a bit bloody, with a freshly cut umbilical cord. Don't let that distract you. Take her, not the blanket, and whisk her away to the marina office. Get her out of earshot as fast as possible."

"Meanwhile, I place my son into the same blanket," said Chris.

"Yes," said Zelde. "It will be covered in fluids from the birth, so—"

"Is that really necessary?" asked Julia. This was the part of the plan she most disliked. Her newborn son being wrapped in a filthy blanket.

"I grew up on a sheep farm," said Zelde. "If a lamb is orphaned, the farmer will give it to a ewe that had a stillbirth, but the ewe will reject the lamb unless it smells like her offspring. The farmer rubs the orphaned lamb in the stillborn lamb's scent, and the mother accepts it. Trust me."

"Ugh," said Julia. "Can we stop obsessing over these details? Everybody knows their job."

"Fine," said Zelde. "Let's get started."

Zelde, Chris, and Julia headed for the summerhouse.

Inside, Julia led the way upstairs. "Do you know, Chris, Eve noticed my bump had dropped? I had to make up a story to explain it."

"So, when you said Sarah had commented that you'd dropped, that wasn't true?" Zelde asked, fishing her key out of her medical bag.

Julia tittered. "No, Sarah didn't say anything about my bump. She didn't ask the name of my obstetrician, either. I made the whole story up on the spot."

"You've always been adept at thinking on your feet." Zelde

unlocked the door to the birthing suite. "I'm glad to hear Sarah won't be leaving."

"Oh, I have to fire Sarah," said Julia, "or Eve might wonder why I didn't. A pity. It'll be hard to replace her. Anyway, I get the feeling Sarah and Eve might become chums otherwise. They're pretty close in age, and Sarah's so friendly. We don't want Eve getting too close to anyone, or she might overshare."

"Good thinking," said Chris, "although you'll find it hard to find another maid as hardworking as Sarah."

"I'm glad the lies will be over soon," said Julia.

Zelde raised an eyebrow. "I don't think they will be. As long as Eve lives here, you'll always be lying to her."

Zelde always made such depressing comments, but Julia refused to let the old woman spoil her mood. Her pregnancy was finally ending today. She was giving Chris a son and getting Silas out of her life for good.

Zelde patted the hospital bed. "Hop up."

"One thing I'm doing first," said Julia. She took off her maternity blouse and pants, exposing the flesh-colored garment beneath. It looked exactly the same as the fake bellies she had shown Eve all those months ago, but there was one crucial difference. The part that covered her belly was merely a thin layer of silicone with no padding beneath.

Julia wrenched off the garment and threw it to Chris. "I never have to wear that uncomfortable thing again!"

Standing in the birthing suite in her bra and knickers, she pressed her hand to the bare skin of her distended abdomen. *Imagine if Eve could see me right now. What a shock she'd get.* But there was no need to worry. Eve wouldn't be brought back to Paradise Bay until Julia's baby was safely born and ready for the swap.

Eve will never find out the truth. Julia found the thought so com-
forting. *Eve will never suspect she's been given the wrong child. Silas
will never suspect he's been given the wrong child.*

No one will know.

THIS CONTRACTION WAS something else. Julia felt as though a
demon was about to burst from her belly. She had been pacing
the floor of the summerhouse as daylight faded and night set in,
but now she froze in place, doubled over. Chris rushed to her
side.

She gripped him. "Surely this can't go on much longer."

Zelde, sitting with a notebook, shook her head. "Your contractions are still quite infrequent. This is going to be a long night."

"Nooo," Julia moaned. "I'm going to be awake all night *and* tomorrow night holding Eve's hand through her labor." She flopped
into an armchair. "Then we have to hold a goddamn christening
just to get Eve to make a public declaration that we are the baby's
parents."

A knock at the door downstairs.

"Who's that?" asked Julia. "I thought nobody was here except
Joseph."

"I'll see." Chris disappeared downstairs. He reappeared a moment later with a deep frown. "Joseph says Breaksea Light is out."

There was silence.

"You and Joseph had better go," said Zelde. "I'll stay with
Julia."

"Are you joking?" cried Julia. "Chris isn't going anywhere!"

Another contraction hit. Julia clutched her belly.

Why had Joseph come to bother them with trivia? It wasn't as though one light on the blink was a danger to shipping in these days of satellite navigation.

Chris took her hand. "Julia, those lights don't go out by themselves. Eve must have broken the light. I can think of only one reason she would do that."

"No, surely it doesn't mean . . ." Julia couldn't say the words. Could Eve be in labor?

Julia's heart fluttered, seeming to rise out of her chest. She didn't want to think about this news. How could Zelde manage two labors at once? What would happen if Eve's baby was born first?

Julia buried her head in her hands. She didn't want to do anything more. She wanted to fall asleep here in this armchair, but Zelde and Chris were buzzing around the room, exchanging frantic whispers.

Zelde handed Chris a number of medical items, giving hurried instructions on their use. She pointed at Julia's thigh. "This is where you inject the sedative into Eve."

"Why can't *I* have the sedative?" Julia asked.

Zelde handed Chris the syringe. "The drug should slow Eve's labor and sedate her. Give it the moment you arrive. Hopefully, Eve won't realize I'm not there. If worse comes to worst and you have to cut the cord, remember to clamp it first."

With a terse nod, Chris dropped the items into his bag.

Zelde turned to Julia. "If we're going to get your baby out in time, we need to pull out all the stops. First, we need to vacate the summerhouse. Eve expects to give birth here. You have to move."

Julia could hardly believe her ears. All that money spent on the birthing suite to make her labor more comfortable, and she had to give it up to Eve. Leaning on Zelde, she limped all the way from the summerhouse to the mansion. Each step she took seemed to intensify her contractions. By the time she reached the master bedroom, she was ready to die.

JULIA LAY SPRAWLED on her bed. Time passed in a blur of pain, resentment, indignation. She heard the helicopter leave and return, but Chris didn't come to her. Now Zelde had gone to check Eve's progress. Everybody was so concerned about Eve. Julia was all alone.

The bad luck of being in labor at the same time made Julia want to scream, but she couldn't make a sound, not even during the most agonizing contraction, in case Eve heard. Paradise Bay was like an amphitheater—sound traveled over the water. As another brutal wave hit, she stuffed a pillow into her mouth.

Footsteps on the staircase. Julia turned, hoping for Chris, but it was only stupid old Zelde.

"Eve's labor is moving fast." Zelde sounded grim.

Julia gasped for words. "Can't you—slow—slow it down?"

"I've tried. Sometimes birth is unstoppable. All we can do is speed yours up." She fiddled with Julia's drip. "This may increase the pain."

"I can't," panted Julia. "It already hurts so much."

Zelde set her mouth firmly. "The more pain the better. We need this baby out. Try harder."

Julia's body was on fire. The next contraction hit like a bolt of lightning.

Try harder. But pushing made the pain worse. What was this baby doing to her body? It felt like she was being ripped apart.

Julia writhed. She closed her eyes, waiting for the pain to pass.

A clawlike hand caught her chin. Startled, Julia opened her eyes. Zelde's haggard face was inches away.

"Don't you understand?" the old woman snarled. "If you don't do your job and push this baby out, we'll have a serious problem on our hands, and your husband will have to fix your mistake!"

Julia gasped. How dare she—

But Zelde was right. Julia had to get her baby out first. The backup plan was for Eve to disappear.

Chris had stood by her so far, but he had his limits. If he was forced to take part in getting rid of Eve, he would hold it against Julia. He'd never feel the same toward her.

When the next contraction came, Julia took a deep breath and pushed. She pushed with every ounce of strength she could muster. She was being tortured by this baby. White-hot pain spread through her body to her fingers and toes. She was dying. She was going to die this minute.

Now, at last, she saw him. A head of red hair emerging between her legs.

"One more push!" cried Zelde.

Julia closed her eyes and pushed as if it were life or death. The baby came out in a rush.

He's here. I've done it. It's over. Julia opened her eyes and reached for him. "My son!"

But Zelde had already picked up the baby and was dashing out of the room. Something fell to the floor with a clunk. Julia glanced down and saw a pair of bloodied scissors. Zelde had cut the cord, literally cut her baby away from her.

"Stop!" Julia hissed. "Bring him back!"

Seconds counted. Eve's daughter might be born any moment. It could make the difference between the plan succeeding and failing. Yet Julia couldn't bear not to see her baby, not to hold her baby.

"Come back!"

Zelde's feet clattered down the stairs. She was gone.

To think that her son was being given to Eve, that Eve would hold him first. Julia would never forgive the girl for that.

CHAPTER 37

Eve

I'm sitting in *Squall*'s cockpit gazing unseeing at the horizon.

I remember my baby leaving my body. I was drowsy, sedated with painkillers I didn't want, confused. Why was I giving birth in the dark? Where was Zelde?

My baby didn't cry. *Where was she? Was she okay?*

And then she was in my arms—she was he, she was Alec. He was beautiful, and he smelled so right, and I never questioned that he was the baby I had just pushed out of my body. Alec was my son, Xander's son.

The idea that a baby existed who was my daughter is unreal. And Alec isn't mine. How can I claim him now?

Joseph is talking about the Hygates' financial problems. "What with the drought and the pandemic, Chris lost a fortune. Now the borders are open again. Julia's restarted her business."

I couldn't care less about anything except my child—whoever *my child* is. But I have to pay attention. I have to understand. "Julia has a business? Not Chris?"

"She's a smuggler."

I blink. I want to say, *Aren't you the smuggler?* but I refrain.

Something's off about the way Joseph is talking. Moments ago, Chris angrily ordered me off the property, but Joseph's acting as if we're buddies having a cozy chat. I was gone for a few days, and it feels as though I've come back to an alternate universe. Someone called Ruby is visiting. A schooner is coming. Julia is a smuggler. I have a *daughter*. *Alec* is not my son.

But this isn't an alternate universe. Nothing's changed. It's just that they always kept these things hidden from me. Now they're not bothering.

Why not? Why hide so much from me for years and now tell me everything?

One other thing is troubling me. We're well clear of the reefs. We could have turned south ten minutes ago. Instead, Joseph's still heading east. Out to sea.

"Who's Ruby?" My question comes out at random.

"There's no such person." Joseph smirks as though he's made a clever joke.

It's weird how even a crook like him will tell the truth sometimes. He thinks it's safe, that I won't guess what he means, but if Ruby's not a person, then what is she? What else would have a woman's name?

A yacht.

Joseph said the schooner would arrive at nine. He doesn't know I've seen this schooner before. I suspect it's the one that entered the marina with its lights off the night I saw the empty terrariums. That schooner was red, so it would make sense for its name to be *Ruby*. It's coming back tonight.

The Hygates' recent business travel, the venture to recoup their fortune—they're smuggling wildlife. The bundle I saw Julia carrying when she climbed out of the helicopter must be an animal. That explains why she was cradling it like a baby. Not a gecko, but a rare species of koala perhaps.

Is this why Alec is on a sleepover? To keep him away from the criminal arriving on the schooner?

Joseph was told to be back before *Ruby* arrived. He's meant to be back at Paradise Bay in a couple of hours. There's no time to drop me in Hobart and return.

The world seems to slow down and stop. My blood pulses fast and feverish as the truth dawns.

This is why Joseph is telling me everything. He isn't taking me to Hobart. Joseph is heading out to deep water, and then he's going to turn around and come back—without me on board.

I CAN'T LET Joseph know I've guessed the plan. If he thinks I'm going to start fighting for my life, he might attack at once. Perhaps he's armed. Even if he isn't, he could easily overpower me.

I look around for something to use as a weapon. There are always a couple of steel winch handles in a cockpit, but not today. Joseph has removed them.

We're at least three miles from land. Too far to swim. Joseph could simply push me overboard.

My only chance against him is with words. If only I hadn't told Chris that nobody knew I was coming to Paradise Bay today.

I need to get Joseph talking. I need to make him feel we share a bond.

"Can you tell me about the night you rescued me?" I ask. "I can't remember much."

"You were out of it," says Joseph. "Would never've found you if Alec hadn't cried out. He was all right, but I thought you'd carked it."

"The doctor said you knew how to treat hypothermia."

"You don't hang round these waters for years without learning a thing or two about the cold. You keep the victim horizontal, don't jostle them. I put you in the cabin with a hot water bottle and blankets and radioed for a rescue chopper. It was waiting when we got to Paradise Bay."

"I was hoping I'd get a chance to thank you. I owe you so much. To think that I'll never see you again. I've decided to move to Italy—permanently. That's where my nanna was from."

Joseph eyes me suspiciously. "Thought you wanted to hang around near Alec."

"I was already thinking of leaving. Nothing ever happens on Breaksea. I want to meet new people, see the world. Now that I know Alec isn't my kid, there's nothing stopping me."

It hurts to say this. I want to claw my words out of the air and set them on fire, but I have to be convincing. "Truly, Joseph, I want you to know how grateful I am. I'd do anything for you, anything you asked, if it weren't for the fact that I'm leaving right away."

"Even if you feel that way about Alec, you're gonna want to find out where your daughter is."

His words pierce me like arrows to my heart. My daughter. He knows where she is.

I can't speak. If I do, I'll scream. *Where the hell is my daughter? What did you do with her?* I want to punch him and kick him. *How dare you take my baby!*

I can't say any of this. I can't show that I care. I can't even ask where she is. If Joseph tells me the answer, there's no way he'll let me live.

At least I know she's somewhere. Joseph said "is"—present tense. She's alive.

I give a nonchalant shrug. "I've never met this *daughter*. She's not my child any more than Alec is. Whatever happened, it's too late to undo. What I want is a fresh start. Live my life a little."

"Nice try," says Joseph.

He shoves the engine into neutral and hits the kill switch. The silence of the sea settles around us. There's not a breath of wind.

"Please," I say, "wouldn't you rather not do this? Just drop me somewhere. Anywhere."

"I have my orders."

"Just let me go. I'll never come back. I promise. Chris will never know. Why would I tell him?"

"I don't care about Hygate. He can't do anything that might upset the missus. He thought about killing you years ago, soon as you'd had your baby, but he didn't want to worry her. He decided as long as you didn't know about your daughter, there was no need."

"Why did Chris want to kill me?"

"Because of Silas. He's the real boss. He's one scary bastard, and he doesn't know you exist. It's my job to keep it that way."

Silas. The name triggers a memory from years ago. I overheard Joseph talking on the ship's radio about a guy called Silas who would take "creative revenge" if he found out what Joseph was up to.

He sounds ominous. I thought it was bad enough I had to deal with the Hygates and Joseph, but there's someone else? Someone *Joseph* thinks is scary?

Does this Silas have my daughter?

"I'll get on a plane. I swear."

"Words are cheap," says Joseph. "I'm not stupid. You'll make fancy promises and then go straight to the cops. There's only one way to do this."

"You're right," I say. "Nobody feels obliged to keep a promise made under coercion. But things are different between you and me, Joseph."

Joseph has lied to me for six years, letting me love Alec as my son, not telling me about my daughter. He's treated me like dirt, like *Hygate's whore*.

I need to forget all that.

"Joseph, you pulled me from this very patch of water. You didn't have to rescue me, but you did."

"Hygate said I shouldn't have. Could've left you there, spared us all the trouble."

"Yet you chose to save me. I owe you my life. That's why you know I won't go to the police. Besides, what could I say to them? I have absolutely no proof I was pregnant. I never saw a doctor, and the only people who ever saw me looking pregnant were you, the Hygates, and Zelde—four people who would all tell the police I was lying."

As I'm speaking, I realize my words are not just a story to convince Joseph. They're true. Zelde will have destroyed her medical notes relating to my pregnancy. I told the Blairs about the baby, but then I wrote to them saying I had miscarried. Officer Maxwell already thinks I'm a crazy lady for claiming Alec is mine. He probably wouldn't have even listened to a new round of "allegations" from me.

I guess Maxwell wasn't corrupt. The Hygates didn't need to

bribe anyone, because they had nothing to fear from a DNA test. No wonder Maxwell was looking at me strangely. He'd met three people who were utterly convinced they were Alec's parents.

"It isn't just the cops," Joseph says. "Chris doesn't want you making a fuss, drawing attention to the smuggling. He can't afford that with Silas on the scene. If Silas thinks the cops are sniffing round, he'll take action. The kind that leaves no witnesses."

"I've got no interest in stirring up trouble."

Joseph looks unmoved. He opens the lazarette and reaches for something.

A length of chain.

A shudder goes through me. I have to try a different angle, and fast.

"People will notice I'm missing. I made friends with another patient at the hospital. I promised to meet up with her in the village tomorrow. And I told my family in Italy to expect me in a week or two." I'm lying, of course. "When the police investigate my disappearance, can you be sure the Hygates will stay silent? They might rat you out to save their own skin."

"They would never," says Joseph. "Hygate's in as deep as I am. And the missus doesn't know anything about it. She doesn't even know you came back today."

"What about Zelde? She knows I came back. And she saw us leave together on the boat. She was watching from the house."

Joseph is sitting perfectly still. His eyes drill into me.

"You and Zelde aren't exactly close, are you?" I ask. "If she cut a deal with the police, you'd be glad you'd let me live. It's a life sentence for murder."

Joseph is quiet for an eternity. The sun burns down on me.

Sweat trickles down my back. At last, he starts the engine and pushes the tiller to starboard. The yacht describes a wide arc as it turns toward land.

I THOUGHT TIME could never pass more slowly than it did during the hours I spent in the cold, dark ocean with Alec, but the journey back to land with Joseph seems to take longer.

We travel in silence. I keep opening my mouth to repeat my assurances that Alec means nothing to me and nor does the daughter I've never met, but I stop myself. I might say something that makes Joseph change his mind.

At last Joseph speaks. "There's no time to take you to Hobart. I'm dropping you at the lighthouse. The key's under a white stone by the door. There's no bedding or anything, but tinned food's in the kitchen."

I should be relieved, but I don't feel I can breathe. Tinned food? How long am I going to be stuck there?

"I'll come back and take you to Hobart when I get a chance. Then you go straight to Italy. If I ever see you again round these parts, you won't get a second chance."

We motor into the cove.

"Listen up," says Joseph. "Julia doesn't know you're dead." His words make my skin prickle. "Hygate knows you're at the bottom of the ocean with weights chained to your ankles, but Julia thinks you upped and left Tassie. I don't think she'll try to track you down, but you need to lie low just in case. I'll be in deep shit if Hygate finds out you're alive."

"He never will."

"What would be a thousand times worse is if Silas got word of this debacle."

"He won't."

Joseph doesn't drop anchor. He tells me to untie a kayak from the side deck and place it in the sea. I attach a long rope to the kayak's stern while Joseph steers *Squall* in circles.

I have nothing but the T-shirt and pants the hospital gave me, nothing in my pocket but a bank card, a few dollars, and a ferry ticket. I want to ask for warm clothes, some water in case the tank's empty. I want to ask for a dozen things that would render my survival on this rock more likely, but I don't dare.

I climb into the kayak and paddle ashore. As soon as I'm out, I stow the paddle in the kayak, and Joseph hauls the rope hand over hand until the kayak is back beside the yacht. He lifts it on deck, tying it in place, and heads off without a word of farewell.

I watch *Squall* exit the cove and disappear. I'm alone in this beautiful, cursed cove as the sun dips below the ridge and seabirds gather for the night.

At the lighthouse, I find the key and let myself in. As the adrenaline wears off, my stomach grumbles. In the ground-floor kitchen, I find some dusty cans. I wolf some tuna and beans cold. I search for painkillers—my burn is aching—but come up empty-handed.

I can't believe I'm back on this rock, a prisoner once more. But I'm a different person from the naïve girl who lived out her pregnancy here six years ago. Back then, I trusted Julia. I never suspected Chris had plans to harm me. Now it turns out my life was in danger all along.

They stole my baby. *My daughter.* The thought of her sends an ache through my body so intense I almost collapse on the floor. They took a newborn baby from her mother, and nobody knew she was gone. Nobody would ever come looking.

I didn't get to hold her, not even once.

They fooled me completely. Now I know not to trust anybody. Even Joseph might have a change of heart.

Last time I was here, I couldn't try to escape in case I hurt my unborn child. But I'm not pregnant now. Conditions are ideal. There's no wind, no ocean swell.

I'm going to swim for it.

CHAPTER 38

Windless days on Breaksea are rare. I need to seize the moment. It's now or never.

First, I mount the spiral stairs to the light room and survey the water stretching to the horizon. To the east, the nearest land is New Zealand, a week's sail away. To the south, the ocean stretches unbroken to Antarctica. Yet there's no groundswell. I've never seen the water so still.

I spy *Squall* already well on her way back to Paradise Bay. In the vast blue, she looks like a child's toy.

I lived in this lighthouse for months, but what I remember most vividly is my labor. I was sure I was having a girl. How deeply I yearned to give birth here and hold my baby in my arms. If I'd done that, everything would have turned out differently. I would have seen my daughter. They could never have fooled me into believing Alec was my baby. What would have happened?

They would have killed me.

I have to get out of here. I can't think beyond that. All I know is that if I stay, I'll be at Joseph's mercy once more.

I leave the kitchen as I found it, hiding the empty cans at the back of the shelf. I lock the lighthouse door and place the key under the white stone. At the beach, I take off my sandals and link them through the belt loops of my pants. Time to go.

THE BURN ON my neck stings when I enter the salt water. As I swim out of the cove into the open sea, each stroke pulls at the flesh. Despite the hot weather, the water's cold. I'm growing numb already. It's not a good sign.

It takes only a short time to swim to the base of the cliffs of Breaksea Island, but as I foresaw, I can't land. The sea is calm enough for me to clamber ashore, but I'd be stuck, unable to climb the sheer rock face.

I continue along the coastline, swimming freestyle. I must make the most of daylight. Once it's dark, it will be difficult to judge where to come ashore. There are beaches further north, but no way can I swim that far.

I try to fall into a rhythm, but I have to come up and check my direction every few strokes. Each time, I've veered off course. My swimming stroke is uneven. The burn on my neck, worse on my left side, is affecting it.

The cold seeps into my bones. My ears hurt. I want to huddle in a ball. I feel as though I've spent the last week in the water, as though I never fully warmed up.

Daylight is ebbing as I round a rocky outcrop and approach a lower cliff. Could I climb that? It's hard to tell in the gloom.

I have to chance it. I'm shivering violently. I can't stay in the water.

Despite the apparent calm, when I get close to the rocks, the water is surging and retreating. Every surge threatens to drag me over razor-sharp barnacles. I hang back, trying to choose my moment, but the sea decides for me. With a great rush it picks me up and washes me over the rocks. I grab hold, and as the water recedes, I'm left high and dry.

Pain sears through my limbs. I glance down. Blood is washing away with the water. I scramble up the cliff face as fast as I can, afraid the next wave will suck me back out to sea. My legs are clumsy with cold, but I fumble a little higher before the next surge hits. I hold tight until the water recedes again. No way could I have done this if there had been any breeze.

I'm safe for the moment, a few feet above the surge line. I don't really want to look at my injuries, but I must. The barnacles tore my pants and grazed my knees, but the deepest gash is on my forearm from when I tried to grab hold while washing across the rocks. Blood oozes from the wound.

I reach for my sandals, but they're gone. The flimsy stitching on the belt loops has torn through.

What with my burnt neck, my shaven head, and the blood dripping from my arm, I must look like someone from a war zone. I yank the dressing off my neck and press it against my arm. The adhesive tape has lost its stickiness, but I manage to tie it in place, stemming the bleeding.

Now to climb the cliff. I cling to the rock and clamber upward, finding first a foothold, then a handhold, slowly gaining height. Xander and I would climb for fun sometimes when we were spending an afternoon ashore at a remote beach. Tonight, it's anything but fun, but I'm glad I've done this before.

I make it to the top at last, heave myself onto the scrubby grass and roll onto my back. I never knew grass could feel so welcoming. I rake my fingers through it. I feel like kissing the earth, making a vow never to enter the water again.

A buzz attracts my attention. A helicopter.

Chris said he was leaving in the helicopter at eight. I'm not wearing a watch, but I'd guess he's running late. The sun sets closer to nine in summer.

I scramble to some shrubs and take cover. Christopher's un-likely to spot me from the air, but I haven't made it this far to take risks now.

The helicopter comes into view. I recognize its yellow paint-work. The craft heads into the western sky. How strange to think that the man in that helicopter believes my drowned corpse lies at the bottom of the ocean. What does he feel? Guilt? Relief? Satisfaction? Whatever it is, I must take care never to cross paths with him again.

I'm not home free. I'll pass Paradise Bay on my way to the ferry. It would make sense to board as inconspicuously as pos-sible. The late ferry is the safest bet. It's usually pretty deserted. Once off the ferry, it's straightforward to disappear. Buy some new belongings and an airline ticket. Live out my days overseas.

It's the only sensible thing to do, but I'm not going to do it. I was never going to do it.

I told Joseph I owed him my life and that was why he could trust that I'd disappear. But there's more to it than that.

Joseph's the kind of guy who knows nothing about women and doesn't care to learn. At times I've found his indifference rude, but tonight I'm grateful for it. If he knew me at all, I'd never have managed to convince him that I would leave my children.

Children. Even though he grew in Julia's womb and Chris is his father, Alec still feels like my child.

Alec is living among criminals. His mother is a smuggler. His father ordered my death. Chris and Julia wouldn't hurt Alec physically, but they're harming him in different ways. What kind of person would they raise him to be? Dishonest? Ruthless? Mur-derous? I can't abandon Alec to that destiny.

There's another person I can't abandon. Someone I've never met, yet we are not strangers. She spent nine months inside me.

I am her mother.

As soon as the helicopter is far enough away, I stand and head into the bush. I'm wet, bleeding, barefoot. Night is upon me. I need to move to get warm. I need to move to stay alive.

Chris said Julia was angry with me, but of course he'd say that to persuade me to leave. According to Joseph, Julia knows nothing about the plan to kill me.

Julia will know where my daughter is. The time to ask is tonight. Chris has left, and if I can slip past Joseph and Zelde, I'll get Julia to myself. I'll find a way to get the truth from her.

CHAPTER 39

I'm struggling through the bush. The forty-minute walk to Paradise Bay is taking me a lot longer thanks to my lack of shoes. No starlight penetrates the canopy. I'm traveling blind. I can't even find the trail.

Despite my impatience, I force myself to take care. I can't afford to trip and hurt myself. The heat of the day has vanished with the light. In Tasmania, people lost in the bush overnight can die of exposure even in summer.

My wounds throb. Blood seeps from my burn and from the deep gash on my arm. I'm almost glad of the pain. It keeps me focused, awake.

I stumble into a tree. I press my forehead against it and close my eyes. Sleep lures me. I'm part of the tree, part of the land. We're breathing together. Through the soles of my feet, the leaf litter is soft and crackly. It would be easy to sink down . . .

You can't rest. You can't stop until you find her.

I jerk away from the tree. I must not close my eyes.

At last, I find the trail and the going becomes a little easier, but it's still tomb-dark and I barely gain speed.

By the time I emerge onto the ridge, my limbs are leaden. Outside the bush, the night is bright. The moon has risen, and Paradise Bay is laid out before me in ghostly splendor. All the lights are out in the marina, and the mansion is dark apart from a soft glow emanating from the third story—the master bedroom.

Squall is back in her berth, and a new yacht has arrived in the marina—a big one. I can't tell her color, but I recognize the double-masted rig and the distinctive hard chines of her hull. The red schooner.

I'll go to the summerhouse first and quickly bandage my arm. I've already lost a lot of blood.

Which route should I take? I don't want Julia to see me creeping past the mansion. The vineyard wouldn't provide much cover. Better to descend on this side of the mansion, where thick vegetation reaches to the shoreline. I'll emerge at the marina parking lot. Julia and Chris's cars are always parked there. I'll scuttle behind them and then behind the big gum tree between the marina and the beach.

I'll be in plain sight when I cross the beach in front of the house, but it will take only a few seconds to reach the blackwood trees surrounding the summerhouse.

Once I've stanched the bleeding, I'll head to the mansion and sneak upstairs to Julia's bedroom. At this late hour, Joseph should be asleep, as should Zelde.

When I've learned my daughter's whereabouts from Julia, I'll take Joseph's pickup and drive to the police station. Joseph parks the truck by the summerhouse, and everyone at Paradise Bay leaves their keys in the ignition—on a small island, people don't steal cars.

Officer Maxwell might not believe me at first, but at least I'll be safe. All hell will break loose when Joseph finds out I returned to Paradise Bay—let alone when Chris discovers I'm alive—but hopefully they'll both be in police custody by then, along with Julia and Zelde. Once Maxwell uncovers evidence of the wildlife smuggling, he'll give my story more credence.

With a new burst of energy, I creep down the valley, reaching the shoreline close to the marina. I cross the parking lot, and I'm about to head along the beach when I hear the front door of the mansion open and close. Someone strides down the path toward the beach.

I dart to the gum tree and press myself against the trunk.

The figure crosses the beach in darkness, no flashlight in hand, but she's surefooted. She knows her way well. It's Julia. She's breathing hard. I freeze as she passes me. She's carrying a bundle. Is this the animal she took out of the helicopter?

Now I hear another sound. A quiet, tiny, unmistakable whimper. The murmuring of a newborn.

Julia is carrying a baby.

My body seems to catch on fire.

Julia is not smuggling animals onto that yacht. Julia is smuggling a baby. And this is the yacht that came into the marina the night after my daughter was born.

I can't let this happen. I'm about to leap out of the shadows and wrench the baby out of her arms when I hear a male voice.

"Get a move on, Julia. The tide's turning." The voice is deep, commanding.

I press closer against the tree and swivel my eyes toward the voice. Two figures stand on the pier, only a few meters away. The smaller man holds a lantern. It's Joseph, but he's not the one who spoke. The man who spoke is taller, more muscular.

I observe the stranger's confident stance. He's middle-aged

but has a strong, youthful build. A scar runs across one cheek. Despite his casual sailor's shorts and jacket, it's obvious he's in charge. *The real boss.* I feel as though he's a predator waiting in the darkness—a wolf or a lion.

This is Silas.

I hold my breath. I'm within the men's line of sight, but it's dark under this tree, and their attention is focused on Julia.

"I'm sorry, Silas." Julia's voice is full of fear. "I had to quiet the baby. Zelde's asleep in the house."

I feel as though I'm going to be sick. Silas, the guy Joseph described as *one scary bastard*, is right here. He owns the yacht. He takes the babies. He took my daughter.

The three figures walk along the pier and board the schooner. As Joseph's lantern light sweeps over the crimson hull I read the name *Ruby* and the home port, Bluff, New Zealand. The group disappears below deck. A low rumbling tells me Silas has kept the yacht's engine running. He's here for only a short time.

What should I do? Rush to the summerhouse and call the police? There's no cell reception, but I can call over the Wi-Fi.

No. Chris said Julia couriered my phone to the hospital, and there's no landline in the summerhouse. I could use the phone in the mansion, as long as Zelde doesn't catch me. Is she really asleep? Why would Julia not want to wake her? Zelde knows what's going on. She's neck-deep in it.

Before I can make up my mind, Julia and Joseph reappear. They step off the yacht and approach along the pier. I shrink back behind the gum.

At the end of the pier, they part ways without a word. Joseph heads for the marina office, while Julia turns toward the mansion. Her arms swing empty by her sides. The trade is done.

I hear the door of the office shut behind Joseph. This is my chance. Julia is alone.

I emerge from beneath the gum and run along the beach after her. I'm almost upon her when she senses me and wheels around.

"Who's there?"

"It's me."

"Eve?" Julia's eyes sweep over my shaved hair, my bleeding limbs, my salt-encrusted clothes. "What in Heaven's name happened to you?"

I want to shout at her. *I'm bleeding because your husband wanted to kill me and I ended up swimming for my life and being dashed across rocks.* But I can't let her know how high the stakes are for Christopher, or she'll try to stop me from leaving. If she calls Zelde or Joseph for help, I'll be in deep strife.

"Shh," I say. "Neither of us wants Silas to know I'm here, right?"

Julia looks aghast. "How do you know about Silas?"

Damn, I shouldn't have let his name slip. "Here's the deal, Julia. You get to keep Alec. No more visits from the police. I'll go away forever. I just want one thing."

Julia's eyes narrow and she gives an understanding nod. "How much?"

"Keep your money. I don't want it. I want the truth about my daughter."

Her eyes widen. Her mouth forms an O.

"I know about her, Julia. I've had time to think, and you know what? I feel liberated that Alec's not my kid." The lie burns my mouth. "I miss city life. I'd like to travel. I don't care what you're doing with that baby." I point toward the schooner, forcing myself to sound sincere. "I just need to know what happened to my daughter. Tell me, and you'll never see me again."

Julia casts a fearful glance toward the marina and lowers her voice. "After all this time, it would be a relief to tell you. Once you hear the pressure I was under, you'll see why I did what I did." She takes my arm. "We can't go into the house."

"Why not?"

She gives me an uncertain look. "It's Alec."

"What about him? Please tell me he isn't here."

"His sleepover fell through. I had to pick him up. Everything's fine. Silas is leaving, and Alec's sound asleep in bed. I gave him Phenergan. But I don't want to risk any noise."

So, it's not Zelde whom Julia doesn't want to wake. It's Alec. I sure don't want him to wake up, either. This isn't the first time Julia has used a sedative on her child, to my dismay, but she seems to have forgotten that Phenergan has a paradoxical effect on Alec. Far from making him sleepy, it keeps him awake.

"Fine," I say. "Let's go to the summerhouse."

Together, we stalk to the end of the beach and through the dark grove of blackwoods. As we pass Joseph's truck, I pretend to stumble. I lean against the driver's door and peer inside at the ignition. The key glints silver. My exit strategy is sound.

We approach the summerhouse, my home for so many years. I once thought it pretty, idyllic, but tonight it seems to crouch like a crab on the shoreline. This is the place where my daughter was stolen from me.

Inside, we head upstairs. We both know we're not turning on a light lest it attract Silas's attention. Through the window, I can see the great yacht in the milky moonlight, slipping away from the marina.

"I need to bandage my arm." I pull off the tattered dressing. Blood wells up in the wound. Barnacle cuts turn septic, and I used up the last of my antiseptic recently, so I step into the kitchen and dig out an unopened bottle of whiskey.

Julia follows me, watching as I stand at the sink and pour the liquid over my arm.

"Is there a first aid kit anywhere?" she asks.

"In the bathroom cupboard."

She disappears, and I hear her ferreting around in the bathroom. "Got it. Come and sit by the window."

I join her at the table. Outside, the yacht is leaving the bay. Julia takes some gauze and presses it into my wound.

This is surreal. Chris wants me dead; Julia is giving me first aid.

"How did you get hurt?" she asks.

"I was in hospital, remember."

"This looks fresh."

"I walked here from the village, and I—I tripped."

"You had no shoes?"

"I lost them. It's a long story."

"Chris said you phoned in your resignation, that you were too ashamed to show your face here, but I want you to know I don't blame you for the fire. Alec told me you kept him warm in the water. You saved his life. I'm very thankful."

It's true, then, that Julia didn't even know I came here earlier today. Good. I'll let her believe I'm still on amicable terms with Chris.

I force myself to use a friendly tone. We're just two mothers having a heart-to-heart. "I wouldn't exactly say I resigned, but if you prefer me to leave, I will. I'll keep quiet about everything that's going on between you and Silas. All I ask in return is an explanation."

She takes a deep breath. "So, this is the deal. I tell you everything I know about your daughter, and in return, you leave us alone. You can't ever repeat this information to anyone, and you can't try to contact Alec ever again."

"Absolutely," I lie. "Suits me."

Julia shifts uncomfortably. "Eve, you loved Alec like a son. I hope you can understand that everything I did was to protect him. Any mother would do the same. You've no idea what I've been through in my life."

The night is so bright that I can see creases lining her forehead. Our moon shadow lies across the floor.

"My parents were alcoholic, violent deadbeats," she says.

I sit up straight. This doesn't sound like the privileged upbringing I thought Julia had enjoyed. How does Margareta fit into this picture?

"I ran away from home at sixteen," she continues, "and for the next decade I struggled to make my way in the world. I was so vulnerable. When I met Silas, I thought my troubles were over. He gave me a job delivering exotic pets. Easy money."

"Smuggling."

"I didn't realize it was illegal. When I found out, I tried to get out of the trade. That led me to make a big mistake. I tried to make some money on the side so I could go straight." Julia shakes her head. "Silas got wind of my side deal. He took advantage of the situation and framed me for murder. From then on, I was one phone call away from going to prison. But Silas let me go free as long as I gave him one thing." She looks directly at me.

Julia's jasmine perfume is cloying at this distance. It's hard to maintain the pretense of friendliness when she can see every twitch, every eye movement. I force myself to hold her gaze.

"Silas said he had clients who wanted a very precious animal—the most valuable animal of all. They were willing to pay a premium for a product made to order. Silas had met the man through the wildlife trade. He was sterile, and his wife carried a gene for some dreadful disease. The man also had a conviction. Just a minor thing in his past. Nothing that would affect their ability to provide a good home, but it was *technically* a felony. The wife had blue eyes, a pale complexion and dark red hair. The father was a redhead, too, tall and blue-eyed. The problem was he was under government surveillance."

I can't help my alarmed tone. "He sounds like a hardcore criminal."

"No, Silas said he'd gone straight, but the police can be so suspicious, apparently. They were perfectly nice people, but they'd been rejected as adoptive parents, so if a baby had suddenly appeared in their home, the authorities would have known they hadn't adopted legally. The woman had to pretend to be pregnant, and the child had to look like it belonged to them. That's why Silas chose me." She points at her hair. "Silas told me to find a tall, blue-eyed, redheaded man and . . ." She trails off.

The blood seems to drain from my body. "You agreed to this?" I can't keep my horror out of my face.

Fortunately, Julia has glanced away. She takes Steri-Strips from the first aid kit and begins taping them across my wound. "I had no choice. Besides, you know how it is when you're young. I mean, the idea of sleeping with a stranger was ghastly, but pregnancy didn't seem like a big deal. Plenty of women give up babies for adoption, and they're not even paid. Everything would have worked out fine if I hadn't met Chris. That was when I made my second big mistake. I tried to hide from Silas. Next thing I knew, he was pointing a gun at my head—on my wedding day no less. And it was one thing to be rid of some brat conceived during an anonymous one-night stand, but no way was I giving up Christopher's child."

CHAPTER 40

I feel as though insects are crawling over my skin. I barely know which way is up. At last, I'm getting the truth, and I can almost excuse Julia's choices. She was fighting to keep her baby out of the hands of criminals.

"Running from Silas could have cost me my life," Julia says, her eyes wet with tears.

I can't keep up this friendly manner, being the docile patient while Julia tends my injuries. I stand, almost knocking over my chair. "I need to sit somewhere more comfortable. I feel a little faint." I sink onto the sofa, grateful to be in shadow.

"Where's that whiskey?"

"In the kitchen."

Julia heads into the kitchen and returns with the whiskey bottle and two glasses. Is she for real? Does she think we're drinking buddies now?

"I'm not meant to mix alcohol with my meds," I ad-lib.

"Well, I need a drink."

Julia's always been a drinker. She couldn't even stay off the wine when she was pretending to be pregnant. Wait. She *was* pregnant. Did she drink alcohol while carrying Alec?

The answer comes to me. The Hygates gave me fake wine to drink to fool the servants. No doubt Julia did the same to fool me.

The evening she invited me to the mansion to see the false bellies, Chris ostentatiously poured her a Chardonnay. They drank a toast to me, "the cleverest girl on the island." Looking back, I see there was something theatrical about the whole performance.

There's nothing fake about Julia's desires now. She pours a finger and drains it. "Seeing Silas tonight brought back awful memories. My wedding day was the worst day of my life. I got married in a ten-thousand-dollar dress, patched up just in time for the ceremony after Silas tore it, but I was trembling so much I felt like the breeze would knock me down. That night, I told Chris everything. I was sure he would leave me, and I think he came close. If it weren't for the embarrassment of telling a Supreme Court judge and a key business associate that the marriage was over the day after the wedding—Philip and Spencer were our witnesses, our only guests—well, Chris might have walked away. But then he came up with a plan to keep our child safe."

The hair stands up on my neck. That's how I came into the Hygates' lives. This is why I can't excuse Julia. In order to keep her own child safe, she handed over my baby.

"Luckily, Silas set sail for Asia soon after to meet with reptile collectors," Julia continues. "He was gone for months. Chris and I had time to carry out our plan. We set up a nursery—an absolute treasure of a room. We wanted our target to take one look and covet it for her baby."

"Your target?" The word tastes sour in my mouth.

"Eve, we didn't know you at the time. Don't take it personally. We had to treat the matter as a business transaction. There was no room for sentiment. First, we created the illusion that I'd suffered a miscarriage. Chris said people believe a story more readily if they work it out for themselves. So, we pretended to go off to Mongolia to ride horses, and when we returned, we acted bereaved."

"Wait." My head jerks up. "Angel never existed?" I'm rattled. All the sorrow I felt for that baby, the pity I felt for Julia. That was a lie, too?

"Who?" Julia looks baffled. "Oh, Angel. No, I never miscarried. We just made a headstone. We needed a sob story to explain my 'infertility.' Next, we hired that social worker. We were lucky to find her. She had money problems and was desperate to make a quick buck. What was her name again?"

"Yasmin."

"You're good with names. We had a stroke of luck with Zelde, too. I read an old newspaper article about a midwife who lost her license for making mistakes in her paperwork. *Perfect*, I thought, *paperwork's one thing we don't need or want!* Chris tracked Zelde down and made her a generous offer. The funny thing is Zelde loved living here so much that she wanted to stay after the babies were born. She's been such a godsend."

"Right," I say in an even tone. So Julia employed an incompetent midwife? "Paperwork" might sound trivial, but if Zelde lost her license over it, she must have made a serious mistake. "I remember you told me Zelde was appalled by your plan."

"Did I? Oh, that was probably just to make you think she was *honest* and *trustworthy*." Julia pronounces the words with a sarcastic tone. "Zelde was all in. Once she was hired, we started trying to conceive, which fortunately happened quickly. I'm sure you can see the plan was designed so nobody would get hurt. We were looking for someone who wanted to give up her baby for adoption anyway. When Yasmin told us about you, you seemed perfect with your auburn hair. Your boyfriend was blond—not a strawberry blond like Chris, but close enough. Best of all, you had no husband and no money. But when we offered to adopt your child, you acted like we'd asked you to cut your heart out of your body. In desperation, I invited you to be our child's nanny. I know you were asked to come to interview as a nanny, and Chris thought it would be great to have a nanny who believed she was our child's mother, but I'd actually hoped you'd hand over your baby, take the money, and leave."

A buzz. Julia pulls her phone from her pocket and looks at the screen. My heart lurches. *She has her phone with her. What if she tells Chris I'm here? What would he do? Would he tell her he'd ordered Joseph to drop me overboard?*

"It's Chris saying he landed safely in Hobart." Julia sighs. "I wish he were here, but he's taken the helicopter to create an alibi for us. I'm on the flight manifesto as a passenger, so it looks as though we weren't here tonight, just in case someone intercepts Silas's yacht."

To my relief, she puts her phone face down on the table without typing a reply. "You obviously know what was happening tonight. You must have noticed our cash-flow problems."

"You're trafficking babies."

"Please don't use that word, Eve. I admit we deceived you back when Alec was born, but with these mothers everything's open and aboveboard. They know their babies will be adopted. Okay, we pose as the adoptive parents in order to gain their trust, but like your daughter, their babies are going to good homes. Two babies have been delivered so far, and we've got four more due this year. That will be enough to get us back on our feet. It may not be strictly legal, but nobody's harmed. We're all consenting adults."

"I'm not judging you." The lie is so brazen, I can barely get it out. *Good homes? All consenting adults? What about the babies? They sure don't get a say.* "Why are you in financial trouble? What happened to the inheritance from Margareta? The castle?"

Julia shakes her head. "Eve, don't you remember, in the beginning you were always on the point of leaving? One time you even pulled out your suitcase and started packing. We were out of time to find someone else. My belly was sticking out a mile, and I couldn't hide it anymore." She lets out a brittle laugh. "There's no inheritance. There's no castle. 'Margareta'"—she makes air quotes—"was an actress. We hired her to pose as my grandmother. We told her it was an elaborate prank, like a murder mystery weekend. She was pretty good, if a little over the top with the crown and the curtseying."

"What? So, is Margareta not dead?"

Julia shrugs. "The actress? I haven't a clue."

My jaw falls open. The lengths this pair went to. I'd begun to suspect the castle wasn't real, but I had no idea Margareta wasn't Julia's grandmother.

I'd like to say the pretense of wealth had no effect on me, but deep down, I know otherwise. Yes, I did want my child to inherit that castle. I may have been more difficult to persuade than the Hygates foresaw, but in the end, their lies worked. I took the bait.

Julia refills her glass. "That charade when Joe opened the door on me wearing the fake belly while Margareta was nearby—we staged the whole thing. Joe knew everything before you arrived at Breaksea. We didn't want you to know how close we were with

him, since it's pretty obvious he's an ex-con. Anyway, we got Joe
to pretend to believe Chris had got you pregnant. The purpose of
the 'near-miss' was to show you the need for you to hide better so
you'd be willing to live at the lighthouse. Chris had had enough
of you living close by. He ordered Joe to move you. What a relief
when you agreed to stay there! Finally, everything settled down."

I'm glued in place on the sofa. I'm glad I'm in darkness. If
Julia could see my face right now, she'd know exactly how I feel
about her.

I hate Silas, who buys and sells babies. I hate Christopher, who
tried to have me killed. But what makes Julia's part worse is that
she doesn't think she's done anything wrong. She's so caught up
in her story—a story in which Silas is the villain, Chris is the
hero, and she is the victim—that she doesn't even stop herself
saying her darkest thoughts. In her mind, I'm an inconvenience,
an obstacle. She almost expects me to be grateful that she let me
believe Alec was my child.

"I need the ladies' room," she says. "My nerves have been shot
to pieces this evening. Don't take this personally, but I'm glad
you're leaving." She slips into the bathroom and shuts the door.

A buzz from the table. Julia's phone again. I dart to the table and pick it up. A message shows on the lock screen. It's from
Chris: *All OK? You were supposed to call.*

Holy hell. I've got to stop Julia replying.

I tap the screen. *Swipe up for Face ID or enter passcode.* Can I
guess her passcode? I tap in Alec's birthday. The phone jiggles.
That's a no. I try Julia's birthday and Chris's with no luck.

I can at least clear the message from the lock screen. I swipe
left and hit *clear.* The message disappears.

I've bought some time. As long as Julia only looks at her lock screen and doesn't open her messaging app, she won't see Chris's message. But what if he messages again—or calls? He's likely to, since he's clearly concerned by her silence.

Hang on. There's no cell reception. Julia's getting these messages via the Wi-Fi. If I turn it off . . .

The toilet flushes. I put the phone down and scurry to the router. I grab it from the bottom shelf of the bookcase, yank out the plug, and replace it on the shelf as the bathroom door opens.

Seeing me bent over the bookcase, Julia throws me a questioning look. "What are you doing?"

"Where is my baby now?" I demand. "Tell me!"

"Don't use that tone," Julia snaps. "Don't you understand the sacrifices I made to keep you happy? You were fine, Eve. *I* was the one who suffered. So many lies, so much stress. Anyway, I've told you everything now, although I guess Joe might know something more about your daughter. Good old Joe." Julia's voice almost sounds wistful. She returns to the table but doesn't sit. She picks up her phone. My heart nearly stops, but she glances at the screen and puts it down again.

I can't believe how flippant Julia is. She hasn't told me the thing I most need to know. She cares so little about my baby that she's never bothered to find out where she ended up. How else can I possibly find out? Seeking information from Joseph is obviously out of the question, and I can't imagine Zelde would tell me anything.

Julia pours herself yet another whiskey, which she drinks standing. "Joe was our saving grace. It was a stroke of luck Silas hired him to run the marina. Joe had done time for Silas and kept his mouth shut, so Silas trusted him. Silas never realized Joe cared about me. We'd met years earlier when I was delivering animals for Silas. When I told Joe that Silas was making me give up my baby, he flipped out. So, while Silas believed he had a man on the ground keeping an eye on me, Joe was secretly helping us. But there was one last job I had to do myself."

Julia is staring into the middle distance. She shudders, as though still fearful of that final hurdle. "The night after the children were born, I had to meet Silas one last time. My goal was to extract a promise from him that would secure my child's safety, but I had to take extreme care. Silas had warned me: *Cheat me a third time, and no fortune on earth will save you.* And here I was lying to his face."

CHAPTER 41

Julia

Julia stood over the crib, watching her sleeping baby. He was perfect. All those dreadful feelings she'd suffered last night during the birth—that disturbing sense that her baby was inflicting pain on her on purpose—had melted away today. She had a son. She had given Chris the child he longed for.

Christopher entered the nursery, binoculars in hand. "You're still here?" His voice was stern. "I can see the yacht from the upstairs window. It's almost here. You'd better get down to the marina."

Julia's phone buzzed in her pocket. She pulled it out. Another message from Joe. *What's the hold up?* She quickly put the phone away, but not before Chris caught a glimpse of the screen.

"What's going on, Julia? You know you've got to do this."

Julia turned to her husband, beseeching him with her eyes. Surely Chris would relent. He'd told her she would have to hand the child over to Silas herself, but she'd do anything to avoid having to see that man again.

Christopher's eyes were stony. Julia could see he'd made up his mind.

"I'm going." Julia picked up the vial of sedative that Zelde had obtained for her and hurried out of the room.

Inside the marina office, Joseph was pacing up and down with the baby in his arms. The crying was nerve-jangling, and the dark circles under Joseph's eyes suggested he'd been kept awake all night. "Better double the dose, I reckon," he said, holding the baby still while Julia administered several drops of sedative.

The crying abated almost at once, and within a minute, the child was quiet.

Julia took her outside and stood on the pier, taking deep breaths to calm herself. It was a still night, but dark and cold. The yacht glided into the harbor, a solitary male figure at the helm. The only sound was the cawing of gulls disturbed by its arrival.

Ruby bumped gently against the pier, and Julia watched the man leap down, rope in hand, and tie the yacht up. Silas. Her heart beat fast.

It was time to speak with him one last time. Julia approached the yacht.

Silas spotted Julia and jumped back on board to flick on a deck lamp. His gaze focused on the bundle in her arms. "So, you've kept your word for once, Julia."

Julia nodded.

"It looks dead," he muttered.

Julia glanced down. The child's eyes were open, but her face was a mask of stillness.

"I sedated her. A baby's cry is very loud." Julia's voice came out as a croak.

"I thought no one was around."

"Uh, there isn't, but . . . I didn't want to take any chances." Her

cheeks grew warm. Could he see she was flushed and anxious?
Would he hear the tremor in her voice and realize she was hiding
something?

"Remember, there's no point begging, Julia."

"I know." Julia stepped close to the side of the yacht and handed
the bundle to Silas. As her hand grazed his rough skin, she forced
herself not to recoil.

He prodded the baby's cheek. The child squirmed.

"She looks healthy enough," he muttered. "She's a girl?"

"Yes. Listen, Silas, I have something to say. We're even now."
Julia gripped a stanchion, trying to look stern. "Any children
born after this one are mine. You have no further claim over me."

"The cops still have your fingerprints. All I have to do is phone
in an anonymous tip and you'll be in the slammer."

"If you do, I'll reveal you blackmailed me into giving up my
baby. I won't be the only one who ends up behind bars."

"You don't need to tell me how it works. You can keep any
other kids you have."

There. He'd said it. Julia wanted to sink to her knees with relief. Instead, she spoke firmly. "I never want to see you again. It's
not safe to bring the yacht in here. We have so many people living
on the property—servants and the like. In future, stick to meeting Joseph at Lighthouse Rock."

"Fine, but I need to see Joe while I'm here. I've brought some
geckos from New Zealand. He needs to bring the cages down to
the boat and help me unload."

"I'll tell him." Julia started to move away.

"Don't you want to say goodbye?" Silas gestured at the child.

Julia couldn't fake the emotion. The baby had felt like a lump of coal in her arms. If she held it again, surely he'd see she felt nothing for it, that it wasn't her flesh and blood.

"No," she said.

"Suit yourself. I'm setting sail tonight back to New Zealand. The parents will meet me there. What about your cover story? Have you told people you had a stillbirth? I don't want anyone looking for this kid."

"No."

"You're gonna have to, Julia. Stage a funeral or whatever. It would've been easier if you'd hidden the pregnancy in the first place. Joe tells me you didn't."

She folded her arms across her chest. "You'll be pleased to hear that won't be necessary. I gave birth to twins."

This was the crucial moment. The lie had to be convincing. Silas was bound to find out about her son's existence at some stage.

"Twins? Where's the other one?"

"None of your business. I gave you my firstborn. You said yourself, any children born after her are mine."

"Is the other one a boy?" he asked.

"What does it matter?"

Silas's eyes narrowed. Julia was sure he was about to leap onto the pier and grab her, demanding an answer, except that he was holding a baby. A baby whose red hair and blue eyes matched the client's requirements perfectly.

"I want the boy."

Julia met his gaze. Her voice was steely. "I never promised you a son. You've got my firstborn. The end."

"You'd better think again, Julia, or I'll be calling the cops first thing tomorrow!"

"Do your worst."

Silas took a step back. His expression betrayed his surprise. He could see that, despite her fear, Julia meant it. She had called his bluff.

She turned and strode along the pier toward shore. She didn't look back once. She couldn't risk Silas seeing her smile.

CHAPTER 42

Eve

Hearing Julia describe handing over my baby to this evil man is almost too much to bear, but I let her speak in case there's a clue in her words—and there is.

"Silas was sailing to New Zealand? So my daughter must be there!" My heart leaps. It might be possible to find her in such a small country.

I'm sitting on the floor by the bookcase. Julia's slouched on the sofa. I've lost count of how many whiskeys she's downed.

"No," she says. "The parents traveled to New Zealand for the handover. I don't know where they were from."

I let out a despairing sigh. This is hopeless. "Did Silas tell you *anything* about where she ended up?"

The door opens downstairs.

A heavy tread on the staircase. Joseph? He'll have heard my voice. He'll be furious that I came back. *If I see you again, you won't get a second chance.*

My God. I can't get away. I shrink back into the shadows.

The man who appears at the top of the stairs isn't Joseph.

It's Silas.

My pulse races. I can't take my eyes off this man who steals babies. Here he is, walking around, not a care in the world, in the process of committing a heinous crime.

Julia's eyes widen. "I thought you'd left."

"My headsail tore."

"What, just now?"

"Yeah. It caught on a stanchion as I was raising it." Silas spots me in the corner. His expression is indifferent. He has no idea I'm the mother of a child he stole. "I knew Chris had sail-repair tape, so I came back to get some. I was heading to your house when I heard voices. I thought it was strange you were having a midnight chat with the lights out. Who's this? She looks like she's been run over by a truck."

"This is my son's nanny," Julia says. "She, uh, came back to-night unexpectedly."

Julia's covering for me. I nod, trying to look relaxed. I'm a random person who has inadvertently stumbled upon the scene. I don't know what's going on. Silas can safely leave me here.

But now Silas says, "This is Eve."

What?

Julia starts. "You know her?"

"Chris phoned me earlier, said one of the mums had turned up. Joseph had to take her out on a boat and deal with her, which would make him late for our meeting."

I'm rooted to the spot. This is bad.

Julia's jaw drops. I can see what's going through her head: *How much did Chris tell Silas? Not everything. Silas doesn't know that I passed off Eve's baby as mine.* And now Julia's figuring out what Jo-seph "dealing with" me means. Her gaze passes over my injuries, my salty clothes. She's joining the dots.

"Where's Joseph?" she asks.

"In the office."

"You've left the product unattended?" Julia stands, frowning. "That isn't safe. It's barely a day old."

Silas emits an ugly laugh. "If you want to seem like you care, Julia, don't call it *the product*." He sneers. "People are so precious about babies needing to be watched all the time, yet nobody ever guesses that their kid spent a week lying alone in a crib while crossing the Tasman. I'm too busy sailing to do anything except feed and change them every now and then, but I've had no complaints from the buyers. The little brats are toughened up. Maybe they'll grow up to be serial killers." He shrugs.

"I don't want to think about it." Julia shudders.

"Don't give me that bullshit, Julia. You know I'm sailing single-handed. Hell, you knew when you gave me your own kid. Did you think she was going to get cuddles and lullabies?"

Julia's eyes dart to me. I can see what she's thinking.

They're talking about my daughter. My daughter was taken aboard that red yacht with this devil of a man. She was neglected, left crying in her crib as he crossed the Tasman to hand her over to her *buyers*.

My fists clench. I want to leap up and attack him like a ferocious mama bear. I want to scream, but I force myself to stay silent.

"If you need anything done, you've got to do it yourself," says Silas. He crosses the room, raises his hand and hits me open-handed across the face. Stars explode inside my skull as I hit the floor.

"Don't hurt her!" Julia cries. "We can let her go. She won't talk."

"Are you fucking kidding me?" Silas replies. "Jesus, talk about the power of denial."

I try to stand, but he kicks me in the stomach. Pain pulses through me. I groan and writhe on the floor.

"You're soft in the head, Julia." Silas yanks an extension cord out of the wall. He grabs me and drags me to the top of the stairs, where he jerks my arms behind my back and wraps the cord around my wrists. In a moment, I'm stuck fast to the balustrade. The metal digs into my spine.

"Silas, Alec adores Eve," Julia stammers. "He'll be distraught if she's hurt. Eve has become a good friend."

"Wait a minute," says Silas. "Why did you get your son's nanny to give you a baby?" He studies my features. "When was your baby born, Eve?"

I have no idea what to say.

"Is this the one who had the baby you just gave me, Julia? Or the one last month?"

Julia is silent.

"You've given me three babies. The one on board now, the one last month, and the first one, six or seven years ago. But that one was *your* baby, right, Julia?" He turns to me and asks again. "When did you have your baby?"

I stare up at him, my brain on fire. If I tell the truth, he'll know Julia deceived him. He'll know the first baby he took wasn't hers but mine. I don't know how that would work out for me, but I can't imagine it would help.

Silas raises his hand to my face and I flinch, but instead of striking me again, he runs his hand over my close-shaved head, inspecting my hair. It's not much more than stubble, but it's long enough for Silas to see that my hair is red.

"You didn't have twins, did you, Julia?"

Julia gasps. "Please forgive me, Silas. I—"

"That first baby, the one I thought was yours, *this* is the mum?"

"Tha—that's right."

"I thought you were oddly chill about handing over your kid," says Silas, "even for a cold-hearted bitch like you."

I'm waiting for his rage to turn on her. Instead, he throws back his head and laughs.

"Well played, Julia. God knows how you swung that. Quite an achievement. You kept the mum as a *nanny*? What did you tell her?" He takes my chin and looks into my eyes. "Did you know your baby ended up on my yacht?"

His gaze is chilling. I can't think of anything to say except the truth. "Not till tonight."

"Where did you think she was?"

"I thought Alec was my son."

Silas snorts. He starts patting down my pockets. "No phone. Good." He turns to Julia. "No wonder you were confident you could persuade pregnant women to give up their babies. I wondered where you got the idea of posing as an adoptive mum. You'd done it before." His voice has a sinister edge. "Julia, for a smart woman, you sure are stupid. You've got rocks in your head if you think we can let this girl go. She knows you stole her baby. You think she's your friend? She hates you."

My life is in Julia's hands. She needs to convince Silas that it's safe to let me go, that I'm a friend who won't go to the police. He's not going to listen to me.

I'll forgive Julia everything if she saves me from Silas. She just needs to persuade him to leave me alone.

Julia averts her eyes. "Fine. Do what you have to do."

CHAPTER 43

I don't need your permission, Julia." Silas speaks in a languid tone. "What's more, you're going to help me. We have two problems. We have to get rid of her, and we have to deal with Joe."

"Joe won't care what you do to Eve."

"Julia, you're not thinking straight. Your husband told Joe to drop the girl overboard, but Joe didn't follow instructions."

"Joseph didn't let me go," I lie. "I escaped. I swam ashore."

Silas's response is to backhand me so hard my head crashes against the balustrade.

"Please don't hurt me!" I cry. "I just want to leave. I promise I'll never come back."

Silas hits me harder. My head strikes the balustrade again.

Every part of me wants to scream, yell, struggle, but I force myself not to. Begging may have worked with Joseph, but it won't with Silas. I let my eyelids droop and my head hang forward.

"No more trouble from her for a while," Silas mutters.

"Did you hear what she said?" Julia asks. "Joe didn't let her go. She swam ashore. Look, she's been in the water."

"Bullshit. How could she escape from a boat? If she jumped overboard and tried to swim away, Joe could've run her down. It was his job to get rid of her. He failed, and he didn't tell anyone. Why'd she come back here?"

"She wanted to know where her daughter was."

"Exactly. She's a liability. Jesus, all these years I've kept secret from you what happened to that kid after I handed her over, thinking you'd freak out if you knew."

My body is rigid.

"Huh?" Julia's tone is one of idle curiosity, a little thick from the whiskey.

"The father was huge in the wildlife trade. He ran the biggest operation in America. That's why I went to such lengths to get the right kid for him, the right shade of hair and everything. He's not the kind of guy you want to annoy. A couple of years back, he was taking animals across the Mexican border when the deal went sour. He killed someone, and the FBI nabbed him. He went back to prison. They pinged the wife, too. The kid ended up in an orphanage. Easy come, easy go, I guess." He lets out a short laugh as though the whole story tickles him. "Anyway, we've got to get Joe out of the office. We can't have blood in there. Forensics will be all over it."

I can barely process what I'm hearing. My daughter's buyer was a murderer? And now she's in an orphanage?

"Forensics? We can't— What?" Julia stammers.

"Tomorrow you report Joe missing. It'll be bloody suspicious if you don't. Tell you what, I'll tow his boat behind *Ruby* when I leave. I'll scuttle it in deep water, well away from the bodies."

"Bodies?" Julia's voice trembles.

"Yes, Julia, I'm going to be taking two corpses out to sea and dropping them overboard. As if I didn't have enough to do solo-sailing to New Zealand with a baby on board. Tomorrow, you report to the coast guard that Joseph took this girl out on his boat and didn't return."

"Not Joe!" Julia's voice catches. "Isn't there some other way?"

"Julia, are you with me or not?"

Julia sniffs. I can almost hear her inner struggle, but I know which side she's coming out on. "I'll do whatever you need me to do."

"I'll get my rifle from *Ruby* and wait behind that gum tree near the office. You lure Joe outside. You'd better put on a good performance. If you give him any warning, well, there are six rounds in my rifle. Plenty for everyone. Zelde's asleep in the house, right? Anyone else on the property?"

"No," Julia squeaks.

Alec. My heart stops. Please don't let Silas find out Alec is here.

"We leave Zelde where she is," Silas says. "The old bird'll stay put. We go and hit Joseph first, otherwise he'll skedaddle when he hears me shoot the girl." He taps my head. "Whereas *she's* not going anywhere. Come on. Move it."

What will Alec do when he hears a gunshot? It's bound to wake him. If he comes out of the house and Silas sees him . . .

"What if Eve comes to?" asks Julia. "Are you sure she's tied up securely?"

"I'm a sailor. I know how to tie a knot."

Two sets of footsteps descend the stairs.

My heart is racing. I can't believe what I just heard. A plan to commit two murders, outlined as casually as if we were cattle due for slaughter. Julia is going along with it.

The door shuts below. I start trying to wriggle free. Pain courses through my head, my wounded arm, my burnt neck, my belly where Silas kicked me.

In the movies, people who are tied up always shake themselves free, but I can't move an inch. Is there some other way to escape?

Could I pull the balustrade out of the wall or get hold of a knife? I look around with desperate hope, but the balustrade is bolted securely and there's nothing sharp within reach.

I slump against the balustrade. I'm going to die. I'll never see Alec again. He'll be raised by those criminals, never knowing what happened to me. My daughter will spend her childhood in an American orphanage.

A sound in the playroom. A rustle.

My eyes flick to the door. The handle is turning.

The door opens.

CHAPTER 44

A small figure stands in the doorway of the playroom, pajama-clad, bleary-eyed. Alec.

"Evie, you're back!" he exclaims. "I thought I was never going to see you again. Why do you look like that? Your hair's cut off."

My eyes must be as round as portholes. "What are you doing here, Alec?"

"I missed you, Evie. I asked Mummy if I could sleep here like the old days. She said no, but I couldn't get to sleep, so I snuck here. Am I in trouble?"

"No, Alec, but—"

"Why are you tied up? You're hurt. Are there robbers?"

"Yes, but we can get away if you do as I say."

Fear rises in his face. "I'll untie you." He leaps to my binds.

"It'll be quicker to cut me free. Grab a knife from the kitchen!"

Alec runs to the kitchen and returns with my fishing knife. He unsheathes it.

"Watch out. It's very sharp." I pull tight to make the cord taut.

"There," says Alec, stepping back.

A jolt of pain as I shake my arms free. I scramble to my feet.

Bang! A shot pierces the night.

My God. Joseph. They shot him.

"What was that?" cries Alec.

I press my finger to my lips, my eyes boring into Alec.

Surely Silas wouldn't harm Alec, but I can't take the risk. I must take Alec with me. I sheathe the knife, shove it in my pocket, and seize his hand. We hurry downstairs.

I exit the summerhouse and make a beeline for Joseph's pickup, dragging Alec behind me. I open the driver's door, flick off the interior light, and push Alec in. He scoots over to the passenger seat. I jump behind the wheel and close the door with a quiet click.

"It isn't shut properly," Alec says.

"Shh, honey." I glance toward the marina. Two figures approach through the blackwood grove—Silas and Julia. Silas carries a rifle.

Alec hasn't seen them. I push him down, laying my body over his.

"Stay still," I whisper.

Silas and Julia crunch past on the gravel. The summerhouse door opens and shuts. I peer over the dashboard. The downstairs light comes on.

Any second now they'll see I'm gone. As soon as they're upstairs, I'll start the pickup, jam my foot on the gas, hightail it to the police station. Silas might chase me in Julia's car, but I'll have a head start.

"What about Mummy?" Alec sits up.

There's no time to explain. "Mummy's safe." I reach for the ignition, but I don't turn the key.

I want nothing more than to drive to safety. But what if Silas *doesn't* give chase? If he jumps on his yacht, he'll be well offshore by the time I raise the alarm. The police might never find him.

There's a baby on that yacht.

The light comes on upstairs in the summerhouse. Angry shouting. Silas and Julia are arguing.

I turn to Alec. "We can't leave. You need to do exactly as I say. Follow me."

I open the driver's door, haul Alec out of the pickup, and set off sprinting toward the marina.

"Hey!" Silas's voice rings out from the door to the summerhouse as Alec and I disappear into the blackwoods.

"Run, Alec!" My heart's beating so fast it feels as if it might explode. Alec is almost keeping pace. I'd hoped to grab the baby and get to a car, but that's not going to happen. Silas is hot on our heels.

We tear along the beach. Ahead, the front door of the mansion opens. Zelde steps out and sees us.

"Stop them!" Silas yells.

Zelde seems to understand the situation at once. She sets off at a surprising speed, aiming to cut us off at the gum tree. Her eyes lock on Alec. She's going to grab him—and she's way ahead of us.

"Don't you dare take that boy!" she cries.

A body lies crumpled on the sand in a dark pool. Joseph. He's obviously dead.

"Don't look!" I cry to Alec as we fly past.

Zelde spots Joseph at the same moment. Her gaze is fixed on him, her expression filling with horror. She's not looking where she's going.

Zelde's inches away, her greedy arms grasping for Alec, screeching like some hag sent from hell to snatch children, when she trips on a tree root and goes down hard.

Alec and I reach the pier and pelt along it. I don't dare look behind. Zelde is screaming in pain. I can hear Silas coming like a hurricane. Ahead of us, the big yacht gleams crimson in the moonlight.

Bang!

No! I turn to Alec. He's unhurt. Silas missed us.

"Jump on the yacht!" I cry.

I hear Julia shriek, "Don't shoot my baby, Silas!"

Alec stops. "Mummy's here!"

"Alec!" Julia screams. "Come here! Come to Mummy!"

"Get on board, Alec!" I shout.

Alec looks back to shore with searching eyes. Julia is running along the shoreline after Silas, who's dashing along the pier.

Julia cries, "Run, Alec! Go with Eve!"

A shudder passes through me. Her words can mean only one thing. Silas intends to kill us all.

Alec leaps onto the yacht. "Hurry, Evie! He's shooting bullets at us!"

I jump on board. The engine is thrumming. All I need to do is throw off the ropes and shove the engine into gear.

"Get below deck!" I cry, but instead, Alec runs to the foredeck and throws off the mooring line. I do the same with the aft line. The yacht drifts away from the pier.

Silas is halfway down the pier. He stops and aims the rifle at me. Julia catches up to him and seizes the weapon, yanking it so the barrel points skyward.

Bang!

Now Silas rams the rifle into Julia's chest. She totters backward and falls into the water.

Silas drops the rifle and crosses the distance to the yacht in seconds. I bound to the cockpit and thrust the gear lever forward. The yacht lurches further from the pier.

Silas leaps across the gap of sea.

He slams against the stern. He almost drops into the water, but one arm reaches out. His hand closes over a stanchion. His other hand comes up and grips another. His feet trail in the sea, but he's strong. He'll pull himself up in seconds.

I look around for a weapon. A winch handle is tucked into a pocket in the cockpit. I grab it and dash to the stern. I ram the heavy metal tool onto Silas's knuckles.

Silas yelps and lets go of the stanchion. I pound his other hand even harder, but he's already regained his hold.

"We're gonna hit the rocks!" Alec cries.

"Take the helm!"

I hear Alec jump into the cockpit and grab the tiller. The yacht lurches to port.

I lift the winch handle high and whack Silas's head, but it doesn't slow him down. His foot is on the hull.

"Evie we're gonna crash!"

I glance around. Alec has overcorrected. We're heading back toward the pier.

"Tiller hard to port!" I shout. "Aim for the channel!"

I turn back to Silas, but I'm too late. Silas has pulled himself onto the deck. He grabs the winch handle. I hold on tight. I'm fighting for my life, for Alec's life, but that isn't what gives me the courage to do what I have to do. It's the thought of what Silas has done.

"Let go!" I scream.

"Not a chance, you little bitch."

Silas is grinning. He thinks he's won. But he's focused on wrenching the handle out of my hand. He doesn't notice my other hand reaching into my pocket. My fingers close around my fishing knife.

This man stole my baby.

I shake the knife out of its sheath and plunge it into Silas's chest. Blood spurts out of the wound. His eyes bulge.

It's him or me. If I don't put everything into this, he'll kill us. I pull out the knife and stab again, driving it into his neck.

Silas staggers back clutching his throat. Blood pours from his mouth.

I drop the winch handle. I shove him as hard as I can.

He hits the rails. His head lolls back. The fight seems to fall out of his body. His eyes become dull, unseeing.

He's teetering on the brink. I plow into him with all my strength.

He tumbles overboard.

I watch as his body disappears beneath our churning wake.

I spin around. Alec has brought the yacht out of the bay into open water. Intent on steering, he's oblivious to the bloody scene behind him.

"He's gone," I tell Alec. "We're safe."

"What about Mummy?"

"Mummy's all right. The bad man hit her, but she'll be okay. We'll call the police soon."

I wrap my arms around my son and kiss his forehead. Yes, Alec will always be my son. I have lavished a mother's love on him for six long years. We'll always be family.

The moon, high in the sky, casts a silver path toward the eastern horizon.

"I can't steer this boat," says Alec. "It's too big."

I survey the ocean. No hazards are within sight. "You're doing great. I need you to steer for just a little longer. See the path the moon makes? Sail there."

I grab a life jacket and strap it onto him.

Inside the pilothouse, I spot a ship's radio. It will take only a moment to issue a distress call, but I don't do it yet. One thing is more urgent.

I descend the ladder, where I follow my ears into an aft cabin. I flick on the light.

Lying in a makeshift crib, dressed in a pink onesie, is a newborn baby, plump and downy and perfect. She has a full head of dark hair and beautiful brown eyes. She squirms, her little face contorted with sobs.

I gather her into my arms. "Hey, baby girl," I whisper, rocking her. "You're safe."

I carry her back up on deck, where Alec stands at the helm, gazing at the horizon with fierce concentration. The night breeze is wafting the yacht away from land. Behind Alec, the jagged silhouette of Breaksea is receding into the gloom. I would happily never set foot on that cursed island again.

Off the starboard quarter I spy the great, pulsating light of the lighthouse, and I think of Xander. We were so young when we were together, and it's been so long since he died, that sometimes I feel I've left him far behind, but tonight, he feels near. I feel I will always carry his love within me.

Alec glances at me, and his eyes pop at the sight of the pink bundle in my arms. "Whose baby is that?"

"I don't know, but the police will find her parents. I'm about to radio them. She's the reason we got on this boat, Alec. You helped me to rescue her."

Nobody rescued my baby girl. She was taken by strangers who bought her like a chattel, who lied to her all her life about who she is. My daughter ended up in an orphanage.

I'm going to find her.

EPILOGUE

The guard tosses the mail into the cell. The elderly prisoner scuttles to pick it up off the floor.

"Don't get excited," says the guard. "It's just the newspaper."

Of course it is. Zelde never gets any letters. The newspaper is her only link to the outside world these days. She likes to keep in touch, but it's getting more difficult, thanks to her damned eyes.

Her eyes have been the ruin of her. If her deteriorating vision hadn't forced her to leave midwifery many years ago, she wouldn't have fallen prey to Julia Hygate's lucrative offer. Zelde had originally thought it was lucky that the Hygates didn't know about her eyesight. Julia knew Zelde had left midwifery due to "problems with paperwork" but had no idea what had caused the problems—nor that Zelde's misreading a doctor's orders had endangered a mother's life. Ironically, if the Hygates had found out her disability and dismissed her, Zelde might not have ended up here, behind bars.

Zelde tears the plastic wrap off the newspaper, grabs her Perspex magnifying glass, which she has special permission to keep in her cell, and settles down to read. But the headline makes her blood boil.

Mother and Stolen Baby Reunited, Set Off for Tropical Cruise

That damned Eve. So she has triumphed after all. She's got her daughter back.

Eve always irritated Zelde. Pregnant out of wedlock, poor as a church mouse, yet so precious about giving up her baby. Not to mention nosy. Eve noticed every little slipup Zelde made—handing Eve pepper instead of salt, mixing up medications. And then there was the time Zelde had mistaken Eve for Julia and called her "Mrs. Hygate." Eve had given her such a penetrating look, Zelde had thought the game was up. And finally, Eve did what Zelde had long feared: she uncovered the Hygates' secret and landed them all in prison. Well, all except Julia, who was never caught, having fled the scene by yacht as Zelde, with her broken hip, watched helplessly on. But perhaps Julia had lost almost as much as Christopher. Julia would spend the rest of her life on the run, forever separated from her wealth, her husband, and her son. As for what Christopher had done with Alec, surely Julia must be furious about it.

I won't read this stupid article. I'll tear it up. But then, the days were so long here in prison. Zelde didn't have many friends among the other prisoners. At least the article would give her something to think about.

Perhaps she would just skim it.

The mother of a baby stolen at birth says she and her daughter plan to spend the school break cruising tropical Queensland on board their new yacht. Eve Sylvester was deceived after the birth of her daughter into giving up her baby. Her daughter was taken to the United States and sold but has now been found and reunited with Ms. Sylvester.

Zelde tutted. Newspapers can never get a story straight. But then, how could they possibly know that . . .

She doesn't finish the thought. She can't stop reading.

The crime committed against Ms. Sylvester came to light when the perpetrators, shipping magnates Christopher and Julia Hygate and

yachtsman Silas Carter, made plans last year to traffic more babies.
Their plans were uncovered by Ms. Sylvester, leading to the trio making
an attempt on Ms. Sylvester's life and murdering another employee, Jo-
seph Jones. Mr. Carter drowned at sea after Ms. Sylvester fought off his
violent attack. Mr. Hygate was convicted of conspiracy to commit mur-
der, along with child trafficking charges, and is serving a life sentence.
Mrs. Hygate is still at large. Another employee of the Hygates, Zelde
Finch, was convicted of related offenses. Ms. Sylvester and her daugh-
ter are said to have received a multimillion-dollar settlement from
Mr. Hygate in relation to the abduction.

The article is intensely annoying. No mention is made of
Zelde's cooperation with police. If it weren't for Zelde corrobo-
rating Eve's testimony, the authorities might not have been able
to convict Christopher. And Zelde was the one who provided the
vital clue that enabled Interpol to find Eve's daughter. Zelde had
kept her ears pricked up whenever she was around Silas. Once,
he mentioned the child's name, Celia Mavernick, to Joseph, and
Zelde committed it to memory, knowing if she were ever charged
with a crime, the name would be a bargaining chip. And so it
was. Zelde's sentence was halved.

But the most irritating thing is the way the article makes Eve
sound like an innocent victim. Of course, that *is* how the authorities see it, but Zelde can't agree. The girl's a little minx, too clever
by half.

Zelde flips the newspaper over and immediately wishes she
hadn't. The photo seems to leap off the page: a smiling Eve em-
bracing two children. The children's faces are blurred, but it's
obvious who they are: the redheaded girl wearing a lacy blue garment is the stolen daughter, and the boy is Alec.

Zelde couldn't believe it when she heard that Christopher had asked for Eve to have custody of Alec and that despite his crimes, the authorities took his wishes into account. She could understand the pragmatism behind his request: Eve loved Alec, and with Julia on the run and Christopher in jail, she was the best person to care for him. But didn't Christopher understand how Julia would feel?

Perhaps he did. Perhaps his motive had been to punish Julia for abandoning her child.

The caption reads: *Eve Sylvester says she is delighted to have been granted custody of both the boy she believed was her son and the daughter who was stolen from her. "My love for my two children is equal and infinite. I'm bonded by nature to one and by nurture to the other. The kids are great friends already, and we're working on putting the past behind us and living our best lives together as a family."*

How sickly sweet. The article goes on to state that Eve is working as a fashion designer in Sydney, where the two children are enrolled in school. The other two trafficked babies have also been returned to their mothers . . . An animal smuggling ring is linked to the crimes . . . Investigations are ongoing . . .

Wait a moment. Zelde puts down her magnifying glass and picks up a more powerful one. She focuses on the daughter. The child is wearing the shawl Eve made when she was pregnant. Joseph told Zelde that when he went to the lighthouse the day after the birth to collect Eve's belongings, the shawl bore a girl's name: Skye. The next time Zelde saw the shawl, it had been altered to bear Alec's name. But in the photo, the shawl has been restored to its original state. The child is wearing a shawl with the name Skye.

Has Eve convinced her daughter to take the name she chose for her all those years ago? The idea enrages Zelde. Everything she and the Hygates planned has been undone. Worse, Eve has more money than she could ever have accumulated without the Hygates, and she has ended up with both children. Not that Zelde would want two children, but Eve looks so happy.

Zelde flings the newspaper into the corner of her cell. *Gross* is the word for it. Eve has some weird power over children that makes them love her. Or perhaps it's not so mysterious. If you're prepared to be endlessly forgiving and understanding and oh so gentle, lacking proper discipline, of course the brats worship you. All that silly laughter and messy play and spontaneous running outside to dance in the rain . . . Zelde has no business with all that.

Funny to think the police came so close to DNA-testing Alec, but after Eve found out the truth about Julia's pregnancy, there seemed to be no point. No one disputed that Alec was the Hygates' biological child.

The bell sounds for lights out, and Zelde hurries to brush her teeth and get into bed before the usual ten hours of darkness are imposed. She'll throw the newspaper out tomorrow and never think about the article again.

But, as she lies in the darkness of her cell, Eve's words recur. *I'm bonded by nature to one and by nurture to the other.* Eve thinks she has the perfect balance in her relationship with her children. Her close bond with Alec from years spent together, and her genetic link with Skye. If only Eve knew . . .

Zelde has never told anyone the truth. She has tried to forget it, but as she lies in her narrow, cold bed, she feels as though she's reliving it. The chaotic night when the children were born . . .

. . . Zelde clattered down the stairs of the mansion, Julia's baby in her arms, thanking God that Julia pushed it out in time. Now Zelde just needed to get to the summerhouse before Eve's baby came out in order to secure the fat bonus Chris had promised her if the plan succeeded.

She was getting too old for this. She had thought she missed delivering babies, but not two at once, under so much pressure. Her stress level was off the charts.

In the summerhouse, Chris would be holding Eve's hand through her contractions, trying to cover up the fact that Zelde wasn't there. Joseph, of all people, would be ready to catch Eve's baby.

Reaching the bottom of the stairs, Zelde rushed toward the front door, just as it opened and Joseph leapt inside.

"What's happening?" Zelde cried.

"I've got Eve's baby." Joseph cradled a naked, squirming infant.

"Where's the blanket?"

"You told me not to take the blanket."

How stupid. "Lord, Joseph, things have changed, in case you hadn't noticed." Zelde gestured toward the violet room, where it was always warm. "Put the baby down in there, *run* back to the summerhouse and get the blanket. The one with blood on it! Remember what I told you? Eve must smell her own baby. We can't be taking naked newborns out into the cold!"

Joseph darted into the violet room, plonked the baby down on the nearest chair as though it were a bag of rubbish, and dashed out the front door.

Darn it, there'd be blood all over that nice silk armchair. Zelde hurried into the room and placed Julia's baby, wrapped in a yellow blanket, on the floor. She spread out the blanket, reached to her left, and plucked Eve's baby from the chair, placing it beside Julia's baby. Sure enough, in the moonlight, the lilac chair was smeared with dark shadows. Blood. Zelde spat onto her fingers and rubbed saliva into the worst patch. Important not to let blood dry out. She should turn on a light to see how bad it was.

Footsteps in the atrium. Joseph was back holding a blood-stained white blanket. "Which kid do I give to Eve?" He pointed at the babies lying side by side on the floor.

"The one on the right! The boy!" cried Zelde. Honestly, was Joseph some kind of idiot? She threw him a disparaging scowl. "Give me that blanket."

Joseph handed her the white blanket and she sniffed it. Good. It smelled of birth. At least he got something right. With her back to the babies, she laid it on the floor, folding in the corners, working quickly . . .

Wait. She hadn't checked the sex of the babies.

She'd never admitted it to the Hygates, but Zelde's eyesight wasn't good enough for her to identify the fetal sex with certainty. When she performed Julia's antenatal scan, Zelde had confidently announced the fetus was male, but in truth, she hadn't been sure.

As for the sex of Eve's baby, Zelde hadn't a clue. She had blurred the image when performing Eve's scan, since the Hygates had instructed her to tell Eve she was carrying a son regardless of the truth. Zelde suspected Eve's baby was female, since Eve herself seemed convinced of this, but perhaps both babies were boys? That would explain why Joseph was now standing over the two babies looking baffled.

"The one on the right is a girl," he said.

"Nonsense." Zelde turned and reached for the baby on the right, Julia's baby.

Female.

Zelde stared at the genitals as if willing them to change form, but unlike on an ultrasound scan, no mistake was possible. This was a baby girl.

"Turn the light on!" Zelde barked.

Joseph hurried to the switch, and light flooded the room. Zelde grabbed her spectacles from her pocket and pushed them into place. She didn't like people seeing her wearing such thick lenses, but there was no avoiding it now.

Under the bright light, the two newborns looked remarkably alike—apart from their sex. They were the same size, around seven pounds. Both were covered in blood and vernix. Both had a full head of red hair. The boy's hair was red-blond while the girl's was auburn, but that didn't help any.

The baby on the left was a boy. The baby on the right was a girl.

Zelde *must* have placed Eve's baby on the right. She'd picked up Eve's baby from the chair to her left, lifted it over Julia's baby, and placed it on the right side of the yellow blanket.

The only problem was Zelde didn't remember doing that. She'd put Julia's baby on the right and Eve's baby on the left.

She was sure of it.

Almost sure . . .

She'd just have to tell Chris and Julia she'd misidentified the fetal sex during Julia's scan. That must be what had happened.

But wait. What if she *had* placed Eve's baby on the right just now? After all, she'd been distracted with that bloodstain. She might be misremembering her action. Memory was fallible.

Oh, she was a foolish old woman. How could she get in such a terrible muddle?

Joseph stepped closer. "Aren't ya meant to hurry?"

"Didn't you notice what Eve had? Boy or girl?"

Joseph shrugged. "Didn't *you* notice what Julia had?"

Think, Zelde. If you choose the wrong baby, you'll never be able to correct your mistake.

Joseph was gazing at her with an intent scowl. He was on the verge of realizing she had no idea which baby was which.

If Zelde presented Chris and Julia with a girl after telling them to expect a boy, they'd ask a lot of questions. Joseph might get wind of the issue and tell the Hygates about Zelde's confusion. What if the Hygates DNA-tested their child and found out it wasn't theirs? That Zelde had sent their precious baby away in that awful yacht?

That must not happen. First and foremost, Zelde must protect herself.

She stood and fixed Joseph with the haughtiest glare she could muster. "Of course I noticed. Julia had a boy as expected. I misspoke just now. Take the *boy* for Heaven's sake. He's on the left, in case you can't tell. In fact, I'll take him to Eve myself. You bring the girl down to the marina office and keep her quiet. It's your job to watch her till the yacht comes in tomorrow night."

Zelde picked up the boy and wrapped him in Eve's blanket. She hurried outside and headed for the summerhouse, leaving the girl with Joseph.

Eve had given birth in darkness, and Joseph had taken her baby away at once. Zelde had rushed away with Julia's baby before Julia had even opened her eyes. Neither mother had confirmed the sex of the baby they'd just pushed out.

Everything's fine, Zelde told herself. *I'm sure you've got it right. Regardless, it will never occur to the Hygates that you might have made a mistake. Eve will be handed a boy as expected. The girl will disappear as planned. Christopher and Julia will never suspect a thing.*

No one will know.

AUTHOR'S NOTE

Breaksea Island and Paradise Bay are fictitious. There is an island known as Breaksea Island in Tasmania, but it is uninhabited and is far too small to be the setting of the events of this novel.

Harlequin geckos are a real species endemic to Rakiura (Stewart Island) in New Zealand's deep south. They, along with other endangered animals unique to New Zealand, have been targeted by international criminals. In one notable case, a German poacher was arrested attempting to board a flight leaving New Zealand with no fewer than forty-four geckos and skinks concealed in his underwear.

It is impossible to estimate the number of children who have been the subject of illegal international adoptions. I learned when researching this novel that illegal adoption is often perceived as a victimless form of child trafficking because the child generally ends up being raised by good parents, and yet this practice causes great harm. Most obvious is the suffering of the parents who are deceived or coerced into handing over their children. Adoptive parents also suffer from the disturbing discovery that their child was not freely given up for adoption, and of course, no matter how much they love their adoptive parents, this discovery must be devastating for the children themselves.

I invented the words of the children's book Alec reads aloud in chapter 27, but readers might have recognized elements of the fairy tale "Rumpelstiltskin," first recorded by the Brothers Grimm, in which a desperate mother makes a bargain to give up her firstborn but, through resourcefulness and determination, ultimately wins back her child.

ACKNOWLEDGMENTS

I wish to thank my agent, Faye Bender, without whose guidance, encouragement, and loyalty, I could not have finished this book. Many thanks to my wonderful editors, Liz Stein at William Morrow and Penny Hueston at Text Publishing. It is a privilege to work with you both. Many of the best ideas in this novel came from you. Thank you to everyone at William Morrow and Text who worked so hard on this novel.

Thank you to the scientists who generously gave of their time, including Carey Knox, who advised me about harlequin geckos and the international black market in New Zealand's native fauna. Thank you to Thomas Coyle of Forensic Insight, who talked me through crime scene investigations, and to Henk Haazen for teaching me the three rules of sailing. Any errors are my sole responsibility.

Thank you to the Tasmanian branch of Sisters in Crime Australia for hosting a writing retreat on which I completed an early draft of this novel. It was a joy and an inspiration to be able to visit Tasmania.

Thank you to my beta readers including Eileen Merriman, Jacqueline Bublitz, Cliff Hopkins, Christina Carlyle, Florence Carlyle, Jessica Stephens, Ben Salmon, and Moses Salmon.

Thank you to my sister, Maddie, who worked tirelessly with me on this novel from the time when it was a half-formed idea, through countless early drafts, to the final proofread. You have always believed in me.

I wrote this novel in tribute to my late grandmother, Eileen Celia Mansfield, who like Eve was taken into state care as a child. Eileen gave her four children and many grandchildren all of the love and care she had missed out on herself. I owe so much to her.

Thank you to my wonderful children, Ben, Moses, and Florence, who are everything to me.

Lastly, thank you to all of the mothers of the world who love their children with such courage and devotion, especially my own, Christina. I am proud to call you Mum.

ABOUT THE AUTHOR

Rose Carlyle is a lawyer and keen adventurer. She has crewed on scientific yachting expeditions to subantarctic islands and has sailed with her family from Thailand to South Africa. She is the author of the #1 international bestseller *The Girl in the Mirror* and lives in New Zealand with her three children.

More from
ROSE CARLYLE

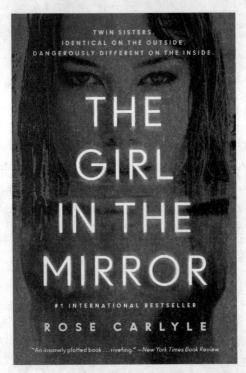

The Girl in the Mirror
The #1 International Bestseller

Identical twins. One wants what the other has. How far will she go to get it?

Here's what Iris knows about her identical twin sister, Summer:

Everything that belongs to Summer is perfect, from her magnificent yacht to her gorgeous husband.

Summer's life will always be better than Iris's.

Nobody—absolutely nobody—can tell the twins apart. Even with $100 million at stake. Now it's Iris's chance to take what she's always wanted—but how far is she willing to go to get the life she's dreamed about?

Against a backdrop of sparkling tropical islands, ocean storms, and outrageous wealth, *The Girl in the Mirror* explores the terrible consequences of greed, deadly lies, and out-of-control jealousy.

DISCOVER GREAT AUTHORS, EXCLUSIVE OFFERS, AND MORE AT HC.COM